Was it an accident, or...?

Vicky lost her balance and staggered backward. Her hip collided with the railing, and she felt the slender metal bars give beneath the impact. Panic filled her throat, and a brief downward glance caused her abdominal muscles to contract violently. She knew with a sickening certainty that she was going to fall.

And then suddenly Cole was on the platform. He yanked Vicky forward, making her fear that in the process of rescuing her he was going to dislocate her shoulders.

At the periphery of her vision, she saw Todd make a fumbling grab for her camera. He swore as it fell under the wheels of the train.

ABOUT THE AUTHOR

Lynn Turner is a warm and enthusiastic person and is a big fan of *Remington Steel*. It's no wonder, then, that she had so much fun writing *Mystery Train*, her first Intrigue. In addition to keeping house for her husband and two sons, Lynn has written books for Superromance and Temptation.

Books by Lynn Turner

HARLEQUIN TEMPTATION
8–FOR NOW, FOR ALWAYS
56–ANOTHER DAWN
75–UP IN ARMS
107–HOOK, LINE AND SINKER

HARLEQUIN SUPERROMANCE
134–A LASTING GIFT
203–DOUBLE TROUBLE

HARLEQUIN PRESENTS
893–FOREVER

These books may be available at your local bookseller.

Don't miss any of our special offers. Write to us at the following address for information on our newest releases.

Harlequin Reader Service
901 Fuhrmann Blvd., P.O. Box 1397, Buffalo, NY 14240
Canadian address: P.O. Box 2800, Postal Station A,
5170 Yonge St., Willowdale, Ont. M2N 6J3

MYSTERY TRAIN

LYNN TURNER

Harlequin Books

TORONTO • NEW YORK • LONDON
AMSTERDAM • PARIS • SYDNEY • HAMBURG
STOCKHOLM • ATHENS • TOKYO • MILAN

Harlequin Intrigue edition published July 1986
Second printing August 1986

ISBN 0-373-22045-6

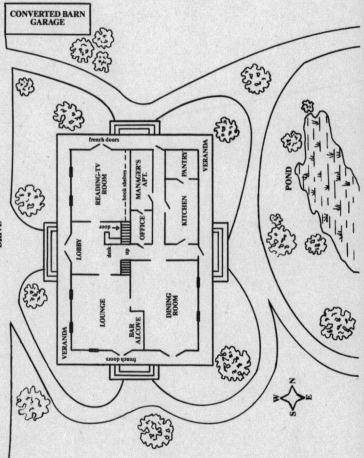

Chapter One

"Did you say one of you is going to be *murdered* this weekend?"

Vicky Rand nodded absently. She'd just noticed a limp Boston fern sitting on the floor at the end of Alicia's sofa. "That's right," she said as she bent to pick it up.

"On the train?"

"Possibly." Vicky frowned as she glanced around the cluttered living room. "It could happen on the train or while we're at the mystery mansion. This fern has to go, Ali. He'll eat it."

"If he nibbles so much as a frond, he's dead meat," Alicia vowed. "You get to stay in a mansion?"

Vicky decided the fern would be safe enough out on the balcony. "It isn't a real mansion," she explained when she came back inside. "It's actually an old country inn about a hundred miles southwest of Indianapolis. The mystery-weekend organizers rented it for Saturday afternoon through Sunday morning. They sent me a brochure describing the place. It's a big, old two-story white frame building surrounded by acres of hilly pastureland and lots of trees, about ten miles from the nearest town—nice and isolated. In fact, the only way you can get to it is by driving down a one-lane gravel road. I suspect the murder will take place there rather than on the train."

Alicia shivered and hugged her arms. "Sounds like the perfect setting for a Stephen King novel."

"Or a Hitchcock movie," Vicky agreed. "I just wish I had a better idea of what to expect. The organizers were adamant that I shouldn't have any more information than the rest of the group. They wouldn't even provide a list of the participants' names. I think they were afraid I'd start digging and find out which of them are actors and blow their covers or something."

"I presume one of the actors will be the murderer."

"Right. There may also be an accomplice or two. Obviously, if anyone could find out ahead of time who they were, that person would have an unfair advantage over the other participants. It's a very clever setup when you think about it. All these mystery addicts have come together for the weekend. They all know that at some point a fake murder will be committed, and they all want to be the one to figure out who killed whom, why, when, where, et cetera. They also know that some of them are the actors who'll stage the murder, but only the actors themselves know who they are."

"So nobody can be sure anybody else is who he claims to be," Alicia remarked. "Which means everybody must be suspicious of everybody else right from the start. Sounds like an interesting weekend."

"It'd better be," Vicky said dryly. "Otherwise I won't have much of a story for next Sunday's edition. Thanks again for keeping Groucho for me this weekend, Ali," she added, collecting her purse. "I really appreciate it, especially since I know you're not a cat lover."

Alicia shrugged. "How much trouble can one neurotic feline be?"

A huge gray cat took that as his cue to pad out of the kitchen. He stared up at Alicia and emitted a plaintive yowl.

"He wants you to come watch him eat," Vicky said as she opened the door.

"You're kidding."

"No, I'm not. He likes to have an audience." Vicky stepped into the hall before Alicia could voice whatever second thoughts she might be having about cat-sitting. "I should be back late Sunday. Have fun, you two," Vicky said with a grin, then quickly pulled the door closed behind her.

The excitement and anticipation she'd been experiencing all week increased as she drove to the station. For the past year she'd been assigned to the newspaper's metro desk, covering stories that had run the gamut from school-board meetings to corporate corruption. It was an interesting job, and she enjoyed it, but most of her work was done after the fact, so to speak. The chance to do a feature article about the increasingly popular mystery-weekend phenomenon had come along just when she was feeling the need for a change of pace. This weekend she would be smack in the middle of things, an eyewitness to whatever happened.

As she'd expected, the station was swarming with people, most of whom were headed for one of the several commuter trains. Vicky had deliberately arrived early to have a look at the three special cars attached to the end of one of them. She was impressed. Evidently the organization that sponsored the mystery weekends had spared no expense to renovate these coaches in their original, opulent turn-of-the-century style.

From the research she'd done, Vicky speculated that the first coach was the "club lounge," or bar car. It was a little shorter than the other two and lacked the raised roof and clerestory windows they both boasted. The middle coach would probably be the dining car; the last, and longest, must be the Pullman, or sleeping, coach, which she knew was divided into five private compartments.

The wooden bodies of all three cars were painted a glossy dark green, with lots of ornamental gold leaf trimming the arched windows and side panels. More gold leaf had been used to print the railway's name—Chicago, Milwaukee and

St. Paul—in extended Roman script on the letter board
above the windows. Compared with their sleek, stainless-
steel descendants, the coaches looked sumptuously elegant.
Not even the wide *Mystery Train* banner suspended beneath the windows of the middle coach could completely
spoil the effect.

Reminding herself that she was there to work, not to stand
around admiring eighty-year-old railroad cars, Vicky deposited her suitcase and camera bag beside the middle car
and slung the 35-mm camera around her neck. Then she
stationed herself next to a large green litter barrel several
yards away, hoping to get some candid shots of the mystery-weekend participants as they arrived.

At first she thought it might be difficult to identify them,
but that turned out not to be a problem. Soon after she arrived, two middle-aged men with paunches and graying hair
spotted her luggage sitting under the *Mystery Train* banner
and placed theirs beside it.

Vicky snapped a couple of quick pictures of them. She
estimated that they were both in their mid-fifties; probably
a couple of close friends who'd read all of Dashiell Hammett's books and seen the movie version of *The Maltese
Falcon* at least a dozen times.

Before she could go over and introduce herself, another
couple joined the men, depositing their bags on the other
side of Vicky's. *Married,* she thought as her shutter clicked
three times in rapid succession. *To each other.* They touched
and smiled at each other with the casual affection that only
long time lovers or very good friends—or both—displayed.
They were both strikingly attractive, and judging by their
clothes and luggage, fairly affluent. The man was well over
six feet tall, with thick dark brown hair and an enviably lean
frame. His companion's shoulder-length page boy was a
rich, deep auburn.

With that face and figure, Vicky thought, the woman
might well be a model, or perhaps an actress. She grinned

as she framed a shot of the foursome. Trying to identify the actors among the group might turn out to be the most interesting part of the trip.

Within minutes three more people had joined the first four. The row of luggage now extended halfway down the car. A petite strawberry blonde with big blue eyes and a chest measurement that caused Vicky to dislike her on sight was the fifth person to arrive. She was followed closely by two swarthy men Vicky assumed were father and son. If not for the hint of silver at the older man's temples and the slight thickening at his waist, they might have been brothers.

She had only four shots left on this roll of film, and a glance at her watch showed the time to be 5:19. According to the literature she'd received, mystery-weekend participants were to board the train at precisely 5:30. She wondered if the seven people assembled were the entire group. If so, she probably ought to go over and introduce herself now, before they boarded, and explain that she was coming along to gather information for a newspaper article.

She cast a quick look around to see if any late arrivals were approaching the three special cars. A blond man was hurrying toward her, his head bent as he read a scrap of paper in his hand. He looked like a typical businessman-commuter, though—sport coat and tie, garment bag, brown leather attaché case—so Vicky dismissed him. Then she noticed the woman.

She'd probably come to the station to meet someone, or perhaps to see someone off, because she wasn't carrying any luggage. She was of average height, with average brown hair and an average sort of face. Even her neat skirt and blouse were a nondescript khaki color.

Vicky might not have spared the woman a second glance except for the exquisite blood-red lizard handbag dangling from her hand and the matching lizard-and-suede pumps on her feet. Vicky had scoured half the stores in Chicago for shoes and a purse to go with a gray suit she'd bought the month before, but so far she hadn't found anything she liked half as well as these. She lifted the camera impulsively to snap a quick shot, thinking she could take the photo with her the next time she went shopping.

Since the shoes and purse were all she was interested in, she lowered the viewfinder to the level of the woman's knees, focusing specifically on the purse. The lens picked up the tiny diamond pattern of the lizard skin and even the fine stitching where the handles had been sewn to the bag. There was an elaborately scrolled monogram near the bottom that Vicky didn't take time to decipher. She depressed the shutter release, then immediately advanced the film to take another picture just in case the first one didn't turn out.

Before she could shoot again, a pair of long legs encased in brown gabardine slacks moved in from the left and halted abruptly, blocking her shot. Vicky lowered the camera with an irritated frown. It was the blond man she'd noticed a few moments before. The paper was still in his hand, but he was no longer looking at it. Evidently having realized that he'd stepped between Vicky and her subject, he'd promptly stopped dead in his tracks. A couple of seconds elapsed while he considered whether to continue on or beat a hasty retreat. By the time he made up his mind, Vicky had forgotten what she'd been preparing to photograph.

He was the most gorgeous man she'd ever seen in her life—golden hair shot with streaks of silver, bronzed skin, eyes the color of a rain-washed sky and a trim, compact build that made her hormones sit up and take notice. He muttered an embarrassed apology as he dodged out of her way. Vicky impulsively lifted the camera again.

"Hey, wait a minute."

When he glanced back in question, her index finger was poised above the shutter release, ready to strike. Through the viewfinder she saw surprise flicker across his face as he realized she was taking his picture.

"Why—" he started to ask, then apparently cha
mind.

*Because you're the most magnificent example of m
line pulchritude I've ever laid eyes on, and when I get
picture developed, I'm going to have it enlarged to poster
size and tack it to the ceiling above my bed.*

"I'm a reporter," she said aloud, as if that should explain everything.

He blinked owlishly. "A reporter? Oh, I see—you must be here to cover the mystery weekend."

It was Vicky's turn to be surprised. "Yes, as a matter of fact, I am. Are you one of the participants?" She fully expected him to say no. She'd already pegged him as a commuter rushing to catch the train that would deliver him to the wife and 2.5 kids who were waiting at a split-entry ranch house in the suburbs. But he surprised her again.

His boyish grin made him even more attractive as he repeated the words she'd used a moment before. "Yes, as a matter of fact, I am." Depositing his attaché case on the pavement, he held out his hand. "The name's Cole Madigan. Will you be joining us on the train, Miss . . . ?"

"Rand," she supplied as his fingers closed around hers in a warm, firm clasp. "Vicky Rand. Yes, I'll be tagging along for the entire weekend."

"Terrific!" The enthusiasm in his voice seemed to startle them both. He hastily withdrew his hand and bent to collect his attaché case. "I guess I'll see you on board, then," he said as he turned away.

He was heading in the wrong direction. Without thinking Vicky grabbed his arm to stop him. "Wait! It's almost five-thirty. That's when we're supposed to get on the train."

He glanced down at her fingers, which were frantically clutching his sleeve. She snatched her hand from his arm as if she had no idea how it had got there.

"Yes, I know," he said. "But I have to make a quick phone call first." His mouth slanted in another appealing grin. "Don't let them leave without me, all right?"

He hurried off before she could respond. Vicky gazed after him for a moment or two, then reminded herself that she had a story to cover and turned back toward the train. While she'd been talking to Cole Madigan, the woman with the lizard shoes and purse had disappeared, and a man dressed in a conductor's uniform had started checking the passengers' gold-embossed tickets prior to boarding. Vicky dug hers out of her purse and hurried over to get in line. She noticed that the son half of the father-son pair was missing from the group. Maybe he'd had to make a last-minute phone call, too.

SEVERAL YARDS AWAY, a couple hurried toward the last car of the commuter train. The woman walked slightly ahead of the man, taking long, determined strides. Determination was also stamped on her face, while her companion's expression was impatient, slightly irritated. As soon as they entered the baggage car, he turned on her in accusation.

"What do you mean, you're not coming? You can't just pull out at the last minute, for pity's sake. The entire script revolves around you."

"Then you'll just have to revise the script," she replied coldly. "Improvise, darling. That's what you're so good at, isn't it—ad-libbing, rewriting each scene as you play it?"

His eyes narrowed at the venom in her voice. "All right, what's going on? Did they really offer you the commercial, or is canceling out at the last minute just a petty way to get back at me for something you imagine I've done?

The woman inhaled a sharp, angry breath. "I got the commercial, all right. Call my agent and check if you don't believe me. And as for what I 'imagine' you've done…" She withdrew a small manila envelope from her purse. "Look at these and then tell me what an overactive imagination I have.''

The man accepted the envelope with a wary frown. He removed four grainy black-and-white photographs from it, stiffening in surprise as he examined them one by one. ''Where did you get these?''

''That doesn't matter. What matters is that I have them. Did you honestly believe I wouldn't find out about you and that phony redhead?''

He shrugged as he slipped the photographs back into the envelope. ''Okay, so I've been sleeping with her. It doesn't have anything to do with you . . . with us. She's a means to an end, that's all. Her old man has the money and the connections I need. He could open a lot of doors for me.''

''Right.'' The woman's tone was openly derisive. ''I'm sure he'd be only too happy to help further the career of his wife's lover.''

''Don't be an idiot! He'll never know. She realizes what a fantastic setup she's got, and she's not about to jeopardize it. But she's willing to put in a good word for me now and then, so why shouldn't I make the most of the situation?''

''And you're an expert at making the most of whatever opportunities come your way, aren't you?'' Now the woman's voice was laced with bitterness. ''Or perhaps I should say you're an expert at using people.''

The man's mouth curved in a complacent smile. ''Only people foolish enough to allow themselves to be used, darling,'' he countered smoothly.

She paled. ''You bastard.'' Both her voice and her expression were taut with the effort of maintaining control. ''You've humiliated me once too often.''

''Is that so?'' he mocked softly. ''And what, pray tell, do you intend to do about it?''

The swiftness of her reply told him she'd anticipated the question. ''I'm not going to do anything. You are. You're going to stop seeing her, as of now. If you don't, I'll make sure that you no longer have a career to worry about. I'll send those pictures to her husband.''

A long, charged silence preceded the man's quiet reply. ''I'm afraid I can't allow you to do that, darling,'' he said as he ripped the envelope and its contents in half.

Chapter Two

Vicky was eager to see the interiors of the renovated cars but felt reluctant to board the train until Cole Madigan reappeared. Michael Espinoza, the man who'd been absent when she joined the group, had returned a couple of minutes ago; except for the buxom strawberry blonde, the others had already gone aboard to locate their compartments. The other woman also seemed to be waiting for someone. She confirmed it when Vicky asked.

"Yes, my sister. She was supposed to meet me here. I can't imagine what could be keeping her."

"Maybe she got hung up in traffic," Vicky suggested.

"Mmm, that's probably it. I just hope she doesn't miss the train. We've been looking forward to this weekend for months."

The woman had one of those slightly breathless, little-girl-lost voices that always set Vicky's teeth on edge. She was ultrafeminine, from the soles of her stylish high-heeled sandals to the improbably long lashes fringing her china-blue eyes. Vicky wondered who colored her hair. It was too blond to be called auburn, too red to be called blond and too subtly shaded to be anything but a very expensive dye job.

"My name is Paula Danvers." The hand she proffered could only be described as dainty, and her smile displayed a mouthful of small, perfectly straight, perfectly white teeth.

As Vicky provided her own name, it crossed her mind that Paula Danvers and Cole Madigan would make a well-matched pair. No doubt Paula would think so, too, once she'd seen him.

"Excuse me, ladies." They both glanced up at the conductor, who had come out onto the platform between the last two cars. "We seem to be missing three of our passengers. Would either of you happen to know a Mr. Hamilton, a Mr. Madigan or a Ms. Wagner?"

"Ms. Wagner is my sister," Paula told him. "As far as I know, she's planning to be here."

"And Mr. Madigan's already at the station," Vicky added. "I spoke with him about ten minutes ago. He said he had to make a phone call."

Frowning, the conductor consulted a large gold pocket watch, muttered something about schedules and disappeared back inside the Pullman car.

"What time does the train leave?" Paula asked anxiously.

"Five forty-five, on the dot. They've got exactly four and a half minutes to get here."

Cole Madigan made it with two minutes to spare. Vicky spotted his golden head when he was still about fifty yards away. She waved to get his attention, then urgently pointed to her watch. He nodded to let her know he'd got the message, slung his garment bag over his shoulder and broke into a jog.

There were two frames left on the film in her camera, and she couldn't think of a subject she'd rather use them for. She didn't bother to change the f-stop setting, which meant the pictures would probably be cluttered with a lot of background detail. That was all right. These particular shots weren't intended for publication.

She lost him for a moment when he swerved to avoid colliding with an elderly couple. The second she picked him up in the viewfinder again, her finger hit the shutter release. A shock of hair had fallen onto his forehead, the front of his sport coat was flapping open, and his mouth was curved in an amused grin as he looked straight into the camera's lens. Vicky snapped the second shot just as he passed the green litter barrel she'd been standing beside when she'd first seen him.

He slowed to a brisk walk for the last couple of yards. He was still grinning. "Could I get a copy of one of those?"

Wonder of wonders, he didn't appear to have noticed Paula Danvers. "For a souvenir, you mean?" Vicky asked. "Sure, I guess so."

His grin widened as he reached up to push his hair back into place. "Actually, I thought I'd send it to my mother. She's always telling me I should get more exercise. Has everyone else boarded already?"

"Everybody but us." As she introduced him to Paula, Vicky reflected that his mother needn't worry that he was out of shape. His fifty-yard sprint hadn't left him even a little short of breath.

Cole shook Paula's hand and murmured a polite "Pleased to meet you." Then, apparently oblivious to the admiring glint in her eyes, he turned back to Vicky. "Do I need to check in or something?"

Before she could answer, another man bustled up, dropped his suitcase and released an explosive breath. "Thank goodness! I was afraid I'd missed the train."

Evidently Paula didn't believe in playing favorites. She gave the newcomer an appreciative once-over as he took a moment to smooth a hand over his stylishly cut, light brown hair. "You must be Mr. Hamilton."

After they'd all introduced themselves, Todd Hamilton reached into the pocket of his burgundy blazer and produced a folded piece of paper. "I stopped at the information desk to make sure I wasn't headed for the wrong track, and they asked if I'd bring this message to a Miss Danvers." He handed the note to Paula. "I hope it's not bad news."

Her forehead creased in a troubled frown as she read the handwritten note.

"Is it from your sister?" Vicky asked.

"Yes," Paula murmured. "Her nine-year-old fell out of a tree and broke his arm this afternoon. They're keeping him in the hospital overnight." She refolded the paper and shoved it deep into her purse. "Looks like I'm on my own for the weekend," she said in a woe-is-me little voice.

As they gathered their luggage and climbed the steps to board the train, Vicky thought that Paula Danvers was one woman who would never be on her own for long. Cole Madigan might not have succumbed to her obvious charms—yet—but judging by the way Todd Hamilton hurried to take charge of her suitcase, Paula needn't worry about feeling left out or lonely this weekend.

The passengers who'd already boarded were dodging in and out of their own and one another's compartments, admiring the luxurious accommodations and speculating among themselves about what to expect during the weekend. Cole and Todd stopped to show the conductor their tickets and find out which compartment they'd been assigned. Since Vicky already knew she would be in the last one, she started down the corridor to stash her suitcase and camera bag.

One of the middle-aged gentlemen smiled and politely backed through an open door to make way for her. Vicky smiled back and murmured a quiet "thank you." As she passed him, his friend stuck his head out of one of the doors down the aisle to remark that the petit point on the pillows was simply darling. Vicky halted for a second in surprise. *Simply darling?*

By the time she reached her compartment, she'd learned that Michael Espinoza and his father, whose name was Fred, both lived in St. Louis and owned a small but thriving chain of Mexican fast-food restaurants and that the married couple were Jayne and Gary Kayser, from Detroit. Jayne casually took possession of Vicky's camera bag and carried it the rest of the way, for which Vicky was grateful. She'd brought along three different lenses and an assortment of film, and the thing weighed almost as much as her suitcase.

"I wish we'd thought to bring a camera," Jayne said as she deposited the bag on one of the bench seats that would later convert to berths. "Maybe if you get some really good pictures, we could have copies made."

"You'll have to take a number and get in line," an attractive male voice remarked. Both women looked around to see who had spoken. Cole Madigan stood in the aisle, leaning one shoulder against the door frame.

"Oh, my," Jayne fairly purred. "Where did *you* come from?"

"Dubuque, originally," he answered. "But I've lived in Chicago for the last six years."

Vicky searched his face for an indication that he was joking, but she could find none. Jayne seemed amused by his straight-faced response. Vicky wondered if he was always so dense. Twice in the last ten minutes a good-looking woman had displayed overt interest in him, and both times he'd acted as if he hadn't even noticed.

Paula suddenly appeared at Cole's shoulder, announcing in a perky voice that she and Vicky were going to be roommates. Cole stepped aside to let her enter.

Terrific, Vicky thought as Todd followed Paula in with her suitcase. She'd hoped to have a compartment to herself so she could start putting together her story. She didn't really expect the action to begin until they reached the inn, but in the meantime she wanted to get some of the background material roughed out.

"That's nice," she said with all the sincerity she could muster.

"Isn't it?" Paula agreed. "When my sister had to cancel, I was afraid I'd be stuck in a compartment all by myself. As it turns out, they had all three of us assigned to this one, anyway."

"And Cole and I are right next door," Todd put in.

"How convenient," Jayne remarked. "I don't suppose any of you would admit to being an actor."

Todd grinned, revealing laugh lines at the corners of his hazel eyes. "Don't look at me. I'm an ordinary bookkeeper by day and a struggling CPA student by night."

Vicky decided that this would be a good time to start spreading the word about who she was and why she was there. She explained that she was only along to gather material for a newspaper article and that she would prefer everyone to think of her as an impartial observer rather than an active participant.

"A reporter, huh?" Todd murmured. He gestured at the camera, which she'd placed beside the camera bag on one of the benches. "Does that mean we can all expect to see ourselves on the front page?"

"I doubt my editor will feel this story rates a spot on the front page," Vicky said dryly. "More likely you'll find it sandwiched between Pet Care and Gardening Tips in next week's Sunday supplement."

She suddenly remembered that Todd was the only member of the group she hadn't managed to get a picture of. She was about to mention the fact when a deep voice called a question from somewhere up the aisle.

"Is there a luscious redhead among the mob down there?"

Cole glanced from Jayne to Paula and called back, "Two, as a matter of fact."

"Well, if one of them's missing a husband, tell her he's gone to the bar car with the Espinozas."

"Not without me, you don't!" Jayne yelled. Cole hastily stepped out of her way as she made for the door. She started to pass him, then stopped. "How about the dreamboat from Dubuque?" she teased with a smile. "What's your story?"

Cole looked puzzled. "I beg your pardon?"

"Assuming you're not one of the actors, what do you do for a living?"

"I assure you, I'm not an actor." From the tone of his voice, he might have been assuring her that he wasn't a child molester. Vicky ducked her head to hide a grin. "Since you asked, I'm a physicist."

Paula gaped at him in speechless awe. Todd rolled his eyes in a way that conveyed extreme skepticism.

"How interesting," Jayne murmured. "What kind?"

"I beg your pardon?" Cole said again.

"What kind of physicist are you—bio, nuclear... what?"

"Oh, I see. My field is molecular physics. I'm presently attempting to develop a new family of liquid crystal polymers."

Vicky wondered if he was putting them on. Jayne didn't appear to have any doubts. She shook her head confidently.

"Bull. No man with your looks and sex appeal would shut himself up in a dull old laboratory with nothing to play with but test tubes and Bunsen burners. You must be one of the actors."

Without further comment, she breezed past him to join her husband and the Espinozas. Vicky watched Cole's handsome face, intrigued by the expressions that chased one another across it. He'd looked startled at Jayne's succinct "Bull," then embarrassed by the remark about his looks and sex appeal, and finally mildly insulted when she'd concluded that he must be one of the actors. Vicky thought that if in fact he was, he was an extremely talented one.

Cole glanced around and caught her gazing at him speculatively. His eyebrows pushed together over the bridge of his nose. "I *am* a physicist." He sounded as if he were daring her to dispute the fact.

Vicky hastily squelched a grin. "Bully for you. Are you a thirsty one, by any chance? I heard somebody mention the bar car a couple of minutes ago."

His frown cleared, and his mouth relaxed, curving in a slightly sheepish smile. "As a matter of fact, I am. Give me half a minute to stow my things."

Vicky had forgotten that Paula and Todd were still in the compartment. When she turned from the door to collect her purse, she almost collided with Todd, who had picked up her camera and was examining it.

"Nice piece of equipment," he remarked as he handed it to her. "Is it Japanese?"

"No, German," Vicky replied. She checked all the settings to make sure he hadn't inadvertently changed one. "Cole and I are going to join the others in the bar car. Want to come along?"

They both did, but Paula said she needed to stop at "the little girls' room" first. She went to find it while Todd followed Cole to their compartment to deposit his luggage, as well. Remembering that she had to load a fresh roll of film before she could take any more pictures, Vicky rummaged in the camera bag until she found a roll of the high-speed film she'd brought for interior shots. Cole appeared in the doorway just as she'd finished rewinding the exposed roll and popped it out.

"Ready?" he asked.

Vicky dropped the exposed film into her jacket pocket, thinking she'd get around to labeling it later. "Just a second," she murmured as she ripped open the fresh roll. She had the camera loaded and ready to operate in less than ten seconds. "Okay, all set."

When she turned back to the door, she was surprised to find him watching her with a curiously intent expression. *Strange,* she thought as he stood aside to let her exit the compartment. *You'd think he's never seen anybody load a camera before.* Maybe he really was an absentminded genius who'd spent his entire life surrounded by test tubes and Bunsen burners.

Then again, maybe he just wanted everybody to think he was.

They had to pass through the dining car to reach the bar car, and for a while Cole thought they might not see the other passengers again until dinner was served. Vicky photographed everything in sight, exclaiming over the plush maroon velvet drapes, the damask table linens, the crystal, the silverware, the paneling and even the light fixtures, which she informed him were either authentic antiques or excellent reproductions.

"This car alone must have cost a fortune to renovate," she said as she took out a stenographer's pad and made a few notes to supplement the pictures. "No wonder these weekends are so expensive!"

The bar car was just as elaborately furnished, with lots of dark, gleaming wood and genuine leather upholstery. A white-jacketed bartender dispensed libations from behind a massive oak bar equipped with an old-fashioned rail. There were even a couple of brass cuspidors, which Vicky photographed while Cole ordered their drinks.

"Do you always take this many pictures?" he asked as he handed Vicky her drink.

"No, not always. It depends on the story. I doubt the editor will approve more than one or two photos for this particular piece, but I want to have a good selection for her to choose from. Which reminds me—I didn't get a picture of Todd before we boarded. I'd better do that now."

Cole took a quick inventory of the car's occupants. "That might be a little difficult. He doesn't seem to be here."

"That's strange," Vicky murmured. Gary and Jayne Kayser were there, sitting at a table with the Espinozas, and Paula was flirting with the two middle-aged male friends over in a corner. One of the men chuckled at something she'd said, while the other put a match to his pipe and puffed to get it started. "I assumed he'd come on ahead."

"I'm sure he'll be along soon. Why don't we grab that couch in the corner before somebody else does?"

As he made the suggestion, he casually placed his right hand on the small of her back. Vicky liked the subtlety of the gesture. It let her know that he wanted to spend some time with her, get to know her better, but that he was asking rather than insisting. At any other time she wouldn't have hesitated to accept the invitation. Unfortunately, she reminded herself, she was there to work.

"I really should do some mingling," she said with an apologetic smile. "I'd like to get a little background information from each of the participants—what attracted them to the mystery weekend, what they do when they're not playing detective, that kind of thing."

"I'm a participant," Cole pointed out. "Couldn't you start with me?"

"I could," she answered dryly. "But if I did, I might never get around to any of the others."

She saw surprise flicker in his eyes as she turned away, and she expected him to come after her, to follow up on the opening she'd given him. When he didn't, she was more than a little disappointed.

"I can't believe you walked off and left Golden Boy standing there all by himself," Jayne remarked when Vicky took a seat at the table the Kaysers were sharing with the Espinozas. "Are you allergic to good-looking men or something?"

Vicky grinned. "Obviously not. I'm surrounded by three of them right now."

Within five minutes she'd learned that Fred Espinoza had changed his first name from Fernando when he emigrated to the States from Mexico thirty years ago and that it had been Michael's idea for the two of them to substitute the mystery weekend for their annual fishing trip.

"He's the mystery addict in the family," Fred claimed, inclining his head toward his son. "I wouldn't know a clue if I tripped over it."

"Don't be so sure," Jayne told him. "This is our first mystery weekend, too, but we have friends who've gone on similar trips. From what they've told us, the clues should start piling up any time now."

"What do you mean?" Vicky asked curiously. Jayne merely smiled and told her to wait and see.

"Has anyone figured out who the actors are?" Michael wondered.

"I'm fairly sure Jayne is one of them," Gary replied. She punched him on the arm.

"Our blond Adonis is still the most likely candidate as far as I'm concerned," she said. "I mean, honestly, would you expect a molecular physicist to spend his weekends running around the countryside trying to solve phony murders?"

"If he really is a physicist, he'd probably make a better-than-average amateur detective," Michael pointed out. "To specialize in that field of science, he'd have to have an extremely analytical mind and excellent deductive-reasoning abilities."

Jayne shook her head stubbornly. "I reject that hypothesis, Michael. I'd rather think of him as a beautiful but dumb actor than a gorgeous genius."

"Careful, darling," Gary murmured. "Your prejudices are showing. For the sake of argument, let's say you're right and Mr. Madigan is an actor. There's probably at least one more thespian among us. Do you have any other candidates in mind?"

Fred Espinoza spoke up before Jayne could answer. "I do. I may not be Sam Spade, but even I figured out that Bud and Lyle over there are *very* good friends. And I've always thought a lot of actors walk light in their moccasins, if you know what I mean.''

Vicky didn't have the slightest idea what he meant, but apparently Jayne did. Noticing Vicky's baffled expression, she leaned across the table to whisper, ''They're gay.''

''Jayne, for heaven's sake!'' Gary admonished under his breath.

Vicky hastily bent over her notebook to hide her amusement.

''You're not writing that down, are you?'' Jayne demanded in alarm.

Vicky kept her head lowered until she was sure she had her grin under control. ''Don't worry, I won't quote you. What makes you think they're gay?''

''What would give anybody the idea that I'm Mexican?'' Fred countered. ''Some things are obvious.''

''Now *your* prejudices are showing, Dad,'' Michael commented.

His father grimaced. ''Don't start, Michael. I know you think I'm some kind of hidebound old fogy, but in my day certain things weren't—''

''Considered suitable topics of conversation,'' Michael interrupted. The way he said it made Vicky suspect that he and his father had covered the same territory several times before. ''Especially in mixed company. Times have changed, Dad.''

''Don't I know it,'' Fred muttered. ''People seem to feel comfortable talking about anything and everything in mixed company nowadays, from the size of their bank accounts to the newest social disease. But that wasn't what I was going to say. I was about to point out that certain things weren't...*flaunted*. And still shouldn't be, as far as I'm concerned. I'm not as narrow-minded as you make me out to be. What a person does in private is his or her own business, but it makes me uncomfortable to have people parade their . . . peculiarities in public. If that qualifies as a prejudice, I'm sorry, but that's the way I feel.''

Jayne spoke up before Michael could respond. ''I don't think that necessarily qualifies you as prejudiced, Fred. Or if you are, so am I. I'm always a little uneasy around people who are conspicuously different from me in some way.''

''Who's conspicuously different?''

They all glanced up at the question and found Todd Hamilton standing behind Gary, a drink in his hand. While Vicky would have enjoyed hanging around to see what direction the conversation would take next, she decided this might be a good time to move on. She excused herself with the explanation that she wanted to get a few more pictures and spend some time with the other passengers. Todd took her place at the table.

For the next few minutes Vicky busied herself taking candid photos, including several of Todd. While she'd been visiting with the Kaysers and the Espinozas, Cole had wandered over to join the trio in the corner, giving Paula Danvers another male to bat her eyelashes at. *It's a wonder the wind doesn't knock him over,* Vicky thought as she advanced the film for another shot.

Deciding she'd taken enough pictures for one night, she capped the lens of the camera and made room for it in her large shoulder bag. She was zipping the bag closed when a commotion at the bar caught her attention. Michael Espinoza had apparently gone back for a fresh drink and discovered something lying in the dish of salted nuts.

''What is it?'' Jayne asked as she hurried over. The rest of the group quickly followed.

Michael displayed the object on his palm for everyone to see. ''It looks like an earring.''

''It looks like a *diamond* earring,'' Paula corrected in a reverential tone.

Gary Kayser stepped forward. ''May I?'' Michael shrugged and handed it to him. Gary held the earring up to the light, studying it from several angles. "It *is* a diamond. Flawless blue-white, about a quarter of a carat."

"Are you a jeweler?" Fred Espinoza asked.

"No," Jayne replied. "A diamond merchant."

Vicky conscientiously added that bit of information to her notes.

"I'm also the man who bought this particular earring, and its mate, as an anniversary present for his wife." Gary handed the earring to a startled Jayne.

"It must have fallen out," she said as she threaded the gold wire through her left earlobe. When it was securely fastened, she lifted her hair to display a matching diamond teardrop dangling from each ear.

"But why did the person who found it leave it on the bar?" Paula asked with a frown. "I'm not wearing earrings, and neither is Vicky. He must have known it was yours, so why didn't he just return it to you?"

"I imagine it's our first red herring."

The quiet remark had come from Cole. Vicky glanced at him in surprise. "What do you mean? How could Jayne's earring be a red herring?"

"It focused everyone's attention on Jayne," Gary explained. "Which was probably the reason it was left on the bar. As Jayne said earlier, a few of our friends have taken part in these mystery weekends. According to what they've told us, it's standard practice for everyone to plant clues that seem to point to someone else. The problem is, you can never be sure which clues are real and which are merely red herrings."

Paula laughed delightedly. "Oh, I get it! When Jayne lost her earring, whoever found it kept it until he got the chance to plant it in the peanuts."

"Or she," Fred Espinoza pointed out. "It could have been you or Vicky, for all we know."

Vicky quickly spoke up in her own defense. "Wait a minute, Fred. I'm an impartial observer, remember."

Jayne's brows arched speculatively. "So you say. But it's possible that you're actually an actress pretending to be a reporter."

Vicky was taken aback, but only for a moment. "It's also possible that you put your own earring in the peanut dish."

"Or Gary could have put it there for you," Paula added. "Or maybe Michael had it all along and only pretended to find it there."

"This is starting to get awfully confusing," one of the middle-aged men murmured at Vicky's shoulder. She wasn't sure whether he was Bud or Lyle, but she agreed with him.

"We haven't introduced ourselves yet," she said with a smile. "I'm Vicky Rand."

His name was Lyle Skelton. He introduced his friend as Bud Potts. Bud volunteered the information that he and Lyle were the co-owners of a beauty salon in Peoria. When Jayne heard that, she caught Vicky's eye and gave her a "What'd I tell you" look.

It occurred to Gary to ask the bartender if he'd seen someone put Jayne's earring in the dish of nuts. He admitted that he had, then politely but firmly informed the passengers that he'd been instructed not to interfere with the proceedings in any way and could say no more. Everyone fortified himself with a fresh drink, then joined a few of the others to discuss who could or couldn't have planted Jayne's earring in the salted nuts.

Vicky moved from group to group, eavesdropping and frantically scribbling notes that she hoped she'd be able to decipher later. Bud, Lyle and Paula were convinced that the "clue" had been planted by one of the people sitting at the table. The Kaysers and the Espinozas thought it had been Bud, Lyle or Cole. Todd cast his vote for Paula. Cole listened to everyone else's theories and kept his own counsel. None of them seemed to recall that Todd had entered the bar car, apparently unobserved, after everyone else. Vicky considered mentioning that, then remembered her role of impartial observer and decided to keep her mouth shut.

After a while Bud and Lyle adjourned to their corner for a private conference. Bud seemed to be doing most of the talking. Every few seconds he waved the stem of his pipe like a baton, evidently to emphasize whatever point he was making. When Vicky had to flip to a fresh page of her notebook, she glanced around and noticed that Fred Espinoza had also lit a pipe and was puffing away. Normally she didn't object to pipe smoke—in fact, she found it preferable to cigar or cigarette smoke—but two pipe smokers in such a small, enclosed space were a bit much.

Trying to be unobtrusive, she slipped away to open one of the windows a couple of inches, then lingered a moment to inhale deeply of the cool night air. She turned around just in time to see Cole Madigan remove something from the inside pocket of his jacket and place it on the bar.

Chapter Three

Gary Kayser found the pouch of pipe tobacco a few minutes after Cole had planted it. The hubbub had barely died down when Todd discovered the stub of a theater ticket. Either by coincidence or design, the pipe tobacco was the brand Bud Potts smoked, and the ticket stub was for a performance Paula admitted she'd attended with a friend a couple of weeks ago. The way she said "a friend" made it clear that she wasn't talking about a girlfriend.

Speculation flourished, with everyone trying to keep an eye on everyone else as they all hovered within a few feet of the bar. Reminding herself that she was only supposed to observe and report, Vicky kept her knowledge to herself while she circulated among the others.

Evidently no one else had seen any of the clues being planted, which was surprising, considering the size of the car and the number of people in it. Bud was convinced that Lyle was responsible for the tobacco, even though Lyle steadfastly denied it. At first the Espinozas and the Kaysers thought Paula must have planted the theater ticket, since she was the only one to whom it seemed to mean anything. But then Michael pointed out that the ticket itself might not have been intended as a clue. He suggested that maybe they were supposed to concentrate on the name of the theater or the play, or possibly even on the date. Perhaps one of those things would lead them to discover the identity of one or more of the actors.

Before any satisfactory conclusions could be drawn, a waiter wearing a crisp white jacket and black bow tie appeared to announce that dinner was now being served in the dining car. As everyone began to file out, Cole suddenly materialized at Vicky's side.

"You don't mind if we eat together, do you?" he said with a coaxing smile. "The others all seem to be paired off."

Ahead of them, Todd and Paula were preparing to enter the dining car from the connecting platform. Vicky saw Todd's hand slip from Paula's waist to her hip for a moment before she stepped through the door ahead of him.

"He doesn't believe in wasting time," Vicky murmured.

"Neither does she," Cole replied. "Watch your step out here. It's windy, and these railings aren't very high."

She'd noticed that earlier, when they'd made their way to the bar car. A small, square observation platform was built onto the end of each coach, and the platforms were connected by a flat coupling to form a short bridge between the cars. A waist-high ornamental railing at each side was the only safety feature, if it could be called that.

Cole cupped a hand under her elbow to help steady her, for which Vicky was grateful. It had been unnerving enough to navigate the platform, with the wheels clattering against the rails and the scenery whizzing past, in broad daylight. Darkness somehow intensified the sensation of speed and made her even more aware of the rocking movement beneath her feet. Cole must have felt her involuntary shiver, because his fingers instantly curled around her arm.

"Is anything wrong?"

"I just had a horrible thought," she said as he opened the door to the dining car. "What if one of us had had a little too much to drink and lost his balance out here?"

Cole glanced back at the platform. The wind flipped his tie over the front of his unbuttoned jacket and playfully ruffled his hair. His forehead was creased in a slight frown. At that moment, he looked more like a model posing for an ad in a slick fashion magazine than some kind of scientific wizard.

Vicky was admiring his profile when, without warning, he turned to face her. Their eyes met, held, and she experienced a jolt of sexual awareness so unexpected and so strong that it left her feeling slightly disoriented. Cole felt it, too. She saw it in his eyes just before he averted them. A second later he was propelling her through the door and into the dining car.

"You, uh, may have a point. About the platform. It doesn't look very safe."

He sounded as rattled as she felt. Vicky wished he would release her arm so she could put some distance between them. Maybe then she'd be able to regain her objectivity, not to mention her equilibrium. For all she knew, he could be one of the actors. At this very moment he might be planning the phony murder. In fact, it was entirely possible that he'd already selected her to be the victim.

As one of the waiters led them to a table halfway down the car, she told herself she was overreacting. If, in fact, Cole was one of the actors, it was far more likely that he was simply trying to divert her attention from something that was happening elsewhere. She had to admit he was doing a terrific job, so far.

Four places had been set at two of the tables. Bud and Lyle had joined the Espinozas at one of them, while Paula and Todd had elected to take the table for two at the far end of the car, next to the kitchen. Jayne Kayser's mouth slanted wryly as Vicky took a seat across the table from her.

"Isn't it romantic?" she drawled. "The bookkeeper and the gay divorcée have discovered each other."

"How do you know Paula's a divorcée?" Cole asked as he shook out his napkin.

"She told me."

"After you asked her," Gary put in.

Jayne shrugged. "I was curious. She wasn't wearing any rings, and she told us that her sister was supposed to have come with her but had to cancel at the last minute. Face it, folks, Paula Danvers isn't the kind of woman who would go away for the weekend with her sister—not if there was a man she could have come with instead."

Gary heaved a long-suffering sigh. "In case you hadn't noticed, my wife is very outspoken."

A waiter appeared to place a combination salad in front of each of them, then said they had a choice for dinner of roast beef or brook trout. Vicky and Gary ordered the beef; Jayne and Cole chose the trout. Vicky noticed that Cole ate his salad without dressing. When she commented on that, he replied solemnly that one could never be sure what chemical additives processed foods might contain. She frowned down at the thick glob of Thousand Island dressing she'd just ladled out. If he was playing a part, he was certainly doing it convincingly.

The same waiter returned to serve the main course. He placed their plates before them, then started removing the stainless-steel warming covers. He got around to Vicky last. When the contents of her plate were revealed, Jayne emitted a startled squawk, Vicky jerked away from the table so fast that her chair almost tipped over, and the waiter's mouth fell open.

"Good Lord!" Gary exclaimed softly. "What is *that*?"

Jayne leaned forward for a closer look. "If it's the roast beef, I'm glad I ordered the trout."

Vicky cautiously poked at whatever it was with her fork, half expecting the thing to jump up and scurry off the table. "It looks like a dead rat," she said with a grimace. "Smothered in onions and gravy."

Cole calmly took the fork from her and jabbed it into the mess on her plate. Both Vicky and Jayne winced. "It isn't a rat," he murmured, lifting the object to study it. A surprised chuckle escaped him. "It's a hairpiece—a man's toupee!" He sounded delighted by his discovery. Vicky wondered how he would have reacted if the disgusting thing had been on *his* plate.

He used her knife to scrape off most of the gravy, then asked her if she wanted to keep the toupee as a souvenir.

She glared at him incredulously. "No."

Cole looked disappointed. "Are you sure?"

"Positive. Take it away, please," she said to the waiter, who was trying so hard not to laugh that his eyes were watering. He hastily collected her plate and flatware and within minutes had placed a generous serving of roast beef surrounded by asparagus, carrots and tiny new potatoes in front of her.

"Aren't you hungry?" Cole asked when she didn't immediately dig in.

Vicky sighed. "I was. But being served a plateful of matted hair seems to have taken the edge off my appetite."

"Oh, please," Jayne murmured, and reached for her water.

Cole turned aside to cough into his napkin. Vicky suspected he'd choked trying to swallow a laugh. She hoped his trout had bones and was overcooked. When he'd controlled his amusement, he turned back to the table and found himself confronting her level, disapproving gaze. He grinned sheepishly. "It *was* funny, in a way."

Vicky picked up her fork and started eating rather than reply. Of course he was right. If it had happened to someone else, she'd probably have fallen out of her chair laughing. But she couldn't help wondering if it had been merely coincidence that Cole had ordered the fish instead of the roast beef. She knew he'd planted at least one of the clues at the bar. She couldn't be sure he wasn't also responsible for the toupee.

"You know," he said casually, "if you took away the gravy and the onions, it would've been an almost perfect match for either of the Espinozas' hair."

Vicky glanced at him sharply. "So what? Gary has dark hair, too; not that it means anything. This was probably just another dumb practical joke, like all the so-called clues that were dropped at the bar."

Jayne agreed. "I think everybody's just been having a good time getting into the spirit of the weekend. The whole idea is to keep us all a little off balance so that we don't know what to expect next."

"If that's the case, this latest prank would have to be considered an unqualified success," Vicky muttered. "Because I sure didn't see it coming."

"But somebody did," Jayne said with a mischievous grin. "Whoever set you up. Got any suspects?"

Vicky's lips thinned in a tight smile. "Yes, as a matter of fact...and they're all sitting at this table."

Jayne laughed and lifted her water glass in salute. Gary looked startled. But Cole just gazed at her steadily, his expression inscrutable. Eventually the suggestion of a smile touched his mouth.

"So much for your status as an impartial observer," he remarked.

Vicky tried in vain to read the emotion that flickered in his eyes. Was it satisfaction? Disappointment? She'd have given a week's salary to know what he was thinking at that precise moment.

COLE WAS STUMPED. He'd spent the better part of the evening watching Vicky, attempting to analyze what she said and how she said it, the way she walked and sat and cocked her head slightly to one side when she was observing someone else. He'd been convinced that if he watched her closely enough, for long enough, he would eventually figure out what approach to use. He had been wrong.

He supposed the last couple of hours hadn't been a total waste. He'd learned a lot about her just by observing her from a distance—for instance, that she was intelligent and articulate, with a well-developed sense of humor. She was also keenly observant, not to mention thorough; she'd already taken several pages of notes and heaven knew how many pictures.

The way she was dressed provided still more information. Her tailored navy suit and low heels declared that she was a woman who took herself and her work seriously. Yet the creamy ruffles peeking out the front of her jacket added the postscript that she had no intention of totally suppressing her femininity.

She wore little makeup and no jewellry except for a slim gold watch. She'd deliberately set out to create an impression of professional decorum, and she'd almost succeeded. It was her hair that destroyed the effect. A rich, gleaming sable brown, it was randomly streaked with copper and bronze, curling slightly despite the fact that she'd obviously tried to train it to lie flat against her head. She had the kind of hair people had in mind when they referred to it as a mane.

And every time Cole looked at it, he imagined it spread over a white satin pillowcase.

It had been her hair that had first caught his attention, back at the station. Then she'd lowered the camera from in front of her face, and he'd discovered that her eyes matched its sable color perfectly, down to the tiny copper flecks in the irises. He had been aware that she was frowning at him, and why, but several seconds had passed before he'd been capable of voluntary movement. The high-voltage current that had zapped him when their eyes met had left him too stunned to do anything but stare at her like a mindless idiot.

Unfortunately, things had gone downhill from there. Each time he thought he'd gained a little ground with her, something happened to send him right back to square one. He was wary of coming on too strong, too fast, yet he was acutely aware that time was in short supply.

He knew she was physically attracted to him. That was a start, at least. Now if he could just manage to get past her instinctive caution and suspicion . . .

AFTER DINNER everyone congregated in the bar car to discuss the "clues" that had turned up so far, including the one that had appeared on Vicky's plate. The consensus was that they had all been practical jokes or red herrings and shouldn't be taken seriously. Predictably, no one was admitting to anything.

While everyone was still surreptitiously watching everyone else, the atmosphere was relaxed and convivial. Now and then someone went to the bar for a drink or left the car to visit the restroom. Vicky suspected the absences were being timed, but at least no one went rushing off to check on the absentees.

She made an effort to spend some time with each of the mystery-weekend participants, asking questions and taking copious notes. At first Cole stuck close to her side, but after a while he apparently realized that she wasn't going to let him monopolize her attention. He left her talking to Fred Espinoza and went to join Bud and Lyle at the bar.

Fred's shaggy brows drew together as he watched Cole leave. He seemed to hesitate, then blurted out, "Is that young man making a nuisance of himself?"

The question caught Vicky by surprise. "No, not really. He doesn't seem to appreciate that this is a working weekend for me, that's all. Unlike the rest of you, I can't just relax and enjoy myself for the next couple of days."

Fred made a rueful face. "Between you and me, so far I haven't been—enjoying myself, that is. I'm not even sure what's happened up till now, much less what to expect from here on in. I feel like somebody dropped me smack into the middle of an Agatha Christie book and I've already missed all the important stuff at the beginning. To tell the truth, I'd much rather be sitting in a boat in the middle of a lake right now with nothing more important to worry about than whether I'll run out of beer before I run out of bait.''

Vicky gave him a sympathetic smile. "Hang in there, Fred. The weekend's barely begun. I don't think anything really important has happened yet. And it seems to me that the key to being a successful sleuth is simply to be more observant than anyone else. If you're observant enough, who knows? You may turn out to be the one who solves the murder!''

Fred didn't appear to derive much comfort or encouragement from her words of wisdom. He said it was nice of her to try to cheer him up, then sighed resignedly and headed for the bar, freeing Vicky to do some more mingling.

She wandered over to the corner Bud and Lyle had claimed and spent several minutes listening to them wrangle good-naturedly about the pipe tobacco Cole had planted.

"I don't know why you keep denying it," Bud said in exasperation. "It's obvious that you're the guilty party. No one else could possibly have known what brand I smoke.''

Lyle heaved a theatrical sigh. "For the last time, I did *not* leave the stupid tobacco on the bar! Be reasonable, for heaven's sake. Why would I provide you with extra tobacco when I practically begged you to leave that smelly old pipe at home? You know the smoke irritates my sinuses. As a matter of fact, I feel a headache coming on now.''

"There you go again, blaming your bad sinuses on my pipe." Bud's words might have been impatient, but his voice held gruff concern. "If you'd wear those disposable masks at work, like the doctor told you to—"

Vicky didn't think either of them noticed when she slipped away. She eventually ended up sharing one of the scaled-down sofas with Michael Espinoza. Paula and Todd sat facing them across a low cocktail table that was bolted to the floor. They all ribbed Vicky about what happened during dinner, and both men used the incident as an excuse to indulge in a little light flirtation. That wouldn't have bothered her if she hadn't been so aware of Cole Madigan leaning against the bar just a few feet away, watching her like a hawk.

She didn't think he'd taken his eyes off her since he left her talking to Fred. No matter where she moved or to whom she spoke, she'd been conscious of his brooding gaze following her, studying her. It made her nervous, but more than that, it irritated her. Hadn't anyone ever told him it was rude to stare?

He had slowly but steadily worked his way through two drinks, and as she sneaked a quick glance at him, she saw the bartender hand him a third. He'd loosened his tie and unfastened the top two buttons of his shirt, and a shock of dandelion-colored hair had fallen onto his forehead. It required no small effort on Vicky's part to return her attention to the open notebook on her lap. She had a job to do, and she wouldn't get it done if she allowed herself to be continually distracted by Cole Madigan's extraordinary looks.

Cole could barely contain his frustration. With everyone else she was friendly and open; yet the second he got within five feet of her, a guarded look entered her eyes, and she transformed into the proverbial clam. If only there weren't so many other people around. Hell, if only there weren't so many other *men*. Both Todd and Michael had been blatantly flirting with her for the last half hour; worse, she seemed to be flirting back. And stewing about it from ten feet away was getting him absolutely nowhere.

"Is there room for one more?"

Vicky glanced up in surprise, but Paula responded warmly. "For one more good-looking man . . . always."

Cole's fleeting smile looked just a bit self-conscious, which automatically made it suspect in Vicky's eyes. She watched without comment as he appropriated a chair from one of the tables. He moved with the natural, fluid grace of an athlete. A runner, perhaps, or a tennis player. He wasn't tall enough for basketball or hefty enough for football. When she realized that she'd been taking a detailed inventory of his body, she quickly lifted her eyes and was startled to find that he'd been watching her. She felt an embarrassed blush climb her neck.

"Do you play tennis?" she blurted without thinking.

He looked surprised. "No. I swim, though. I try to get in between thirty-five and fifty laps a day."

As he spoke, he stretched his long legs out in front of him, casually crossing them at the ankles. Vicky's blush grew hotter. Evidently he had noticed the special attention she'd been giving the solid muscles of his thighs.

"I also ride a touring bike on the weekends," he added casually.

Vicky's eyes flashed in annoyance. "How interesting." Her tone implied that she couldn't care less what he did on the weekends, or at any other time, for that matter.

"What's a touring bike?" Paula asked.

Cole's attention was temporarily diverted, but the gleam in his eye warned Vicky that he wasn't finished needling her. "Basically, most of the ten-speeds you see people riding on the streets would be considered touring bikes. They resemble racing bikes in appearance, but they give a much smoother, more comfortable ride."

Michael remarked that his uncle had started riding a bicycle after his coronary bypass and was now up to ten miles a day. The comment initiated a discussion about their favorite forms of exercise.

Cole turned to Vicky with a smile. "How about you? Do you prefer indoor or outdoor sports?" The suggestive twinkle in his eye was impossible to miss.

"I jog," she told him flatly. "The last time I rode a bicycle, I was about fifteen years old."

"That's too bad. You should consider taking it up again. Besides being good for the heart and lungs, it's a terrific way to develop your legs."

Realizing that he wasn't going to stop until he'd provoked some kind of reaction, Vicky extended her right leg, which was crossed over her left, and pretended to study it critically. The movement caused the hem of her skirt to ride up a couple of inches. She didn't bother to pull it back down.

"Oh, do you think my legs look underdeveloped?

Cole's mouth slanted wryly. She had the most fantastic legs he'd ever seen outside a Las Vegas nightclub: long and slender, with just the right amount of calf muscle and delicate, fine-boned ankles. He wondered what they would feel like wrapped around him.

"Definitely not." He was encouraged by the glint of amused satisfaction in her eyes. At least she was no longer looking at him as if she thought she remembered seeing his face on a ten-most-wanted poster in the lobby at the post office.

He was well aware that he hadn't exactly bowled her over so far. In fact, she'd probably decided he was a hopeless nerd. He suspected it had been a mistake to tell Jayne Kayser he was a molecular physicist. The word "physicist" alone was usually enough to conjure up an image in most people's minds of an eccentric, absentminded genius in horn-rimmed glasses and a suit that looked as if it had been slept in for five nights straight. Oh, well, what was done was done. He could hardly recant the claim now and tell them all he was really Robert Redford's look-alike cousin from Dubuque. The thought caused his lips to curve in an amused smile.

A deep dimple appeared in his left cheek, and Vicky had to fight an insane urge to lean over and touch the tip of her tongue to it. She supposed she should be grateful he'd left as much space between them as he had. It was unsettling enough to have him lounging less than two feet away, with the soles of his shiny brown loafers resting an inch from her foot. She shifted position, recrossing her legs and angling her body so that she was no longer facing him. Cole's brows rose in mocking query.

He was distracting her again. Deliberately? She glanced around, but there didn't seem to be anything significant happening. Paula's eyelashes—or perhaps her voice—had apparently put both Todd and Michael into some kind of trance. A few feet away, Jayne and Fred were chatting at one of the tables, and Gary had joined Bud and Lyle at the other side of the car.

Vicky told herself she was being unduly suspicious, seeing plots and ulterior motives where none existed. Like everyone else, she'd been caught up in the mood that the mystery-weekend organizers had deliberately set out to create—a mood of expectant anticipation but also of mistrust. Cole Madigan was probably nothing more or less than he claimed to be. Still, it shouldn't be too difficult to determine whether he was actually a molecular physicist or just an actor passing himself off as one. She swiveled to face him again, smiling directly into his eyes.

"I'm embarrassed to admit it, but I'm not exactly sure what a molecular physicist does," she said. "What was it you told Jayne you've been working on—some kind of liquid crystal, wasn't it? Like in digital watches and calculators, that kind of thing?"

Cole stared at her, aware that his expression was utterly blank for the second or two it took him to regain his composure. Her sudden display of interest had caught him off guard, but what really unnerved him was the disturbing effect her smile had on his heart—not to mention his libido. He drew a deep, steadying breath and placed his glass on the table to give himself a few more seconds of recovery time.

"It's a mesogenic, or liquid crystal-forming, polymer, actually. One of a family of plastic fibers that are stronger and stiffer than steel."

Vicky looked interested but dubious. He leaned forward, resting his elbows on his thighs, his hands clasped between them.

"I know it sounds implausible, but it's true. In the lab some mesogenic polymers have exhibited fifteen times the tensile strength of steel. They're also heat-resistant up to seven hundred degrees Fahrenheit. If we can just find a way to fabricate them in forms other than fibers, they could take the place of metal in all sorts of products, from bicycle wheels to certain components of TAVs."

Vicky frowned in confusion. "Pardon my ignorance, but what on earth is a TAV?"

"Transatmospheric vehicle," Cole explained patiently. "Sort of the opposite of a space shuttle. Technically, the shuttles are spacecraft that have the ability to maneuver inside the atmosphere. A TAV is—or will be—an aircraft capable of operating in the lower levels of space, up to a hundred miles above the earth. There are already several on the drawing boards. Because mesogenic polymers are so light and so rigid, it's probable that they'll eventually replace some of the metal components used in TAVs."

Vicky comprehended approximately half of what he'd said, but that didn't prevent her from being fascinated. "But first you have to figure out how to…fabricate them—wasn't that the word you used?"

Cole nodded. "That's right. You see, most plastics are processed through a melt phase and then injection-molded to produce the shape of the finished product. But mesogenic polymers have such a high melting point that they start to decompose before they reach it. The problem is, when we mess around with the molecular structure to alter the melting point, we lose the rigidity that makes them so valuable. What I've been attempting to do…"

Neither of them noticed when Michael, then Todd and Paula, got up and left. During the next hour and a half Vicky heard more about polyamides, esters, olefins and azomethines than she would ever need or want to know. She understood roughly every fourth word he said as he tried to explain the difference between lyotropic and thermotropic formulations and even less when he got around to benzene rings and methylene groups.

Just when she had decided he couldn't possibly be an actor—nobody would put himself through the ordeal of memorizing all this stuff on the off chance that he might be called upon to recite it—his blue eyes would snare her, or that dimple would suddenly flash, and her doubts would resurface. He could have been speaking Serbo-Croatian for all she knew or cared. It wasn't his technical-sounding mumbo jumbo that enthralled her and made her oblivious to whatever was going on around them. She quite simply couldn't drag her eyes away from him, and she was loath to do or say anything that would cause him to stop talking. He had the sexiest voice she'd ever heard.

As for Cole, he lost all track of time. He could have sat there gazing into her copper-flecked eyes for days, maybe weeks. He could hardly believe she hadn't nodded off yet or found some excuse to get up and leave.

She was an incredibly good listener. He supposed that was a prerequisite of her job, but she honestly seemed interested in what he was saying. The wariness and suspicion had disappeared from her eyes. Now they were focused on him with an intensity that made it almost impossible for him to concentrate on mesogenic polymers. He talked until his mouth was so dry that his lips started sticking to his teeth. When he reached for his drink, he discovered that the glass was empty. While she waited for him to pick up where he'd left off, Vicky glanced around and made a discovery of her own.

"Everybody's gone...even the bartender." Checking her watch, she was astounded to see that it was approaching two in the morning.

"I didn't even notice when they left," Cole remarked with a sheepish grin.

Vicky gave him a sharp look as she rose from the sofa. She suspected she'd been had. Thanks to him, the only interesting anecdote she'd managed to acquire for her story was the bit about the toupee—and she had been the victim of that little prank. She didn't speak as she shoved her notebook into her bag and started for the door at the end of the car.

Cole frowned and went after her. When they stepped onto the connecting platform, he automatically clasped her arm to steady her. She stiffened in reaction. He could feel her withdrawing from him again, and it irritated him.

"Are you angry at me for monopolizing your time or angry at yourself for letting me?" he asked tersely.

Vicky didn't answer until they were halfway through the dining car. "Both, I suppose." When she reached the door, she stopped and turned to face him. "Look, I'm sure you've realized by now that I'm strongly attracted to you."

She sounded as if she resented the fact. Amusement glimmered in Cole's eyes, but he managed not to smile. "Just as you must have realized that the attraction is mutual."

She didn't bat an eye. "Of course I have, and I'm glad. Or I would be if I weren't here to do a job." She paused to let her words sink in. "That's why I'm asking you not to do anything about it—the attraction, I mean—for the rest of the weekend."

The request clearly startled him. "What? That doesn't make any sense!"

"It makes a lot of sense to me," Vicky countered. "For all I know, you could be one of the actors."

His forehead creased in impatience. "I've already told you I'm not."

"And I'm supposed to just accept your word for it? If you were an actor, you'd hardly be likely to tell me, now, would you?" Cole opened his mouth to reply, but she didn't give him the chance. "You've already managed to distract me several times."

His frown returned for a moment. "That's bad?"

"It is if you've been doing it deliberately, to make sure I don't notice something important—a clue or something."

"I see," he murmured. "Since you can't be certain I'm not an actor, you've decided to assume I am."

"I didn't say that," Vicky protested.

"Which means that every time I 'distract' you," he continued, "you're also going to assume I have some ulterior motive."

"Well..."

"There's probably a screwy kind of logic in there somewhere," Cole said thoughtfully. "But tell me... How do I know *you're* not one of the actors and that you haven't deliberately set out to distract *me*?

Vicky's mouth fell open. "Wh— That's ridiculous!"

"Now that I think about it, you did seem a little too fascinated by the subject of mesogenic polymers. How do I know you weren't just keeping me occupied while one of your cohorts set me up as the murder victim, or maybe the chief suspect?"

"Cohorts!" Vicky echoed indignantly. "I don't have any cohorts, for heaven's sake. The paper didn't even assign me a photographer!"

Cole reached around her to open the door, then urged her through it with a hand on her back. "But if you were an actor, you'd hardly be likely to tell me, now, would you?"

Vicky didn't respond until they'd entered the Pullman coach. She stopped just inside the door, raking an impatient hand through her hair to get it out of her face. Every time she went from one car to another, the wind played havoc with it.

"You know good and well that I'm a reporter." She kept her voice low in case everyone else had already gone to sleep. "I told you that at the train station, before I even knew you were one of the mystery-weekend participants."

Cole's sandy brows rose a centimeter, skeptical. "So you say. But how can I be sure you didn't know? It's possible that the actors were given a list of our names and a description of each of us. If you're really a reporter, why weren't you mingling with the others at the station? Why were you secretly taking their pictures from fifteen or twenty feet away?"

Vicky released an exasperated breath. "I didn't announce myself right away because I wanted some candid, unposed shots," she said with exaggerated patience. "Would you like to see my press card?"

He shook his head. "It wouldn't prove anything. You can buy one at most novelty shops."

Vicky regarded him in silence for several seconds. "I can't decide whether you're serious or just giving me a hard time."

His lips twitched as he turned her and started her down the aisle. "Maybe both."

They reached his compartment first. Vicky was trying to make up her mind whether or not she wanted him to kiss her good-night when he murmured a casual "See you at breakfast," and slipped inside.

She gave a mental shrug and moved toward her own compartment. When she started to open the door, Paula suddenly blocked her entry. The woman was clutching the front of a semitransparent negligee as she made a ludicrous attempt to cover her ample—and obviously bare—bosom.

"You can't come in," she said breathlessly.

Chapter Four

Vicky scowled. "What do you mean I can't come in?" Her eyes narrowing to slits, she demanded, "Who have you got in there?"

Paula smiled dreamily. "Todd."

"Well, get him out. Now! I'm tired, and I want to go to bed."

Paula turned on the full force of dewy, slightly baffled cornflower-blue eyes, causing Vicky to experience a twinge of sympathy for the hapless Todd. "Oh, but ... you mean you intended to sleep *here* tonight?" Paula's little-girl voice contained an incredible blend of confusion and embarrassment.

Vicky resisted the urge to grind her teeth. "Of course I intended to sleep here! Where did you think I'd be sleeping?"

"Well..." Paula gave her a knowing look. "We couldn't help but notice the way you and Cole sort of latched on to each other after dinner. You were so wrapped up in each other that you didn't even notice when the rest of us left."

Vicky's cheeks burned, but she didn't speak. After all what could she say?

"We figured you'd probably want to spend the rest of the night together, and since we were already thinking along that line ourselves..." Paula let a shrug and an ingenuous smile finish the sentence. "I didn't really think you'd mind, so I moved your two bags into the compartment next door and Todd moved his over here."

Vicky gaped at her incredulously. "You did *what*?"

"You don't have to thank me," Paula said as she backed into the compartment. "Just enjoy yourself tonight. I know I'm going to."

Before Vicky could form a semicoherent response, she found herself staring at the closed door. She raised a tightly clenched fist to pound on it, then reconsidered.

It would appear that she had two choices, she thought furiously. No, three. She could cause a scene and let everyone know that Paula and Todd were sleeping together. She'd probably embarrass herself in the process—and she hated scenes. Or she could go back to the bar car, spend what was left of the night on one of the cramped sofas and risk having someone find her there first thing in the morning. In which case she'd still be embarrassed and probably twisted up like a pretzel on top of it. Or...

Four steps had her standing in front of Cole's door. She closed her eyes and drew a deep, cleansing breath in a futile attempt to get her anger under control. Of all the rude, inconsiderate—   It suddenly occurred to her that Paula and Todd might have been planning this all evening and, furthermore, that Cole might have been in on their plans. What if all three of them were actors and had been manipulating her from the beginning? Maybe it was Cole's job to keep her occupied while Paula and Todd got on with setting up the fake murder. Now they'd have all night to plot in private.

On the other hand, she could be leaping to false conclusions. There was no evidence to show that Todd and Paula weren't exactly what they seemed to be—a man and a woman who had met for the first time that afternoon, been attracted to each other and decided to take advantage of the mystery trip to conduct a weekend fling. But even if that were the case, there was still Cole to consider. And Vicky had a feeling that Cole Madigan was going to turn out to be much more than appearances indicated. She lifted her hand and gave his door three brisk raps. It was opened immediately. Had he been *expecting* a middle-of-the-night visitor?

Vicky took one look at the golden hair swirling across his bronze chest and knew she should have opted for a sofa in the bar car. He was wearing a short brown terry-cloth robe, and judging by the muscular legs showing beneath the hem, little or nothing else.

"I'm sleeping with you tonight." When she realized what she'd blurted out, Vicky felt her entire body turn brick red. Cole's jaw sagged in astonishment, which didn't help. "In Todd's berth," she added hastily. "He's spending the night with Paula, and they moved my stuff over here."

"They did *what*!"

"My suitcase and my camera bag," she explained with a grimace. "Paula said she'd put them in here. Look, I'd rather not make a big scene and wake everybody up in the middle of the night."

Cole made a visible effort to recover from his shock. "No, of course not." He quickly stepped back from the door, gesturing for her to come inside. "Well. I was just, uh, getting ready for bed."

Vicky nodded stiffly. "So I see." This compartment was smaller than the one next door, and he seemed to fill most of it. There was nowhere for her to look except at him. She turned away from the disturbing sight of his chest and stretched up to drag her suitcase off the overhead rack.

"I'll just unpack my nightgown and—"

"Here, let me do that."

Suddenly the chest she'd been trying to avoid was pressing against her back, Cole's arms enclosing her like giant parentheses as he reached to take the suitcase from her. The three-quarter sleeves of his robe fell back to reveal leanly muscled forearms covered by fine blond hair. Vicky's mouth went dry. The breath she'd just inhaled staggered on the way down her throat.

"Thank you," she mumbled when he deposited the suitcase on the berth. "I apologize for inconveniencing you like this."

"Don't be silly. You're not inconveniencing me." He sounded sincere, if a bit agitated. Vicky breathed a little easier when he stepped away to collect a toothbrush and a tube of toothpaste from his open attaché case. "I'll, uh, just go brush my teeth while you change."

He was gone before she could reply. She stared at the door for a moment, her lips pursed. His old-fashioned gallantry surprised her. It also made her feel just a little bit ashamed for having been so suspicious. Obviously he hadn't known anything about Todd and Paula's plans for the night; what was more, he apparently didn't intend to take advantage of the situation. Vicky wasn't sure whether that made her feel more relieved or disappointed. She tugged on her Garfield nightshirt and headed up the aisle to the ladies' room.

When she returned to the compartment, she found that Cole had already made up both berths and was lying under the covers on his. A sheet and a lightweight blanket covered him to the waist and not a centimeter beyond. Vicky refused to allow herself to speculate about what he was or wasn't wearing beneath the sheet, and she managed not to stare at him for more than a couple of seconds as she thanked him for making up her bed.

"It was no trouble," Cole replied. "Cute nightshirt."

Vicky couldn't tell if he was serious or making fun. Just in case it was the latter, she quickly climbed into bed and pulled the covers up to her chin, then reached up to turn off the light.

"Good night," she said in a low, self-conscious mutter.

In contrast, Cole's voice was a soft, incredibly sexy murmur that caused goose bumps to sprout on the back of her neck. "Good night, Vicky. Sweet dreams."

She was so acutely aware of him lying nude or nearly nude just a few feet away that at least an hour passed before she was able to get to sleep. She lectured herself about the importance of maintaining her professional objectivity. She reminded herself that she was there to work, not to play, and also that it was entirely possible that the hunk occupying the other berth was planning to "murder" her sometime during the next couple of days.

Eventually she fell asleep, but it was a sleep disturbed by dreams of a handsome blond man wearing a white lab coat and horn-rimmed glasses—and absolutely nothing else.

Several hours later she was jolted awake by the piercing screech of the train's brakes. Before her conscious mind could identify the sound, she was sliding out of bed and onto the floor between the two berths.

"Oh! What the—"

"Vicky! Are you all right?"

Cole's anxious voice came from directly above her. For a moment Vicky couldn't remember who he was or why he was sleeping in the same room with her. When she did, she struggled to sit up before he could take it into his head to climb out of bed and check her condition for himself. Unfortunately, the bedclothes were wound around her legs and lower torso as tightly as a mummy's bindings.

"Vicky?"

She swore irritably as she wrestled with the covers. "I'm okay!" There was a rustling sound above her, as if a sheet were being pushed aside, and she frantically increased her efforts to free herself. "What happened? Did we stop?"

"Not completely. I think we must have switched tracks or something. Are you sure you're all right?"

She finally managed to extricate herself and heaved a huge sigh of relief. "Positive. The only thing bruised is my dignity. Now if I can just untangle these— Oh, Lord, not again!"

The train lurched forward as precipitately as it had slowed. This time it was Cole who tumbled out of his berth. He landed solidly on top of Vicky, forcing the air from her lungs on a pained grunt. He muttered several succinct swear words as he levered himself up on his elbows.

"I hate to keep repeating myself, but are you all right?"

"I . . . think so," Vicky wheezed. "You just knocked the wind out of me. Listen, do you think you could move to one side or the other before my ribs cave in?"

He murmured an earnest apology and heaved himself over so that he was only half covering her; then he swore again, with surprising fluency.

"What's wrong?"

"The damn covers are all tangled around my legs."

Squelching a smile, Vicky reached out to help him free himself. When her palm made contact with what was unmistakably a bare buttock, she choked on a gasp. An instant later, three things happened in quick succession: Cole jerked in reaction to her touch, she snatched her hand away, and somebody knocked on the compartment door.

"Is everything okay in there?"

Vicky automatically opened her mouth to reply, but Cole quickly clamped his hand over it. "Fine," he called back. "I got thrown out of bed, is all."

There was a deep masculine chuckle from the other side of the door. "So did Jayne. She's swearing a blue streak. It looks as if no one is seriously hurt, so I guess I'd better get back to our compartment and try to calm her down. See you in the morning."

Even when he was sure Gary Kayser had gone, Cole didn't immediately remove his hand from Vicky's mouth. He could feel the tension radiating from her; she was positively stiff with it. He suspected she was furious about the way he'd shut her up. But he thought—he hoped—that part of the tension was caused by the same electrifying awareness that was making it difficult for him to breathe normally.

"I didn't want him to know you were in here," he explained softly. He felt her muscles go slack and risked lifting his hand from her mouth.

"Thank you." Vicky was embarrassed by the husky note in her voice, but there didn't seem to be anything she could do about it. "That was very...considerate."

Cole didn't reply. He hovered above her, so close that she could both hear and feel each disturbed breath as it left his body. Her mouth and throat felt parched, and suddenly there didn't seem to be enough oxygen in the compartment. Her fingers itched to reach up and touch his face. The reaction was totally insane. She didn't even know the man, for heaven's sake. He could be married with five kids or some kind of warped sexual pervert or...

He whispered her name, an ache in his voice that echoed the one in her body. The next thing she knew, his warm, hard mouth was fastened on hers, and her arms were lifting to clasp him to her.

Spontaneous combustion.

The phrase flashed through Vicky's mind as Cole wrestled with the yards of percale and flannel keeping them apart. When he didn't free them from the bedclothes quickly enough, she reached down to help him. Somehow, despite all the twisting and turning, their mouths never broke contact. He muttered impatient curses against her lips between deep, hungry kisses, and when the only thing between them was a pair of beige bikini panties, he moaned into her mouth.

"Oh, Vicky!" His voice sounded strained as his palms skimmed the outer curves of her breasts. He placed tiny, nibbling kisses at the corners of her mouth, over her chin and down her neck. "I've been wanting to do this for hours...ever since I looked up and saw you taking that woman's picture back at the station."

His lips closed softly on an erect nipple. Vicky's hands plunged into his hair, then clenched as his cheeks and tongue began a gentle tugging that sent heat surging through her. She gasped for air. This was happening too fast. Much too fast. He wasn't giving her time to think, to consider. To choose. Her mind objected strenuously. Unfortunately, her body didn't seem to be listening.

"Cole! No, Cole. Stop."

She pulled at his hair until he reluctantly lifted his head. The only illumination in the compartment came from the moonlight slanting through the venetian blind at the window. It created bizarre silver stripes across Cole's face as he gazed down at her. His chest heaved with his agitated breathing; his erection pressed into her hip like a brand. Vicky called on every scrap of willpower she possessed to keep herself from moving against him.

"Why should I stop?" he whispered. "We're adults, and we both know what we want." One of his hands slipped inside her panties, his fingers curling in a possessive clasp. Vicky's breath lodged in her throat. "We want each other." His voice grew hoarse as he thrust against her with restrained but unmistakable urgency. She moaned helplessly.

"I need you." His fingers slipped inside her, wringing another tormented moan from her throat. She tried and failed to prevent her hips from lifting. "And you're ready for me," he murmured against her neck. "In fact, you're more than ready, aren't you, sweetheart? You want me as much as I want you. Tell me . . . let me hear you say it."

Vicky struggled to resist his seductive voice and the promises his talented fingers were making. She knew instinctively that making love with him would be a glorious experience for both of them. She was tempted. He would never know how tempted. But in the end, plain old common sense won out over the heated, exciting pulse and throb of desire.

"Yes." Even as she made the admission, she was tugging his hand away. Next she pushed against his chest, and though Cole tensed, he let her shove him away without offering any resistance. "I want you. If I said I didn't, you'd know I was lying." She took a moment to steady her voice. "But I'm not going to make love with you. Not now, and certainly not like this."

She was careful to avoid his eyes as she rose to her knees and started searching for her nightshirt among the sheets and blankets. Cole raked both hands through his hair, then moved to sit with his back against the compartment door, arms wrapped around his knees. His robe was hanging from a hook just above his head, within easy reach. He could have yanked it down and put it back on, or reached out and pulled part of the bedclothes over to cover himself. He did neither. Vicky could have hit him for his total lack of self-consciousness.

The ensuing silence started out strained and quickly became nerve-racking. Finally locating her nightshirt, she hastily pulled it over her head, then realized she had it on inside out. Swearing under her breath, she yanked it off and started over.

"I think I understand the 'not now'," Cole said quietly. "We've known each other approximately—" he paused to glance at his watch "—nine and a half hours. But I'd like to know what you meant by 'and certainly not like this'."

He sounded coolly composed, almost remote, while Vicky was seething with embarrassment and frustration. She pushed her hair out of her face and gave him a resentful glare that was probably wasted, since her back was to the window.

"What I meant was, not on the floor of a moving train, with all the romance and...and finesse of two animals in heat," she snapped. "Is that plain enough for you?"

Not waiting for an answer, she jumped up and began trying to separate one set of bed linens from the other. The sheets were fairly easy to untangle even in the dark, but the blankets were another matter altogether.

"The hell with it," she muttered after several futile attempts. She was bent over her berth, doing her best to smooth out the rumpled sheet, when something that felt like a giant pillow bounced off the back of her head.

"Here's your blanket," Cole announced belatedly.

Vicky stooped to retrieve it from the floor. "Thank you." The words were forced past stiff lips.

"You're welcome. In case you're interested, you've got your nightshirt on backwards."

Vicky gritted her teeth and didn't deign to reply. She climbed into bed, yanking the sheet over her head before she attempted to rearrange her nightshirt—again. As she performed the necessary contortions, she could have sworn she heard a throaty chuckle from the other berth.

A PALE GRAY LIGHT was visible through the slats of the venetian blind when Vicky woke up. She turned her head on the pillow to sneak a quick look at Cole. One of his arms was folded across his bare chest; the other dangled over the edge of the narrow berth. Slowly she eased out of bed and reached for her suitcase. She'd prefer not to confront him just yet. Not until she'd at least washed her face and brushed her teeth and her hair.

Cole lay absolutely still, watching through one slitted eye as she hauled her suitcase down and fished around in it for a change of clothes. She looked good first thing in the morning—damn good, he thought. Her hair was a riot of soft, undisciplined curls and waves, but it looked terrific that way. For a moment he was tempted to tell her so. Then she stretched up to replace her suitcase on the rack, and he forgot all about her hair.

The bottom of her nightshirt rode up at least six inches, baring the entire length of her heartbreakingly beautiful legs and the seat of her beige silk panties. Cole had to make a conscious effort to keep his breathing slow and regular. Unfortunately, there wasn't a thing he could do about his accelerated pulse or the fact that an increased supply of blood was suddenly rushing to a certain area of his anatomy. Without warning, Vicky turned toward him. He instantly lowered his left eyelid that last millimeter.

Vicky had intended to slip out before Cole was awake, then go dress in the ladies' room. But when she turned for the door, she made the mistake of glancing at him to check that he was still asleep. He was sprawled on his back, his gold-dusted chest rising and falling rhythmically. The top edge of the sheet formed a straight line between the twin points of his pelvis, barely preserving whatever modesty he possessed. The temptation to feast her eyes on him for a minute or two was too great to resist., After all, he was asleep. He would never know.

What was she doing? Why hadn't she left? Cole didn't dare open his eyes to find out. If she realized he'd been awake all along, she'd probably be furious with him for playing possum. He tried to concentrate on keeping his muscles relaxed and his breathing regular. The trouble was that no matter how convincingly he feigned sleep, there was a very strong possibility that his body was about to give him away. The heat in his groin was reaching a critical level. If she didn't leave soon, he was going to have to roll over. He just hoped the damn sheet didn't slip any lower when he did.

Vicky indulged herself a few seconds longer, then reluctantly turned away. Just as she opened the door, Cole mumbled something in his sleep and flopped onto his right side. Glancing back, she noticed that the movement had dislodged the sheet and exposed his left buttock. For a moment she considered tiptoeing back to peek over him and see what else might have been exposed. Then she decided not to push her luck. What if he woke up and caught her leering at him? Grimacing at the very thought, she slipped out of the compartment and closed the door behind her.

She had finished dressing and was standing in front of the small lavatory mirror, trying to coax her unmanageable curls

into manageable waves, when she heard voices. Evidently a
man and a woman had stopped in the corridor just outside
the restrooms. Expecting the woman to enter, Vicky made
a face at her reflection and started cramming her things into
a small cosmetic bag that had *Stuff* printed on one side.

"I still say it was damned inconsiderate of her, canceling
out at the last minute like that," the woman said tersely.

Vicky's hands stilled. That didn't sound like Paula's
slightly breathless, irritating-as-hell little-girl voice. But who
else would be complaining about a "her" who'd canceled
out at the last minute? Setting the bag in the marble wash-
basin, Vicky crept to the door and pressed her ear against it
just in time to catch the man's response.

"Don't fret about it, darling. We'll manage. And you
can't really blame her for jumping at the chance to do this
commercial. The product's practically a household word.
The network exposure alone will be invaluable to her career."

Vicky tensed. *Commercial? Network exposure?*

"I suppose you're right," the woman said with a sigh.
"But not having her along is certainly going to complicate
things. The entire script revolved around her role. I don't see
how we're going to carry it off without her."

Script! Vicky could hardly contain her excitement. If only
she could see the couple outside. Their conversation made
it obvious that they were actors, but somehow their voices
were too distorted for her to identify either of them.

"We'll just have to improvise," the man murmured.
Vicky could imagine him shrugging carelessly. His voice
deepened as he added, "And we excel at improvisation,
don't we, darling?"

His companion gave a husky laugh. "I'd say it's our spe-
cialty." There was an extended silence that made Vicky
wonder if they might be locked in a clinch, and then the
woman spoke again. "We'd better join the others before

they start to wonder where we are. I think our little reporter is already beginning to get suspicious.''

"She's suspicious of everybody," the man said dismissively. He chuckled softly. "It's a shame Erica couldn't make it. She could have done her radical social-reformer routine and kept everybody busy wondering if she might have planted a bomb in the luggage."

Their voices started to fade, but Vicky managed to catch most of their last exchange.

"By the way, I liked what you did with the toupee last night. That was a nice touch . . . very dramatic."

"Wh—Good Lord, I didn't plant that disgusting thing. I thought you did."

"Me? Heavens, no! But if you didn't, and I didn't, then . . ."

"Who did?" Vicky finished aloud.

Cautiously, she eased the door open, but the corridor was empty. Oh, well, she would just have to hope that sooner or later someone would slip up and say or do something to identify himself or herself as one of the actors she'd just overheard.

The woman had to have been either Paula or Jayne. If it was Jayne, the man with her was probably Gary; and if it was Paula, the man was probably Todd. Then again, maybe not. Both Paula and Todd were attending the mystery weekend alone, as was Cole Madigan. Could the man have been Cole?

When Vicky returned to his compartment, it was empty. His blanket and sheet were neatly folded and stacked at one end of his berth. It would appear that he was a tidy, well-organized man. That would seem to lend credibility to his claim that he was a scientist . . . wouldn't it?

She quickly folded her own bedclothes, then collected her purse and headed for the dining car. She was anxious to see which members of the group were already there and which ones hadn't yet left their compartments. She was especially eager to find out if either of the other women hadn't shown up for breakfast, and also whether one of them had exchanged her partner for Cole this morning.

Both Paula and Jayne were there. So was Cole—and Todd, and Gary. *Terrific,* Vicky thought. At this rate, the weekend would be over before she figured out who the actors were.

She studied the five of them surreptitiously as she made her way along the buffet table. Once again Paula and Todd had taken a table for two, while Cole shared one with the Kaysers. Vicky was trying to convince herself that she didn't really want two croissants when the door at the end of the car opened and the Espinozas entered. They were followed closely by Bud and Lyle.

Michael Espinoza smiled warmly and made a beeline for the buffet table. Vicky saw Cole frown and start to rise from his chair, then apparently change his mind. She was relieved. After what had happened—or almost happened—during the night, she'd rather not have to make polite conversation with him across the breakfast table. When Michael invited her to join him and his father, she accepted gratefully. She didn't even mind that he deliberately moved his chair closer so that his leg rested against hers or that he started flirting outrageously the minute they were seated. Well, actually she did mind; but at the moment she felt better able to cope with his unwelcome attentions than with Cole's disturbing blue gaze.

Michael's smile was dazzling as he held a dainty china pitcher poised above her cup. "Cream?"

Her lips formed an answering smile that was friendly without being encouraging. "Just a drop or two, thanks."

She'd met enough men like Michael to know how to handle him. He was still young enough—under thirty, she'd guess—to believe that good looks, charm and sex appeal were a combination few women could resist. Unfortunately, he was well aware that he'd been blessed with impressive amounts of all three attributes.

"Have I told you how delectable you look this morning?" His knee pressed against hers as he spoke. Vicky shifted away from him, not bothering to disguise the movement as anything other than withdrawal. She had tried being pleasant but reserved. He'd refused to take the hint and back off. She didn't want to risk offending his pride, especially in front of his father, but at the same time she was determined to get the message across that she simply wasn't interested.

"As a matter of fact, you have." Although she spoke lightly, her smile hinted that she found his flattery boring.

A dark flush spread upward from Michael's collar. His eyes darted across the table. Luckily, his father didn't appear to have noticed the exchange. Not surprising, Vicky thought in amusement. Fred's attention was focused exclusively on his own side of the table.

Lyle Skelton had joined Vicky and the Espinozas, while Bud had claimed the vacant chair across from Cole. It was obvious to anyone who cared to look that Lyle's presence made Fred more than a little uncomfortable. After observing the two of them for a few minutes, Vicky began to suspect that Lyle had taken the seat beside Fred for that very purpose. Her first inkling came when Lyle complimented Fred on his "divine" taste in clothes. Fred was wearing brown twill trousers and a lemon-yellow polyester knit shirt. She squelched a smile and sat back to enjoy the show.

"Tell me, Fred—is the food served in your restaurants prepared from your own recipes?"

"Yes, it is," Fred answered without thinking, then hastily added a qualifier. "That is, they're family recipes. I got most of them from my mother."

"How interesting!" Lyle exclaimed. "That's something else we have in common."

Fred almost choked on his coffee. "I beg your pardon?"

"I have quite a few of my mother's recipes, too. As a matter of fact, one of my favorites is for Four-Alarm Chili. Of course, I've had to adapt it to accommodate Bud's sensitive tummy. The old dear simply cannot tolerate highly spiced foods. I've also found that adding a spoonful of brown sugar neutralizes some of the acid in the tomatoes and gives the chili a much more civilized taste."

Fred mumbled that he'd have to try that sometime. Vicky had to give him credit. Despite his obvious discomfort, his manners couldn't be faulted. Michael might consider his father a "hidebound old fogy," to use Fred's words, but as far as she was concerned, the junior Espinoza could learn a few things from the senior about tolerance and forbearance.

Fred seemed to hesitate for a moment, absently stirring his scrambled eggs with the tines of his fork. "You, er, said that was something else we had in common," he muttered, not quite meeting Lyle's eyes. "Our mothers' recipes, I mean. What was the other thing?" He sounded as if he weren't at all sure he wanted to know.

"Why, fishing, of course. I understand you're quite an enthusiast."

Fred stared at him in amazement. "You like to fish?"

"Do I like to fish? You might as well ask if I like to eat," Lyle said with a grin. "Set me down on the bank of a lake with a bucketful of night crawlers and a cooler of beer and I'm in heaven."

Before long the two of them were swapping stories about the one that got away and comparing recipes for filet of sole. Vicky dabbed at her mouth with her napkin to cover a smile. At precisely that moment, Lyle glanced up, caught her eye and slipped her a sober wink.

She was too distracted by the activity at her own table to notice the brooding expression on Cole's face as he watched her. She was doing it again, he thought—shutting him out, deliberately ignoring him. The hell of it was, he knew he had no one to blame but himself. He'd felt her start to withdraw from him again after that fiasco in his compartment last night.

He allowed himself roughly ten seconds to indulge in self-disgust for his stupid loss of control, then switched off the part of his brain that dealt with emotion and let the coldly analytic part take over. There had to be a way to undo the damage he'd done and allay her suspicion and mistrust. He'd done it last night for a short while; he could damn well do it again.

The schedule called for the train to arrive at a small country depot in southwestern Indiana shortly after lunch. From the depot, the passengers would be transported to the inn—or "mystery mansion," as it was dubbed in the literature they had received—where they'd stay until Sunday morning, when they would once more board the train for the return trip to Chicago.

After breakfast the group lingered in the dining car for a while, but eventually the comfortable sofas and armchairs in the bar car beckoned. Thinking it would be a good idea to get some more pictures before leaving the train, Vicky excused herself to fetch her camera from Cole's compartment.

There were still a couple of frames left on the high-speed film she'd used the night before, but she decided to go ahead and reload now with a fresh roll of all-purpose film. She labeled the exposed roll "Bar Car, Fri. nite" and dropped it into the bottom of the camera bag, then picked up the camera by its neck strap and started back to rejoin the others.

Just as she reached the bar car, the door was yanked open, and Todd Hamilton hurried out onto the platform. Vicky tried to make way for him, but the platform was too narrow for her to move more than a few inches to either side. His chest caught the point of her left shoulder, knocking her off balance, so that she staggered backward and to the right.

She heard Todd swear softly. A second later her hip collided with the ornamental railing and she felt the slender metal bars give beneath the impact.

Chapter Five

Vicky's arms instinctively flew up as she tried to regain her balance and reverse direction. She knew at once that her effort wasn't working. The flimsy railing bowed outward another half an inch.

Panic filled her throat, so that even if she'd tried, she couldn't have uttered a sound. A brief downward glance caused her abdominal muscles to contract violently. The grass beside the tracks was a bright green blur: the rail itself, an endless, gleaming silver blade. She didn't notice when the camera strap slipped from her hand. And although her fingers frantically sought something to wrap themselves around, they encountered only the wind. The railing shifted another fraction of an inch beneath her weight.

She knew with a sickening certainty that she was going to fall. In another second, maybe two, the damned railing would break apart, and over the side she would go. If she was lucky, she'd clear the tracks and the train's wheels and get off with no more than a concussion and a few broken bones. If she wasn't lucky...

Some morbid impulse drew her gaze back to the rail streaking past beneath her feet. It gleamed as brightly as the chrome on her father's restored '57 Chevy, sending sharp white needles of sunlight into her eyes. The strength left her legs. Her knees trembled, then started to fold.

And then suddenly Cole was on the platform, reaching for her, his lean fingers locking around her wrists. The strength in his hands and arms startled her as he yanked her forward, making her fear for a second that in the process of rescuing her he was going to dislocate both her shoulders. She registered movement at the periphery of her vision when Todd made a fumbling grab for the camera she hadn't even realized she'd dropped. He swore as it fell between the bars of the railing and under the wheels.

Cole's bruising grip didn't ease until he'd hauled her through the door and into the bar car. He was pale, his expression grim, his body taut with barely restrained anger. Vicky unconsciously retreated a step. Her wrists were instantly released.

"Whew, that was close," Todd said behind them. He looked as shaken as she felt.

"Too close," Cole agreed. "What happened?"

Vicky's voice wobbled a little as she explained. "I tried to come in as Todd was going out. I guess he didn't see me."

"I didn't," Todd confirmed. "Not until it was too late to stop. Are you okay?"

She assured him that she was but didn't mention that she would probably have black-and-blue marks on both her hip and her shoulder by lunchtime. Why make him feel even more guilty? she reasoned. It had been an accident, after all. Or, to be more accurate, a near accident.

She considered asking why both men had been leaving the car almost at the same time, then thought better of it. No doubt they would each have a perfectly plausible explanation, which would be impossible either to prove or disprove. Her mouth twisted in self-mockery as she realized the direction her thoughts were taking. What did she think—that they were both coming after her to do her in? Maybe they'd planned to strangle her with the strap of her camera and then toss her off the train. Oh, brother, her imagination was really working overtime this weekend!

Paula came over to see what had been going on. After she and Todd ambled off, Cole slipped a supporting arm around Vicky's waist and guided her to one of the chairs. He left her there while he got a glass of water from the bar, then held the glass to her lips when her hand shook so badly that a couple of drops landed on the front of her short-sleeved shirt.

"Thanks," she murmured with a feeble smile.

He smiled back and perched on the arm of the chair. He was closer than he'd been all morning. So close that every time she inhaled, she caught a whiff of his woodsy cologne; so close that she could see the cuticles of his neatly trimmed nails and the fine blond hairs covering his arm; so close that if she shifted a scant inch to the right, her elbow would be nudging his thigh.

She quickly averted her gaze and resisted the urge to bolt to her feet. *Good grief, Victoria. Get hold of yourself, for heaven's sake.* She was behaving like a goggle-eyed teenager in the throes of her first big crush. He was only a man, after all. Which was a little like saying the Cathedral of Notre Dame was only a church.

"Are you sure you're all right? You're still trembling."

"Delayed reaction," she muttered, and was annoyed when her voice emerged as a hoarse croak.

Cole contented himself with a noncommittal "Mmm," but Vicky could have sworn she detected a knowing gleam in his eyes.

Her annoyance was instantly transferred from herself to him. Just because he had the face of a movie star and the body of a Greek god, he probably thought he could drag her from the jaws of death, flash his dimple at her, bring her a glass of water and *zap!* she'd melt like butter on a warm day. Well, he could damn well think again. She was still ticked off about the way he'd come on to her in the middle of the night. At least that was what she told herself, ignoring the sly inner voice that suggested she just might be a little ticked off at herself for the way she'd responded.

Cole leaned across her to place the water glass on a table. The movement brought his shoulder within scant inches of her breasts. Vicky held her breath until he'd straightened again. Lord, what was wrong with her? She wasn't the type to be bowled over by a handsome face, and normally she didn't look twice at blue-eyed blond men. So what was it about this particular man that caused her heart to flop around like a beached carp every time he got within a few feet of her? Maybe she should ask him. If he really was some kind of scientific genius, he might be able to explain the chemistry between them.

Cole bent his head for a moment. When he lifted it, Vicky saw that the humor was gone from his eyes. "I owe you an apology," he said quietly, "for my crude behavior last night. You were right to be offended."

She frowned. Offended? Was that what he thought? The primary reason for her anger had been acute embarrassment; the secondary reason had been a bad case of frustration. She'd been sure he knew that. Good grief, what woman in her right mind would be offended because a man she was attracted to was overcome with passion for her?

Her frown wasn't exactly an encouraging sign. Cole impulsively reached out to clasp one of her hands. It twitched in surprise, but at least she didn't pull it away.

"Will you accept my apology?"

His expression was earnest and solemn. So was his voice. Vicky thought it was a shame he was always so serious. That dimple and those glittering blue eyes begged for a boisterous, fun-loving personality to go with them.

She knew she had to let him off the hook, but first she glanced around to make sure none of the others were close enough to overhear. The Kaysers and the Espinozas were seated around a table in the middle of the car, engrossed in conversation. Paula had settled on one of the sofas, from which she was actively flirting with Bud and Lyle; and Todd—

Now that was strange. A few minutes ago he'd been in such a hurry to leave the car that he'd almost knocked Vicky off the platform. Yet now he was lounging beside Paula, smiling indulgently as he watched her charm the socks off the two older men. Realizing that Cole was looking at her expectantly, Vicky forced her attention back to him.

"There's no need to apologize. You weren't crude, and I wasn't offended. It was just that...well, things were happening too fast. In the first place, I didn't expect you to—"

"Make a move on you?" His tone was still solemn, but the gleam was back in his eye.

Vicky prudently decided to ignore both the remark and his gently teasing gaze. "What happened was as much my fault as yours. If I hadn't let you kiss me in the first place—"

"Didn't you want me to?"

"Hasn't anyone ever told you it's rude to constantly interrupt—"

"Didn't you?" His voice was softly insistent. He leaned closer, holding her gaze as he rested an arm on the back of the chair. The top two buttons of his polo shirt were unfastened, allowing her a tantalizing glimpse of swirling golden hair and smooth bronze skin.

"Obviously, I did," she admitted with reluctance. "Otherwise I wouldn't have kissed you back."

"And you definitely did kiss me back." He hesitated briefly. "You said things happened too fast last night, that you weren't expecting me to come on so strong."

His voice was now a husky murmur, and his eyes glittered beneath lowered lashes. Vicky thought she could guess what he was leading up to. She placed a restraining hand on his chest. "If you're thinking of warning me in advance this time, don't."

"Don't warn you?" Cole asked hopefully.

"Don't make another move on me."

His expression was a comical combination of disappointment and exasperation. "Not ever?"

Vicky ordered herself not to smile. "I don't like to be pushed or backed into a corner, and I have a strong aversion to being manipulated," she said firmly. Cole looked as if he might be about to protest that he hadn't been trying to manipulate her. Since she wasn't absolutely sure that he had been, she hurried on before he could speak. "I might also remind you that I'm here to work."

She didn't add, "Not fool around," but she might as well have. Cole released a frustrated sigh. It was clear that Vicky was determined to maintain at least a semblance of objective detachment this weekend. What she apparently didn't realize was that he was equally determined to demolish both her objectivity and her detachment, at least where he was concerned.

"Fine," he said in a deceptively casual tone. "How would you like some help?"

Vicky blinked in surprise. "Help? What do you mean?"

His shoulders lifted in a negligent shrug. "As you keep reminding me, you have a story to write. I'd like us to spend some time together, get to know each other. It occurs to me that if we joined forces, we could both achieve our objectives. Besides," he went on before she could think of a reason to refuse, "now that Paula and Todd seem to have formed a twosome, we're the only people still operating on our own, which puts us at a disadvantage. You know what they say about two heads being better than one."

Though she tried, Vicky couldn't find a flaw in his logic. "Exactly what are you suggesting?"

"Simply that we team up for the rest of the weekend— pool our resources. We've both been trained to notice details, the things that everyone else might overlook. With a little luck and a lot of perseverance, we could be the ones to solve the fake murder. That would make your article even more interesting, wouldn't it?''

Of course it would. It might even earn her a spot on the front page. Well, the front page of the features section, anyway. Still, Vicky hesitated. He was suggesting a collaboration of sorts. What if he turned out to be the one who came up with all the clues, put together all the evidence and solved the phony murder with little or no help from her?

Or—and this was still a distinct possibility—what if he was one of the actors and the partnership he was proposing was merely a ploy? It would be the perfect way for him to keep informed about what she knew, at the same time making it possible for him to feed her false leads.

''Well?'' Cole prodded when a full minute had elapsed and she still hadn't responded to his suggestion. ''What do you say? Are we partners?''

Against her better judgment, Vicky nodded. ''Okay, why not? Partners it is.''

WHEN LUNCH WAS ANNOUNCED, Cole requested the table for two before Todd and Paula could claim it. Vicky gave him a suspicious look as the waiter seated her.

''You do realize that I didn't agree to this partnership just so you could play footsies under the table?''

Cole produced an expression of innocent surprise. He tucked his feet under his chair, then crossed them at the ankles, just to be safe. ''I assure you, I didn't have anything like that in mind.''

''I'm glad to hear it.''

He pretended he hadn't noticed the skepticism in her voice. ''I simply thought it would be a good idea to isolate ourselves from the others for a while—to plan our strategy,'' he added impulsively.

Vicky slanted him a wry glance as she unfolded her napkin. ''And how are we supposed to do that when we don't have any idea what to expect?''

"Well, we could start by trying to identify the actors. If we could figure out who they are, at least we'd know which people to keep an eye on."

She pursed her lips for a moment, then nodded. "All right, that makes sense. Do you have any likely candidates in mind?"

Before he could answer, a waiter bearing a tray with two covered dishes appeared. It was the same man who'd served them at dinner the night before. There was an unspoken question in Vicky's eyes as she stared at him.

"Cream of spinach soup," he hastened to inform her. "Followed by a choice of steamed vegetables or stuffed breast of chicken."

Her eyes narrowed suspiciously. "Stuffed with what?"

"Crab," the waiter replied. His tone was perfectly correct, but she thought his thin mustache quivered slightly.

"Did you actually see someone stuff the crab into the chicken breasts?" she demanded.

Cole could hardly believe she was interrogating the man like this. He leaned across the table to murmur, "Vicky, for God's sake!"

"It's quite all right, sir," the waiter assured him. Turning back to Vicky, he inclined his head slightly in affirmation. "As a matter of fact, I prepared the stuffing myself. You have my personal guarantee that any surprises you may encounter during lunch will not have come from the kitchen."

Vicky nodded brusquely. "In that case, I'll have the chicken."

"And I'll have the vegetables," Cole said.

After the waiter had departed, she noticed that Cole was staring into his bowl as though he'd never seen cream of spinach soup before.

"If my behavior embarrasses you, maybe you should move to another table," she suggested.

He lifted his head quickly. "No. I mean, I wasn't embarrassed." She gave him a level, challenging stare. "Well, maybe just a little," he amended reluctantly. "But mostly I was amazed. I don't think I've ever confronted a waiter like that in my life."

"Don't tell me," Vicky murmured dryly. "You're one of those people who's too polite to send anything back to the kitchen."

His mouth quirked in a sheepish grin. "To be honest, I've always been afraid that if I did, the cook would be so offended he'd do something terrible to the food in retaliation."

A startled laugh escaped her before she could stop it. "You're kidding."

"No," Cole said, shaking his head. "I'm serious." He looked it.

"Are you so...cautious about everything?" Vicky immediately regretted the question. She already knew that when it came to lovemaking, he threw caution to the wind, along with patience and self-control.

A smile slid across his mouth as he lifted his spoon. "You almost said 'neurotic.'" Vicky started to deny it, but he stopped her with another shake of his head. "It's all right. Even my own mother tells me I worry too much, and about all the wrong things."

"Such as the chemical preservatives in processed foods, you mean?" she teased. She picked up her own spoon and sampled the soup. It was delicious.

Cole nodded. "And how long the ozone layer will last, and whether there's any asbestos insulation in the building where I work, and, of course, the probability that sooner or later some lunatic will actually push the button that starts a global nuclear war."

Vicky gazed at him solemnly. "Those are things we should all be concerned about. Surely your mother doesn't consider them unimportant?"

"No, it's just that she has a different set of priorities. She's an attorney for the American Civil Liberties Union," he explained. "She's always been deeply committed to the fight for civil rights. She marched with Martin Luther King in Birmingham and was in Washington the day he gave his 'I have a dream' speech. A couple of months ago she was arrested for taking part in a protest against apartheid. She claims we don't have a hope of solving the really big problems facing humanity until we learn to treat one another with decency and respect."

"She has a point," Vicky murmured. "So your mother's a crusading attorney. What about your father?"

"He was what I suppose you'd call an adventurer," Cole said with a fond smile. "He died when I was in high school, during an expedition to the South Pole. He fell into a crevasse, and before the rest of the party could reach him, one of the walls collapsed. He was buried under about fifty feet of ice and snow."

Vicky was appalled. Her hand instinctively sought his. "Oh, Cole, how horrible. I'm so sorry."

His fingers closed gently around hers, as if she were the one who needed comforting. "I still miss him. I guess I always will. But it was exactly the way he would have wanted to go. He'd have hated the process of growing old, slowly losing his strength and vitality."

Vicky felt an odd mixture of compassion, curiosity and envy as she gazed into his eyes. "You must have had a remarkable childhood with parents like that."

Cole released her hand. "You don't know the half of it. In addition to my parents, I grew up under the influence of three sisters and a brother—all older than me—who are what you might call overachievers. One of my sisters is a professor of psychology at Stanford, one's a lawyer and consumer advocate in Washington, and my other two siblings are surgeons."

"My word," Vicky breathed in awe.

"Exactly."

"I would imagine you felt a lot of pressure while you were growing up. Being the youngest, I mean."

"That's putting it mildly. Don't misunderstand—my family has always been very supportive of one another. Our parents encouraged all five of us to pursue whatever careers we wanted." He paused. "They also let us know that we were expected to make some kind of lasting contribution to society. 'We're morally obligated to give back more than we take' is the way my mother puts it."

Vicky experienced an illuminating burst of insight. "And it goes without saying that psychology professors and consumer advocates and surgeons all make important contributions to society."

Her perception startled Cole. For a moment his expression was unguarded and vulnerable, before his mouth slanted in wry acceptance. "Oh, yes. Their contributions are very tangible."

"What about scientists?" she asked. "Don't their contributions count?"

"Certainly they do. The trouble is, unless a research scientist makes the discovery of the century or comes up with a new theory to explain something that's existed for ages, it's difficult to determine the actual value of his work."

"So what?" Vicky retorted indignantly. "There aren't any guidelines for determining the 'value' of an individual's work. You don't earn so many points for being a doctor or a shoe salesman or a housewife. Everyone contributes in his or her own way."

A sudden, breathtaking smile displayed Cole's dimple. "I'd love to get you and my mother together in the same room for fifteen minutes."

Vicky wasn't quite sure how to take that, so she let it pass without comment. They ate in silence for a while, but eventually her curiosity got the better of her.

"Does the rest of your family look like you?" She tried to sound only mildly interested.

The question seemed to make Cole uncomfortable. "I suppose so. We all have light hair."

"And blue eyes?"

"Well, yes, as a matter of fact. My mother's parents were Norwegian."

Vicky gave him a puzzled look, "You sound as if having blue eyes and blond hair is something you feel you should apologize for."

"I wouldn't put it that strongly. It's just that I think too much emphasis is placed on people's physical appearance—what we look like—rather than on what we are."

"You're probably right. And outward appearances can certainly be deceiving." She was thinking of Paula Danvers and her helpless-little-me act. The woman was about as helpless as a barracuda.

The cynicism in her voice made Cole wonder if she was alluding to him. He decided it might be a good idea to change the subject. "How about you—do you have any brothers or sisters?"

"Not a one." Vicky flashed a mischievous grin. "I'm afraid I'm a spoiled only child, the apple of my parents' and grandparents' eyes."

"Don't tell me," he said with a pained expression. "You were one of those overindulged brats who always got anything your little heart desired on your birthday and never had to share closet space until you went away to college."

"Guilty as charged," she admitted cheerfully. The glimmer of amusement in his eyes so disarmed her that she was totally unprepared for his next question.

"And now? Are you currently sharing closet space with anyone?"

Vicky's soup spoon halted halfway to her mouth. For a moment she thought she hadn't heard him right. Then she realized that she had. "That's a pretty personal question, wouldn't you say?"

Cole's direct gaze didn't waver. "I wanted to know."

"Whether I'm living with someone? You don't believe in beating around the bush, do you?"

"I've already told you that I'd like us to get to know each other," he pointed out. "In order to do that, we have to ask personal questions."

Vicky stared at him in exasperation. "But don't you think it might have been more tactful to start out with something like 'What's your favorite color?' or, 'Do you have any hobbies?' Do you always jump right in and ask a woman point-blank if she's living with somebody, for heaven's sake?"

Cole's brows pushed together in a perplexed frown. "No, of course not. I simply wondered if you might already be involved in a relationship, and the easiest way to find out was to ask. I don't understand why you're so upset."

Neither did she, though she suspected it had something to do with the fact that he sounded so reasonable, so logical—so insultingly unemotional.

Her shoulders moved in a restless shrug. "It's just that I wasn't expecting such a personal question," she muttered. "How would you like if I asked you something like that without any warning whatsoever?"

One corner of Cole's mouth lifted in amusement. "I imagine I'd be flattered. Since I presume you're asking now—"

"No!" Vicky shook her head adamantly. "I'm not."

"You don't want to know about my love life?"

Of course she did. But pride and pure ornery stubbornness prevented her from admitting it. She gave him a saccharine smile. "Not particularly."

His eyes told her he knew she was lying, but just then the waiter arrived with the main course so Cole decided to let the subject drop.

"All right, let's back up and start over. My favorite color is robin's-egg blue, and my hobby is collecting and studying various species of arthropods. Arachnids, in particular."

He'd known that would get a reaction. She looked at him as if she suspected he was pulling her leg.

"Did you say 'arachnids,' as in spiders?"

"Spiders, scorpions, mites. I have an especially nice collection of tarantulas," he added with a touch of pride.

"You collect those things?" Vicky could barely keep the distaste out of her voice. *Wouldn't you just know it!* she told herself. Millions of single, good-looking, eligible men running around loose, and she had to be attracted to a guy whose hobby was collecting bugs.

"I'd much rather observe them in their native habitats. Unfortunately, my work keeps me so busy that I don't often get the chance, so I try to maintain small colonies of several different species in my apartment."

Vicky was about to ask how his landlord felt about that when another thought suddenly occurred to her. "Hold on a minute. Scorpions and tarantulas live in the desert, don't they?"

"Not exclusively, though several species are indigenous to hot, dry climates. As a matter of fact, I collect most of my specimens in the Mojave Desert—that is, whenever I can spare a few hours away from the lab."

Always alert for inconsistencies in a story, Vicky detected a glaring one in his. "Your lab is in the Mojave Desert?"

She thought she'd asked the question casually, but something in her voice must have alerted Cole. His eyes narrowed, his gaze sharpening as he answered. "The one where I've been doing most of my work lately is there, yes."

His voice, which had been warm with enthusiasm a moment before, had cooled noticeably. Vicky wondered if he was wishing he'd never mentioned the lab, the desert or his bug collection.

"Yesterday you told Jayne that you live in Chicago." She watched him intently, abandoning the pretense of a merely casual interest. "That seems like an awfully long way to commute."

Cole knew exactly what she was thinking: she was convinced she'd caught him in a lie. The suspicion and mistrust were back in her eyes, and he suspected that she would like nothing better than to pounce on his story and rip it to shreds. He stifled a frustrated sigh. And things had been going so well.

"Chicago is my home base, and I spend most of my time there," he told her, controlling his irritation with an effort. "But I've been at the lab in Arizona for most of the last two months." After a brief hesitation, he added, "Conducting a series of tests and quality-control checks for the government."

Vicky didn't even try to disguise her disbelief. "Of course you have." She leaned forward slightly to whisper, "You're doing undercover work for the CIA, right?"

Cole sent a tight-lipped glare across the table. "No," he said curtly. "For NASA."

She'd been fully prepared to dig until she got at the truth, or as much of it as he was likely to reveal. She had also been fully prepared to discover that the man sitting opposite her was an actor who had slipped up—got his roles confused or something—and unintentionally given himself away. His sudden display of anger stopped her cold and forced her to take another look at her assumptions.

"You've been conducting tests for NASA?" She remembered their mostly one-sided conversation in the bar car the night before. He'd referred to the space program several times. Maybe he was telling the truth.

"That's what I said." The blunt reply was intentionally discouraging, but Vicky wasn't discouraged that easily.

"Does it have something to do with those TAVs you were telling me about last night?"

Cole was surprised that she'd remembered. Surprised, and if he was honest, just a little bit flattered. "I can't answer that question." His tone was a little less sharp than it had been a moment ago. "I can't discuss it with you at all. I've already said more than I should. Anyway, I don't know why you bothered to ask when it's obvious that you don't believe a word I've said."

Vicky felt a twinge of regret. "I apologize if I've offended you."

"I'm not offended," he told her calmly. "I'm ticked off."

The phrase seemed so out of character that she almost smiled. "Try to see it from my point of view—I'm only doing my job."

Normally Cole prided himself on being a reasonable man. At the moment, he didn't feel like being reasonable, and he damn well didn't *want* to see it from her point of view. "Maybe you should get another job," he suggested coolly. "One that wouldn't require you to assume everyone you meet is an inveterate liar."

Indignant sparks shot from Vicky's eyes. "I *don't* assume everyone I meet is an inveterate liar!"

"I see. I must be one of the privileged few, then."

She inhaled a deep breath and made herself count all the way to ten. "This is ridiculous. Are you going to stay mad for the rest of the weekend?"

Cole pretended to give the question serious consideration. Of course he wasn't going to stay mad. In fact, his irritation had already started to slip away. He'd never been able to stay angry for long; besides, it would be an unconscionable waste of time and energy to spend the next twenty-four hours arguing with her when there were so many other more pleasant things they could be doing instead.

His answer was so long in coming that Vicky began to feel a little anxious. Searching for a way to make peace, she said the first thing that popped into her head. "The answer is no."

Cole frowned in confusion. He didn't even remember asking a question. "No?"

"No, I don't share closet space with anyone, and no, I'm not involved in a relationship."

His frown cleared, and a look of pleased surprise entered his eyes. "Oh," he said softly. "I see."

Vicky waited, but he didn't add anything more. There was no way she was going to ask about his love life, not when he'd offered to tell her just minutes ago and she'd denied any interest in knowing.

"How's the chicken?" Cole asked, expending a considerable effort to keep the amused satisfaction out of his voice. Let her stew for a while. It would serve her right for always being so suspicious.

"Very good," she answered with a forced smile. So he wasn't going to tell her. He probably thought that if he didn't volunteer the information, she'd eventually break down and ask. *Don't hold your breath, Blue Eyes,* she thought resentfully. "How about your vegetables?"

"They're excellent—fresh from the garden and perfectly prepared. Would you like a taste?"

Vicky was sure she detected a thread of amusement in his voice. Her smile became strained. "No, thank you," she said primly. "I don't care for rabbit food."

When they finished the meal, he was still amused, and she was still slightly resentful. As they left the dining car, Vicky realized that they never had got around to discussing who the actors might be. For a moment she considered the possibility that the argument had been staged as a means of avoiding the subject. But that theory was so farfetched that she dismissed it almost as soon as it had occurred to her. He couldn't possibly be that devious . . . could he? No, she told herself, trying to shake off her doubts. He really had been angry at the way she'd cross-examined him.

Or acting angry, a sly voice inside her murmured.

THERE WASN'T MUCH TIME—ten or fifteen minutes at the most—before the others would begin to congregate in the bar car. With a little luck, the passenger thought, that should be long enough. It would take only a minute to slip through the door behind the bar and into the baggage car. Another couple of minutes to take a quick look around and make sure nothing had been left behind yesterday that could identify either of them. Then a minute more to get back to the bar car and all would be well. The cook, waiters and bartender had been using the door to move themselves and their supplies back and forth between the commuter train and the three mystery-train cars, so it should be safe to assume that the door wouldn't be locked.

Except it was. *Damn!* The passenger raised a closed fist to hit the solid wood, then thought better of it and let out a savagely whispered curse.

Chapter Six

Vicky stopped to use the restroom and put on fresh lipstick before going to Cole's compartment to tend to her luggage. When she got there, she saw that Cole had already gone. His garment bag was hanging beside the door, and his attaché case sat on the bench seat that had been his bed the night before.

She shouldn't, she told herself as she gazed down at the case. He might have classified documents in there. Opening it to take a peek inside could constitute a breach of national security. What if he was involved in research for the Star Wars project?

That last thought decided her. No reporter worth her salt would pass up a chance like this. Her hands shook a little as she turned the attaché case on its side and placed her thumbs over the latch releases. That it wasn't locked told her there were no top-secret papers inside. Still, there might be some kind of useful information, such as an Actors Equity card or a script.

Instead of a union card, she found socks, plain white Fruit of the Loom underwear, a tube of Crest, a toothbrush, a hairbrush and a comb. She closed the case with a wry smile and turned to drag her suitcase off the overhead rack.

Todd was just coming out of the compartment next door when she left to join the rest of the passengers in the bar car. He was carrying a woman's handbag.

"Paula forgot her purse," he explained. As he followed Vicky up the corridor, he reminded her of the close call she'd had that morning. "I'm really sorry I slammed into you like that. Are you sure you're okay?"

"Fine," she assured him with a smile. "Really, no harm done."

"Except to your camera," Todd said, reaching around her to open the door. He waited until they'd crossed the platform and entered the dining car before adding "I tried to catch it, but . . ." He trailed off with an apologetic shrug. "If your insurance doesn't cover the cost of replacing it, I'd like to make up the difference."

"Don't worry about it," Vicky told him. "It belonged to the newspaper, and I'm sure they have full coverage. If not, they'll write it off as a tax loss."

When they came to the end of the dining car, she opened the door before Todd could reach for it and stepped onto the platform where they'd collided earlier. She didn't dawdle as she crossed it.

"But what about your pictures?" Todd asked behind her.

Vicky stopped with her hand on the doorknob, glancing back at him with a puzzled frown. "What pictures?"

"The ones you took at the station and on the train. I feel terrible that you lost them."

"Oh." She shook her head and pushed the door open. "No, I didn't. I'd just loaded a fresh roll of film. I'll have more than enough shots for the article." Making a conscious effort to be pleasant, she added lightly, "So there's nothing whatsoever to feel guilty about, okay?"

She entered the bar car before he could reply. The first two people she saw were Paula and Cole. They were standing close together—very close together—and Cole's head was bent to catch something Paula was saying.

As Vicky drew within earshot, she was certain she heard Paula murmur, "Leave it to me." A second later Cole glanced up and saw her watching them. Her eyes narrowed suspiciously as he came forward to meet her.

"Talk about dirty looks," he said with a smile. "You wouldn't by any chance be jealous, would you?"

"No," she told him succinctly. "I wouldn't."

"Not even a little bit?" His tone was so hopeful that Vicky felt her mouth start to form a smile. She quickly brought it under control.

"What were you and Paula talking about?"

Cole turned his guilty start into a shrug, but Vicky wasn't fooled. "Oh, this and that. She thinks Bud and Lyle are the actors."

Right, Vicky thought cynically. *I'll just bet she does.* Vicky cursed herself. If she hadn't taken the time to rummage through Cole's socks and underwear, she'd have been here to eavesdrop on their little powwow. She'd give a lot to know exactly what had been said just before she and Todd arrived. Had Cole and Paula been hatching a plot, revising their script?

Before she could think of a way to find out, the train pulled into the small country depot.

Two late-model vans were waiting to ferry the mystery-weekend participants to the inn. Vicky had already lost a five-hundred-dollar camera. She wasn't about to risk having the three lenses—one of which would cost more to replace than the camera—thrown around the back of a van and broken or damaged. She placed her suitcase with the other luggage but kept the camera bag with her. When Cole noticed how the strap was biting into her shoulder, he offered to carry the bag for her. Vicky passed it to him with a grateful smile. While they waited for the drivers to finish loading the luggage, he drew her aside to suggest that they split up and each go with a different group.

"Is this a tactful way of telling me you've changed your mind about our partnership?" she asked.

He looked at her in surprise. "Not at all. It's just that if we split up, between the two of us we could keep an eye on everyone else."

"Surely you don't expect the murder to be committed on the way to the inn?"

"Of course not. But it has to happen sometime today or tonight, which means that someone must already be doing some advance planning."

"Selecting the victim, you mean?"

"That, and staging the murder itself, trying to decide on a time and place, setting up an alibi—who knows what else? Don't forget that after the murder's been committed, the actors will continue to play their parts. They'll be pretending to try to solve the fake crime along with the rest of us."

Vicky nodded thoughtfully. "I think I see what you're getting at. Whoever's going to commit the murder will want to do all he can beforehand to make sure he doesn't get caught. So what are you suggesting—that we should try to watch everybody, all the time, and see if we can catch somebody doing some 'advance planning'? There are only two of us, and we only have two eyes each. We can't be everywhere at once."

"We won't have to be." She thought she detected a trace of impatience in his voice. "All we have to do is use our eyes and ears. Sooner or later someone will invent an excuse to leave the group for an extended period of time. That person will probably be seeing to a few last-minute details before he or she commits the murder."

"Maybe," Vicky said with a marked lack of enthusiasm. "But not necessarily. I hate to burst your balloon, but your little theory or hypothesis or whatever you call it isn't very practical. You can't automatically assume that every time somebody excuses himself to go to the bathroom, he's actually setting up the murder."

Cole looked slightly offended. "I think it's a good plan."

"Plan?" she scoffed. "You call sitting around and watching everybody else for the next twenty-four hours a 'plan'?"

His mouth thinned in irritation. "All right. Fine. You obviously don't agree with my reasoning. If you come up with a better idea, I'll be happy to consider it." His tone implied that he thought the chances of that happening were extremely slim.

"How generous of you," Vicky muttered.

"In the meantime, we have to get to the inn, and I still think it would be a good idea for us to go in different vans."

Vicky didn't for a minute believe that anything significant was likely to happen before they reached the inn. But if she was wrong and they missed an important clue because she'd refused to cooperate, he would probably say, "I told you so," for the rest of the weekend.

"Oh, all right! Lord, you're stubborn."

"Tenacious," Cole corrected with a satisfied smile. Slipping a hand under her arm, he started steering her over to where the vans were parked. As they approached the rest of the group, he lowered his voice to a conspiratorial murmur. "Remember to keep your eyes and ears open."

"Right, chief," Vicky replied. She'd taken two steps toward the nearest van when a sudden brainstorm made her halt. "If I hear anybody talking about scripts or acting jobs, I'll be sure to let you know."

If she'd hoped to startle some kind of incriminating reaction from him, she was disappointed. He merely shook his head with a wry smile, as if he suspected she was making fun of him, then turned and headed for the other van.

Lyle Skelton had just stepped up beside Vicky when a voice shouted a warning off to their right. "Look out!"

"What the devil!" Lyle muttered. He spun on his heel and took off to see what had happened.

Vicky was right behind him as he trotted around the rear of the van. They were just in time to see Cole dive out of the path of the second vehicle. He hit the ground in a tuck, executing a perfect somersault and rolling back onto his feet in one smooth, unbroken movement. Meanwhile, Gary Kayser was racing alongside the van. He grabbed the open door and jumped inside, and a second later the van jerked to a halt.

Vicky was the first to reach Cole. "What happened? Are you all right?"

He nodded as he brushed at the legs of his trousers. "I'm fine, but I'll be damned if I know what happened. I heard somebody yell, 'Look out!' and the next thing I knew, the van was coming straight at me."

Gary hopped down from the driver's seat and came over to where they were standing. "Looks like the gearshift slipped into neutral. You're lucky Bud yelled when he did."

"He's even luckier that he's young and limber," Bud added with a relieved grin. "Are you sure you're all right, Cole?"

He reassured everyone that he hadn't sustained so much as a scratch. "Though I don't think the same can be said for Vicky's camera bag. I'm afraid I dropped it," he told her ruefully.

It wasn't anywhere in sight. They all spread out to look for it, and Michael finally spotted a section of the strap dangling from the front axle. Since Cole's clothes were already dirty, he crawled under the van to retrieve the bag.

"It doesn't look too bad, does it?" he said hopefully as he handed it to her.

Surprisingly, it didn't. One end of the strap had been torn loose from the bag, and the canvas material was streaked with dirt and grease, but at least there were no tread marks. Vicky held her breath and mentally crossed her fingers as she tugged one of the zippers open. When she'd finished checking both compartments, she exhaled a gusty sigh of relief. "All three lenses look okay. I guess the foam padding protected them."

Apparently anxious to get their passengers delivered before anything else could happen, the two drivers began urging everyone into the vans. Vicky relinquished the camera bag to one of them to place with the rest of the luggage. If being dragged under the van hadn't damaged the fragile lenses, she didn't think a short trip over rough roads was likely to.

As they left the depot, it belatedly occurred to her that Cole's near miss might not have been the accident it had appeared to be. The door on the driver's side of the van had already been open when Gary reached it and jumped inside. Why would the door have been standing open when the driver was around at the back, loading the last of the luggage? Was it possible that Cole—or someone working with him—had deliberately moved the gearshift to neutral to make it look as if he were in danger of being run down? Wasn't that exactly the sort of thing the actors might do to create a little excitement and heighten the sense of imminent danger?

Now that she thought about it, trying to provoke him into giving himself away with that remark about scripts and acting jobs might have been a mistake. If he was one of the people she'd heard outside the ladies' room that morning, he would probably go straight to the woman who'd been with him and warn her that "our little reporter" was on to them.

And he'd have ample opportunity to do that during the ride to the inn. Apparently everyone else had been thinking along the same lines as Cole. All five of the established pairs had split up for the trip. Vicky's fellow passengers were Lyle Skelton, Fred Espinoza, Gary Kayser and Todd Hamilton.

Was it merely coincidence that Cole and both women were in the same van? she wondered as she took out her notebook. She made a few hasty entries to bring her notes up to date, then spent the rest of the twenty-minute ride trying to make sense of the conversation Gary and Lyle were conducting behind her. She caught something about a man named Milo who was apparently known to both of them, but the rest was almost as confusing as Cole's lecture about mesogenic polymers.

The room assignments at the inn were the same as they'd been on the train. *Wonderful,* Vicky thought as she and Paula each received a key to the same room on the second floor. Determined not to have a replay of last night's little melodrama, she set the other woman straight about what the sleeping arrangements would be as soon as they reached their room.

"I mean it, Paula," she said firmly. "There won't be any roommate switching tonight. If you and Todd want to sleep together, that's your business, but you'll have to arrange for another room to do it in."

Though Paula didn't argue, she was clearly miffed. She opened her suitcase and began yanking things out of it in a childish display of temper. Vicky wondered if she intended to sulk for the rest of the weekend, then decided it didn't matter one way or the other.

The manager of the inn—a short, stout, balding man whose nameplate identified him as Arnold Hagan—had informed them that afternoon that tea would be served in the dining room at three-thirty. Vicky decided that her pleated burgundy slacks and pink-and-white pinstriped blouse would be acceptable dress for afternoon tea at a country inn. At three twenty-five she descended the stairs and found Cole waiting for her in the lobby. She wished the sight of him coming to meet her didn't give her quite so much pleasure. And while she was wishing, it would be a lot easier for her to remember why she was supposed to be there if he wouldn't smile at her like that.

"Where's your roommate?" he asked when he reached her. He had showered and was now wearing a pair of navy slacks and a light blue V-neck sweater over a white oxford-cloth shirt.

"Up in the room pouting because I refused to play musical beds again tonight."

"I can sympathize with her," Cole murmured as he took her arm. "I may do a little pouting myself."

Vicky refused to acknowledge the remark, much less respond to it. Neither of them spoke again until they were seated at a table in the dining room at the rear of the inn. Vicky noticed that the Espinozas had taken a table to themselves, as had the Kaysers and Bud and Lyle.

"Looks like the debriefing's started," Cole said in amusement. "Everybody's exchanging whatever information he managed to pick up on the trip from the station."

"Well, I hope you don't expect me to pass on any fascinating little tidbits," she told him. "I spent most of the ride listening to Lyle and Gary talk about frozen pork bellies and somebody named Milo."

Cole grinned. "Milo isn't a person. It's a commodity listed by the Chicago Mercantile Exchange. I take it Lyle and Gary were discussing futures trading."

"They could have been discussing Ukrainian folk dances, for all I know," Vicky said with a shrug. "But whatever they were talking about, it didn't have anything to do with planning a murder. How about you?" She deliberately kept her tone casual. "Did you overhear anything suspicious?"

Cole shook his head. "I'm afraid not. The only people I was close enough to hear were Jayne and Paula, and they spent most of the trip carrying on over some Australian actor."

He sounded as if he didn't begin to understand why two mature, reasonably intelligent adults would fritter away their time in such a ridiculous way. Vicky almost smiled. "I told you nothing would happen before we got to the inn."

A stubborn look entered his eyes, but before he could say anything, Todd spotted them from the door and strolled over to their table. Paula was with him.

"Mind if we join you?"

Cole glanced at Vicky in question. She covered her slight hesitation by spreading her napkin on her lap. "Of course not." Whatever Paula had told Todd about the ultimatum Vicky had delivered upstairs, he had apparently decided to be a good sport.

Unfortunately, the same could not be said of Paula. She was still sulking and made no secret of her resentment toward Vicky. Her petulant attitude might have created quite a strain at the table if Todd hadn't tried to make up for it. Even though his charm was a little too lounge-lizard slick for Vicky's taste, at least his enthusiasm for the mystery weekend appeared to be genuine.

"I can't wait to see which of us gets bumped off." He rubbed his palms together with a gleeful grin. "At this point I'd have to put my money on one of the Kaysers. They've got to be the actors."

"How do you figure that?" Vicky asked.

"Are you kidding? Just look at them, for Pete's sake. Have you ever seen two more perfect people in your life?" Vicky had to admit that he had a point. Jayne and Gary were wearing matching gray flannel trousers, tweed jackets and ivory turtlenecks. They looked as if they'd stepped out of an ad in *Town and Country*.

"Wait and see," Todd predicted. "One of them will catch the other in a compromising position and commit what's commonly known as a crime of passion."

"That scenario would require a third party," Cole pointed out. "Are you suggesting there are three actors in the group?"

Todd shrugged. "Maybe. But the two of them could pull it off on their own. For instance, Jayne could lure one of the men off to some secluded, prearranged spot where Gary would discover them *in flagrante delicto*. Then he could kill Jayne, the guy she was with or possibly both of them.''

Vicky shook her head. ''Sorry, Todd, but I can't see it happening that way. For one thing, the Kaysers have been playing the blissfully happy couple ever since we boarded the train.''

''And for another,'' Cole added, ''the scheme would rely too much on timing and the other man's cooperation. What if Jayne chose someone who refused to be lured?''

''I think it would be safe to assume she wouldn't pick Bud or Lyle, if that's what you mean,'' Todd replied. Vicky didn't care for the remark or the smirk that accompanied it.

''No, that wasn't what I meant.'' Though Cole's voice was soft, there was an edge to it that caused Vicky to glance at him in surprise. ''The point I intended to make was that—considering that we know a murder will be committed sometime in the next twenty-four hours and that we have no idea who the victim will be—it would be extremely foolish for any of us to allow himself to be 'lured' away from the rest of the group.''

He hadn't spoken with any particular inflection. He might have used the same tone to ask the correct time. Still, Vicky had the distinct impression that Todd had just been called a narrow-minded jackass.

Todd must have received much the same impression. His smile looked strained as he inclined his head in a stiff gesture of acknowledgment. ''Of course you're right...it would be extremely foolish. But men have been making fools of themselves over women for centuries. Which is why I still say the murder will more than likely fall into the crime-of-passion category.''

A high-pitched giggle suddenly erupted from Paula. ''Sorry,'' she said when three heads swung toward her in unison. ''It's just that you keep using that word. It struck me as funny somehow.''

Todd's forehead puckered in confusion. "What word—murder?"

"No, silly." Paula's cheeks turned a rosy pink. Lowering her eyes demurely, she murmured, "Passion."

Todd chuckled appreciatively. Cole bent his head and hid his pained expression behind his napkin. Vicky, who never would have believed a person could blush at will, ordered herself not to gag. At least Paula had defused the tension around the table. For that reason alone she should try to overlook the woman's idiocy.

From that point on they all made an effort to steer clear of potentially awkward subjects. Waitresses appeared from the kitchen, pushing carts laden with dainty sandwiches, rich cakes, and tarts, and a variety of teas. Vicky tried a bite or two of just about everything, eating with one hand and making notes with the other, at the same time trying to keep track of the conversation. Fortunately, there wasn't much to keep track of. Paula did most of the talking.

When they all rose from the table, Vicky folded her notebook and put it back in her purse, which gave her an excuse to lag behind when Paula and Todd headed toward the lounge next door.

"I hope they've got something stronger than tea in there," Cole murmured dryly. "After an hour in that woman's company, I could use a drink."

Vicky's brows lifted in surprise. "Funny, you didn't seem to mind her company on the train. In fact, I'm sure I saw the two of you having a private conversation just before we got to the depot." She deliberately stressed the words "private conversation."

Cole gazed at her silently for a moment. "We've already established that you aren't jealous. Do you think we were scheming to knock somebody off—is that it?"

"The possibility crossed my mind," Vicky replied as she started after the other couple. She took three steps, then stopped and glanced back questioningly. "Coming? Or do you have some last-minute details to see to?"

Cole released a frustrated sigh. "I don't understand you," he said, following her through the door. "Why did you agree to be partners if you don't trust me?"

"It isn't that I *dis*trust you. But until I figure out who the actors are, I'm not going to trust anybody completely."

"Including me," he muttered.

"Including you," she confirmed.

The old-fashioned furniture in the lounge was arranged in several conversational groupings. Paula and Todd had claimed a love seat in one corner, and Gary Kayser was chatting with Bud and Lyle in front of a set of French doors. From across the room, Jayne waved to get their attention, gesturing for them to join her and the Espinozas. Vicky kept talking as she and Cole wound their way around sofas, armchairs and end tables.

"Look, you shouldn't take it personally. We're all a little suspicious. Can you honestly tell me that you don't have one or two reservations about me?"

"Yes," he said without a second's hesitation. "I can. I have no doubt whatsoever that you're exactly who and what you say you are."

Vicky halted. Since Cole was only half a step behind her, his chest collided with her back. His hands instantly came up to grasp her waist, she presumed to steady her. The trouble was, the light but firm pressure of his fingers had exactly the opposite effect. Her heart gave a startled leap, and when it landed, it seemed to be pumping twice as fast.

Cole bent his head to murmur, "Do you really want to spend the afternoon listening to Jayne Kayser's gossip?" His breath was a warm caress against her ear. "Why don't we slip outside and explore the grounds?" he suggested without waiting for an answer. "It's a beautiful day for a walk, and it would be a good idea to familiarize ourselves with the layout of the place before it gets dark."

Vicky was tempted to say yes. Heaven knew she wanted to. But what if the phony murder took place while they were outside and they missed the whole thing? She could imagine herself trying to explain to her editor that the reason she'd blown the assignment was because, at the critical moment, she'd been dallying in the garden with a mild-mannered molecular physicist.

"I don't think we should," she said reluctantly. "We might miss something."

Cole's grip tightened briefly before his hands fell away. "That's just an excuse. You know nothing's going to happen while everyone's gathered in the same room."

"You're probably right, but why take chances? Besides—" she tossed a mischievous grin over her shoulder "—as someone pointed out not long ago, it would be extremely foolish for any of us to allow ourselves to be lured away from the group."

Cole muttered something under his breath, but Vicky was already moving away from him and didn't catch what it was.

Before long everyone had assembled at one end of the lounge for a lively discussion of favorite fictional detectives. Rather than rearrange the furniture, Cole and Michael Espinoza sat on the floor, and Gary perched on the arm of Jayne's chair.

The first thing Vicky had done when she received this assignment was go to the library and check out as many murder mysteries as she could carry, so at least she was able to keep up with the conversation. She wasn't surprised when Fred, Bud and Lyle all admitted to being Dashiell Hammett fans or when the Kaysers confessed that they'd considered attending the mystery weekend as Nick and Nora Charles.

"That's interesting," Bud said. "*The Thin Man* was Hammett's last novel, you know. Except for the hair, Jayne would make a perfect Nora. I believe Nick described her in the book as a lanky brunette with a wicked jaw."

Jayne seemed astonished. "Really? I've never read the book. For some reason I always pictured Nora as a redhead."

"Isn't it funny how you can form an image of a character in a book you've never read," Fred remarked. "When most people hear the name Sam Spade, they automatically think of Bogart. I suppose that's because he played Spade in *The Maltese Falcon*.

"But Bogey didn't look anything like the Sam Spade Hammett created," Lyle put in.

"You're kidding," Todd said.

Fred shook his head. "He's right. The first paragraph of the book describes Spade as looking like...what were the exact words, Lyle? Something like 'a blond vampire,' I think."

"'A blond satan,'" Lyle corrected with a grin, then quoted the line to which Fred referred. "'He looked rather pleasantly like a blond satan.' Hammett also gave him yellow-gray eyes, a long, bony jaw and jutting chin, and a hooked nose."

"That doesn't sound remotely like Bogart," Todd admitted. He sounded disappointed.

"It doesn't matter," Bud told him. "When Bogey played the part in the movie, he made it his. He *became* Sam Spade to millions of people. I must have read that book a dozen times over the years, but I'll always see Bogart's face whenever I think of Sam Spade."

Michael Espinoza said he felt the same way about Hercule Poirot, Agatha Christie's dapper Belgian detective. "I always associate Peter Ustinov with that particular character."

"Every time I go over to visit my son, he makes me watch his videotape of *Evil Under the Sun*," Fred told them dryly. "I've seen it so many times I could probably recite every line of dialogue by heart."

Vicky paused in her note taking. Had that been a clue? The tip of her ballpoint skipped down a couple of lines to make the terse notation "F.E.—dialogue."

An hour later they were still comparing detectives and detective stories. When the Travis McGee series was mentioned, Cole admitted a bit sheepishly that he'd always secretly wanted to be McGee and live on a houseboat in Florida.

"It figures," Jayne teased. "With your looks, that's just where you belong—on a beach somewhere, surrounded by nubile nymphettes in string bikinis."

"Nubile nymphettes?" Gary repeated in amusement. "Did you get that from a dirty limerick, darling?"

Jayne made a cheeky retort that drew appreciative laughter from the rest of the group. Vicky didn't think anyone else had noticed that the remark about beaches and nubile nymphettes had momentarily disconcerted Cole. After their conversation at lunch, she had finally accepted that his modesty wasn't an act. It was genuine, as much a part of him as his blue eyes and that maddeningly sexy dimple.

Cole glanced up and caught her watching him. A pleased look entered his eyes. Without being conspicuous about it, he inclined his head toward the French doors. Vicky's slight hesitation was all the incentive he needed. He came off the floor in one smooth movement, reached for her hand and pulled her up beside him.

"We've been sedentary long enough," he said before she could object. "Let's go for a walk."

"Good idea," Jayne said eagerly. "Come on, Gary; let's go with them. Anybody else want to come along?"

No one else did. As they left the lounge, Vicky saw Fred take the seat she'd vacated next to Lyle to continue their conversation. She smiled in amusement. Fred had apparently decided that being both an avid fisherman *and* a Dashiell Hammett fan more than compensated for whatever "peculiarities" Lyle might possess.

Jayne automatically took charge of their little expedition, which didn't seem to disturb Cole. Vicky was sure he had intended to leave by way of the French doors, but he followed without comment when Jayne headed off in the opposite direction. The wide archway she led them through delivered them into the lobby, where they found Mr. Hagan sorting mail at the registration desk. He looked up at their approach.

Gary spoke for all four of them. "We thought we'd wander around for a bit, if that's all right."

"Sure, go right ahead," the manager replied. "All the rooms on the first floor are open except for the office and the apartment the missus and I use right behind it. If you'd like to have a look at the grounds, you can get onto the veranda from any of the main rooms." Noticing that Vicky didn't have a wrap, he added the suggestion that she fetch one before she went outside.

"It starts to cool off well before sunset this time of year. Oh, and be sure to watch your step if you go down to the pond. The banks are pretty steep, and there's a lot of moss down there."

Cole and the Kaysers waited in the lobby while Vicky took Mr. Hagan's advice and went upstairs for a wrap. She'd brought an all-weather coat, but she doubted it would get cool enough for that, so she settled for the jacket of the navy suit she'd worn the day before. She threw it over her arm and started out of the room, then at the last minute decided to leave her bulky shoulder bag behind. Out of habit, she set it on the floor of the closet, against the wall and out of sight, should anyone glance inside, then closed the door and tested it to make sure the latch had caught. She was smiling wryly as she left the room and descended the stairs. *Yes, Mom, I remembered not to leave my purse lying in plain view on the dresser.*

On her way past the registration desk, she saw Mr. Hagan pick up a small cardboard box sitting next to the phone.

Ordinarily, Vicky wouldn't have given the box a second glance, and she couldn't have said what drew her eyes to it when he turned to carry it through a doorway beneath the staircase. *Intuition, you dope,* she thought a moment later. Someone had printed PROMO MAT'L in neat block letters on the side.

She didn't share her discovery with the others as they began their tour of the public rooms. After all, she rationalized, "promo mat'l" could refer to promotional material for the inn itself—brochures, maps, that kind of thing. The box didn't *have* to contain information pertaining to the mystery weekend. But it did; Vicky was sure of it. There might even be a list of all the people who'd been involved in putting the event together—including the actors.

She considered telling Cole, at least—they were supposed to be partners, after all—but during the next couple of hours Gary and Jayne were always within earshot, and she didn't want them to overhear. Let them find their own clues.

The inn faced west, toward the Wabash River. The lounge and adjacent dining room took up the entire southern half of the first floor. Occupying the northwest corner was a smaller room that contained a wide-screen television, one entire wall of floor-to-ceiling bookshelves and a billiards table. Behind that room were the manager's office and apartment, and at the rear was a well-equipped kitchen. The registration area was sandwiched between the lounge and the billiards/TV/reading room at the front of the building. A wide veranda ran completely around the first floor, and as the manager had pointed out, French doors opened on to it from every room except the kitchen.

"Lots of potential escape routes," Gary commented when they returned to their starting point.

Cole nodded. "And plenty of nooks and crannies that would make ideal hiding places."

"The people who picked this place sure knew what they were doing, didn't they?" Jayne said in admiration.

The remark seemed to trigger the same reaction in each of them—a feeling of restless anticipation, an excitement they watched grow in one another's eyes. An exuberant grin broke out on Gary's face. "Damn, I can hardly wait for things to start happening!"

Cole's dimple flashed in agreement. "Come on," he urged, taking Vicky's hand and pulling her toward the front door. "Let's reconnoiter the grounds."

Chapter Seven

The large clapboard-sided building was circled by a chain of gravel paths, each of which eventually led back to the veranda. They set out to follow all of them systematically.

To the north, separated from the inn by a wide sweep of lawn and several tall shade trees, was a barn that had been converted to a combination garage-equipment shed. Directly across the gravel drive from it was a fairly large rectangular parking area. Cole remarked that they should add the garage to their list of possible hiding places.

To the east, behind the inn, the ground sloped away to form a miniature valley, where they discovered the pond the manager had told them about. The pond wasn't large, not more than eighty feet long and thirty feet across at its widest point. Its shape roughly resembled that of a human footprint, with the big toe pointing toward the garage. More huge old trees surrounded it, casting deep shadows over the steeply sloping banks and all but a small area of the water. On the other side of the pond the land quickly rose again, so that the path that circled it pitched sharply down and then back up at the northern and southern ends. Trudging up the northern incline with Jayne, Vicky was glad she was wearing slacks and flat-heeled shoes.

Cole and Gary had left them several yards back to take a closer look at the pond. For what reason, Vicky couldn't begin to guess. Since they'd left the inn, the two men had been behaving like a couple of kids on a treasure hunt. She'd been amazed to see Cole's normal reserve give way to a boyish enthusiasm that made him even more appealing.

He fell into step beside her as she reached a fork in the path. The right branch led to the northern side of the inn and from there to the drive, an area they'd already covered.

"Find anything interesting?" she asked, watching Gary lope past them to catch up with Jayne.

If Cole heard the indulgent amusement in her voice, he gave no sign. "Well, we found out that Hagan wasn't exaggerating about the banks being steep and slippery. Gary almost fell in."

Vicky grinned at the thought of the svelte Gary Kayser sliding down the bank and into the algae-covered pond on his elegant backside.

"While you were upstairs, Hagan told us those banks were slicker than goose, uh . . ."

"I get the idea," Vicky murmured.

"Well, he was right. They are." Cole grinned at her and threw his right arm around her shoulders, tugging her against his side. "This is fun, isn't it?"

"A thrill a minute," Vicky said with a straight face, hoping he hadn't felt her agitation when their torsos bumped together. "What else did Mr. Hagan have to say while I was upstairs?" She was wondering whether Cole or one of the Kaysers might have spotted the "promo mat'l" box and asked about it.

Cole slanted her a shrewd look. "Afraid I might be holding out on you?"

"Are you?" Vicky countered.

He sighed. "No. Are you always so suspicious? Never mind; I already know the answer to that." He pulled her a couple of inches closer. She didn't resist. "Okay, let's see. He told us that except for himself and Mrs. Hagan—she's the housekeeper—the entire staff will go home after dinner. Also, once the Hagans have retired to their apartment, they won't come out again unless there's some kind of emergency. Gary and I figure the murder probably won't be committed until the Hagans are safely tucked away in their apartment and everybody else has left.''

Vicky couldn't resist. Letting her mouth fall open, she did a fair imitation of astonished awe. ''The two of you figured that out all by yourselves!''

''Smart ass,'' Cole said mildly.

If he'd suddenly dropped to all fours and started barking like a dog, she wouldn't have been any more shocked. ''What did you say?''

''You heard me. You saw the box, didn't you?''

Vicky's brain scrambled to change direction and keep up with him. ''The box?'' she repeated warily. ''Which box would that be?''

Cole gave her a level stare and started to draw his arm away from her shoulders.

''Oh, *that* box!'' She hastily reached up to clasp his hand. ''I was going to tell you about it.''

''Sure you were.'' He sounded skeptical, to say the least.

''I was,'' Vicky insisted. ''But I didn't want the Kaysers to overhear. Did they see it?''

Cole still didn't look convinced, but evidently he decided not to pursue the question of whether or not she'd intended to mention the box to him. ''I don't think so.''

Vicky thought he was about to say something else, but just then they rounded the corner of the inn and saw a white delivery van pull away and disappear down the drive. The name and address of a local florist were painted on the side, along with a picture of a single long-stemmed red rosebud. The Kaysers were waiting for them on the veranda. Gary speculated that it might be the Hagans' anniversary.

''Or Mrs. Hagan's birthday,'' Vicky suggested.

Rather than continue on around to the front of the inn, they reentered it by way of the French doors on the south side of the lounge. Only three members of the group were still in the room: Fred Espinoza, Bud Potts and Lyle Skelton.

"Where's everybody else?" Jayne asked at once.

Fred claimed that Michael had gone up to their room about five minutes ago to make a couple of business calls.

"And Paula and Todd left shortly after the four of you," Bud added. "We figured they'd gone outside to join you."

Gary shook his head. "No, we haven't seen them since we left."

Cole glanced at his watch. "Almost two hours ago." He and Gary exchanged a brief, meaningful look. "What's your room number, Fred?"

Cole and Gary were headed for the lobby almost before Fred had finished answering. Vicky and Jayne were right behind them as they rushed up the stairs and down the hall to the Espinozas' room. Gary pounded on the door until an obviously startled Michael yanked it open.

"What? What is it?" he asked. "Damn, has it happened already? Did I miss it?"

"Not as far as we know," Jayne answered. "Are you alone?"

Michael just stared at her for a second. "What do you mean, am I alone? Of course I'm alone. What's going on, anyway?"

Behind him, Vicky could see the telephone receiver lying next to the phone on the nightstand, where he'd obviously left it when he came to answer the door. She nudged Cole to get his attention, then mouthed, "The phone." He glanced past Michael, and his mouth twisted wryly.

"Apparently nothing's going on," he said. "We were just checking to make sure you were where your father said you were. Sorry to have bothered you."

"Checking?" Michael repeated indignantly. "You were checking up on me?"

"Don't get huffy," Jayne told him. "For all we knew, you could have been murdered while we were outside."

He glared at her. "Don't give me that. That isn't why you came to check on me. I wanted to make a few phone calls in private, for God's sake. Is that a crime?"

"Of course not," Vicky murmured in a soothing tone. She took hold of Jayne's arm and started backing away from the door, pulling Jayne with her. "We're really sorry we interrupted you, Michael. We'll leave you to finish making your calls."

His response to that was to shut the door firmly in their faces. Vicky didn't blame him for being annoyed, yet at the same time she couldn't help thinking that he'd overreacted just a bit. But on second thought maybe not. If he'd had to interrupt an important business call to deal with a bunch of paranoid mystery addicts, she supposed his irritation was justified.

"One down, two to go," Gary said as they continued down the hall to the room Cole and Todd shared. When they reached it, Cole took out his key and prepared to unlock the door. Vicky laid a hand on his arm to stop him.

"I suggest we knock first," she said dryly. "What if Paula's in there with him?"

"Good point," he muttered. He knocked briskly, waited, then knocked again. "Todd?" There was no answer. Shrugging, he unlocked the door and pushed it open.

There was no one inside, but it was obvious that one of the two double beds had recently been used. Vicky would have been willing to bet that it hadn't been for a nap.

Their discovery made them all a little uncomfortable, and they didn't linger. "I guess your room is the next logical place to look," Cole said as he followed Vicky out.

"I guess so," she agreed reluctantly. It wasn't just that she dreaded the possibility of barging in on Paula and Todd *in flagrante delicto*, to use Todd's phrase. That would be unpleasant enough, heaven knew. But she'd already antagonized Paula once today, and they did have to share the room until tomorrow morning. Vicky had a feeling that if she crossed Paula one more time, Paula would do everything in her power to make the rest of the weekend absolute misery for her.

When they reached her room, Vicky removed the key from the pocket of her slacks, inhaled a deep, fortifying breath and inserted the key in the lock.

"Aren't you going to knock?" Cole asked with a touch of anxiety.

Vicky shook her head. "If they've spent the last two hours hopping back and forth between bedrooms, they deserve to be embarrassed."

"To hell with them," Jayne blurted out. "If we barge in and catch them in bed together, *I'll* be embarrassed. If it's all the same to you, I think I'll go wait by the stairs."

Gary grinned and called her a coward. Jayne made a face at him, but she hotfooted it to the end of the hall just the same.

As it happened, there was nothing going on inside the room that would embarrass anyone. Except perhaps Cole, Vicky thought in amusement. He took one look at Paula—seated on one of the beds and wearing nothing but a couple of bath towels—and hastily averted his gaze.

Paula was also on the phone. She glanced up when Vicky and the two men trooped in, but she didn't appear at all distressed that they'd done so without giving her some kind of warning. *Exhibitionist,* Vicky thought as Paula lifted one dainty hand to check that the towel around her head was secure. It was the other one that was in danger of coming unwound, as she was no doubt perfectly aware.

"Don't let us disturb you," Vicky said. "We'll only stay a minute." Her bogus smile vanished as she turned to Cole and whispered, "Check the bathroom."

He looked at her as if she'd asked him to stand on his head and recite the Declaration of Independence, but he didn't argue. While he was gone, Vicky opened the closet door, half expecting to find Todd hiding inside. He wasn't, but she did make an interesting discovery. Her shoulder bag, which she knew good and well she'd placed against the wall, out of sight, was sitting beside her camera bag, right in front of the open door.

She casually bent down to pick it up by the strap, slinging it over her shoulder as she turned. Her jaw sagged, and she almost burst out laughing. Gary was down on his hands and knees, peering under Paula's bed, while Paula leaned over the edge and stared at him in astonishment. Cole wandered out of the bathroom just as Gary pushed himself off the floor and brushed at the knees of his elegant charcoal slacks.

"All clear," Gary announced calmly.

Paula crooned, "Hold on just a moment, darling," into the receiver, then curled her fingers over the mouthpiece and snapped, "What on earth are you looking for?"

Vicky opened her mouth to deny that they were looking for anything, which would have been such a blatant lie that even Paula would have detected it. But Cole answered the question before she could speak.

"Bugs," he said.

Vicky's open mouth stayed that way. Paula scooted over to the middle of the bed with a horrified gasp. "Bugs?"

"Roaches," Gary confirmed soberly. "The big hard-shelled kind. We saw a couple of them downstairs."

Paula shuddered in revulsion. "Oh, God. I hate bugs!"

"It's all right," Cole assured her as he started across the room. "There's no sign of them in the bathroom."

"Or under the bed," Gary added. He and Cole both looked at Vicky.

"Or in the closet," she reported dutifully, then bit the inside of her cheek to keep from laughing.

"Are you sure?" Paula demanded. "Did you look in my shoes? Sometimes the little bastards crawl inside your shoes."

Vicky was about to explode. "I'll check again," she muttered, and spun around to bury her head in the closet until she could get herself under control. She made a production of picking up a couple of shoes and shaking them vigorously, then banging the soles together and shaking them again.

"Nope, not a bug in sight," she said cheerfully as she backed out of the closet. "Well, I guess this room's clean. Come on, guys; we still have two more to check."

But when she met Cole's eyes, he shifted his gaze deliberately toward the dresser. Vicky stared at him. What was he trying to tell her? That there really *were* roaches in here? Then she saw the vase of long-stemmed pink roses, and it hit her—the van they'd seen leaving the inn had been making a delivery to Paula, not to Mrs. Hagan.

"Paula, what lovely flowers!" Vicky went over to smell them, surreptitiously searching for a card. "Are they from Todd?"

In the dresser mirror she saw Paula's reflection clasp the phone to her bosom. "No, they're not from Todd!" Paula whispered fiercely. "If you're through looking for bugs, would you mind letting me finish my conversation in private?"

Vicky had just enough time to read the inscription on the card before she turned, feigning embarrassment. "Oh! Yes, of course. Sorry," she said as she snagged Cole's elbow and dragged him to the door. Gary hurried into the hall ahead of them. By the time they caught up with him, he was telling Jayne what had happened.

"Bugs?" Jayne said, raising a sardonic brow at Cole.

He shrugged. "I had to improvise. It was the first thing that came into my head."

They went back downstairs to see if Todd had shown up yet. He had. Both he and Michael were with the three older men in the lounge. It wasn't necessary to ask him where he'd been, because when the two couples entered the room, he was critiquing a movie he'd just watched in the reading room on the other side of the lobby. A VCR was hooked up to the TV, and one of the bookshelves contained a fairly large library of videotape cassettes. Todd had spent the last ninety minutes or so watching *The Big Sleep*.

Or so he claimed. It occurred to Vicky that unless someone had happened to wander over to the reading room, it was impossible to know whether Todd had actually been there. And since no one spoke up to contradict his story, she had to assume that no one could.

Whether or not he was telling the truth, Todd's mention of *The Big Sleep* brought about a revival of the group discussion they'd had earlier. This time the topic was their favorite movie and television detectives. The Kaysers found seats and joined in eagerly, but when Vicky would have followed them, Cole grasped her arm to detain her. "Let's talk," he murmured. "Over there."

He led her to the love seat Todd and Paula had occupied earlier. Vicky settled as comfortably as she could on the stiff horsehair padding and waited for him to speak first. She'd realized while they were still upstairs that she had to make a decision about whether to trust him, and if so, how much. The trouble was, knowing she had to make the decision was a lot easier than actually making it—and then following through.

Someone had moved her purse and more than likely searched it. She knew it couldn't have been Cole or either of the Kaysers, because they'd been with her all afternoon. And Bud, Lyle and Fred had apparently been together in the lounge. That left three suspects: Paula, Todd and Michael. Or possibly Paula *and* Todd. Or Paula and Michael or Michael and Todd or—unlikely as it might seem—all three of them.

She released an inaudible sigh. There were too many possibilities and too few clues. She needed help in sorting things out; help from someone who could be objective, someone who possessed better-than-average deductive-reasoning abilities. Cole seemed the most suitable candidate. Now all she had to do was decide whether she trusted him enough to confide in him.

"The bathtub hadn't been used," the object of her thoughts said softly.

Vicky stared at him blankly. "What?"

"Remember when you asked me to check the bathroom? I thought Todd might be hiding behind the shower curtain, so I looked. Everything was dry as a bone—the curtain, the tub, even the bath mat."

Vicky frowned. "I don't get it. Paula wasn't expecting us to pop in unannounced. Why was she sitting around in nothing but a towel?"

"Offhand I can think of a couple of possible explanations. The most obvious one is that Todd had just left and she heard us coming down the hall before she could get dressed."

Vicky mulled that over for a minute. "That sounds a little farfetched. What's the second explanation?"

"She could have been getting ready to take a bath when whoever she was talking to on the phone called."

"Or when the roses arrived," Vicky added. "And she dropped everything to call whoever sent them and thank him."

Cole looked surprised. "I hadn't thought of that."

"Don't be too hard on yourself. You can't think of everything."

He grinned. "That's why I've got a partner—to catch what I miss. Speaking of the roses, did you get a chance to read what was on the card?"

"Yes. It said, 'Took the job. Meet you at the station Sunday. All my love, Jeremiah.' I presume Jeremiah was the 'darling' she asked to hold on for a minute."

"Mmm, probably. I wonder if Todd knows about Jeremiah."

"Somehow I doubt it." A crease appeared between Vicky's brows as she added thoughtfully, "It's an unusual name... old-fashioned. For some reason it seems familiar, though. I have the feeling I've come across it somewhere else, and fairly recently."

"Maybe it was in a news story."

She made a dismissive gesture. "Maybe. I'm sure it'll come to me sooner or later." Even knowing there was a good chance that Cole was one of the actors and that if he was, he was involved in whatever was going on up to his dimple, all her instincts were urging her to trust him. And she almost always followed her instincts. She swiveled to face him, drawing one bent knee under her. "While you were looking for Todd behind the shower curtain, I was checking the closet." She told him about discovering that her purse had been moved.

"You're sure someone deliberately moved it? Couldn't Paula have accidentally kicked it when she was getting something out of the closet?"

"What, a towel?" Vicky scoffed. "She wasn't wearing any clothes, remember, and she hadn't laid anything out to change into. And anyway, I left it sitting against the inside wall, right next to the door. I'm one hundred and ten percent sure about that. Assuming she *did* open the door, she shouldn't have been able to *see* the bag."

"Unless she was looking for it," Cole concluded. "You'd better check to see if anything's missing."

As far as she could tell, nothing was. "But somebody has definitely been pawing through it," Vicky muttered. "I always keep this little pocket zipped just in case the top comes off my lipstick, and I know this pen was clipped to the cover of the notebook.'' Puzzled, she shook her head. ''It doesn't make any sense. All my cash and credit cards are here, and there's nothing else of value.''

''How about your notebook?'' Cole suggested. ''Maybe someone wanted a look at it to see if you'd managed to identify the actors.''

She handed it to him. He flipped through a few pages, then glanced up with a rueful grin. ''Well, that shoots that theory. Is this some kind of secret code?''

Vicky's lips threatened to curve into a smile. ''Smart ass.'' His dimple made a brief appearance as he grinned appreciatively. ''It happens to be shorthand. Well, mostly. When I can't remember the correct symbol, sometimes I compromise by substituting a few letters of the word I want to use.''

He glanced down at the notebook. ''You mean, like 'squiggle, squiggle net exp' or 'squiggle, squiggle Erica'? I won't even ask what 'net exp' means, but who on earth is Erica?''

Vicky plucked the notebook out of his hand and stuck it back in her purse. ''Never mind. You're supposed to be figuring out why somebody went through my things, remember?''

For a second she thought he would insist on an answer to his question, but then he sighed and gave a brusque nod. ''Right. If we assume that someone wanted a look at your notes, we also have to assume that he or she didn't learn anything useful from them. But maybe it was something else....'' He trailed off, his forehead creased in concentration. Vicky waited silently.

''Suppose that someone in the group was looking for something and thought, for whatever reason, that it might be in your purse.''

''But nothing's missing,'' she pointed out.

''Which would indicate that whoever searched it didn't find what he was looking for.

"Obviously," she said in exasperation. "Will you get to the point, assuming there is one?"

Her impatience seemed to amuse him. "Hold your horses; I'm almost there. Whoever searched your purse must have had reason to believe that it might contain whatever he was looking for. The fact that it didn't is irrelevant. The point is that it was *your* purse that was searched. You have something that someone in this group wants—or at least he or she thinks you do. What we have to figure out is what that something is."

He told her to take out her notebook and make a list of everything she'd brought along that would fit inside her shoulder bag. Quickly she jotted down the various items, then asked, "What about the stuff in my camera bag?"

"Didn't you say it was sitting next to your purse in the closet?"

"Yes."

"Then it may have been searched, too. You'd better check when you get back to your room."

"There's no time like the present." She handed him the list as she rose from the love seat. "Besides, it'll give me a chance to see if Paula's still on the phone with 'All my love, Jeremiah.' Be back in two shakes."

When she returned five minutes later, Vicky saw that the other members of the group were still absorbed in their discussion.

"Paula was in the shower," she murmured as she sat down next to Cole. "And the camera bag has been searched."

"You're sure?"

She nodded. "Positive. I always store the lenses in the same pockets, and two of them had been switched. Nothing's missing, though."

The news seemed to disappoint Cole. Vicky gave him a questioning look, and he explained. "This list doesn't contain anything unusual. Jayne and Paula probably brought most of these things, too. But while you were gone, it occurred to me that you're the only one of us who's taken any pictures. I'm probably grasping at straws, but I thought someone might have been looking for your film."

Vicky considered the possibility. "That makes sense. Let's see.... I used a roll at the station yesterday and another roll last night in the bar car. That one's still in the camera bag," she added absently.

Cole's gaze sharpened with interest. "What about the first roll—isn't it in the camera bag, too?"

Vicky had been trying to remember exactly what pictures she'd taken and whether any of them might contain something that one of the group members would rather not be made public. She only half heard Cole's question. "I'm sorry, what did you say?"

"Is that the same jacket you were wearing yesterday?"

She glanced down at the jacket of her navy suit. "Yes, but what has that got to do—"

"Look in your pockets."

"What?"

Rather than repeat the request, Cole reached over and shoved a hand into each pocket. Before Vicky could decide how to react, he held an exposed roll of film in front of her nose and grinned triumphantly. "I saw you put this in your pocket yesterday, just before we went to the bar car. These are the pictures you took at the station, right?"

"Yes." She took the film from him and examined it. "I didn't even take the time to label it. Do you think this is what the person who searched my purse and camera bag was looking for?"

"Probably." Cole tapped a finger against the film. "My guess is that somebody doesn't want this developed. Can you remember who you took pictures of at the station?"

"Everybody except Todd . . . including three of you."

"You're forgetting one minor detail," he pointed out. "You know I can't be the guilty party, because I was with you all afternoon. For that matter, so were Gary and Jayne.''

Vicky knew that his argument made sense, and she hadn't ever truly considered him a suspect. So it must have been sheer perversity that made her retort, ''But any one of you could have had an accomplice—someone who stayed behind to look for the film while we were outside.''

Cole didn't bother to tell her how ridiculous that sounded. He just gazed at her steadily, his eyes narrowed to hide the expression in them. Vicky suspected it might be disgust.

''Of course, I don't actually believe that's the case,'' she added hastily.

''Of course not,'' Cole agreed in a tone as dry as dust.

She went on as if he hadn't spoken. ''Not for a minute. I was merely pointing out that it's one of several possibilities.''

''Mmm'' was his noncommittal reply. ''Another possibility is that neither your purse nor your camera bag was searched and that you concocted the whole story in order to distract me.'' Vicky gaped at him, caught between astonished disbelief and indignant offense. Before she could close her mouth, much less think of a response, he added smoothly, ''Of course, I don't actually believe that's the case. Not for a minute.''

Color flared in her cheeks. ''Touché,'' she muttered with a grudging smile. ''I deserved that.''

''Yes,'' Cole agreed. ''You did.'' Noticing that the group in the center of the room had started to break up, he glanced at his watch. ''Time to go change for dinner. It might be a good idea to stop by the desk on the way upstairs and ask Mr. Hagan to lock the film in the safe until tomorrow morning.''

If Vicky harbored any lingering doubts that he'd had something to do with the search of her purse and camera bag, his suggestion erased them immediately. She and Cole mingled with the other people filing out of the lounge, then detoured to the registration desk.

Perhaps she was being paranoid again, but it seemed to Vicky that Todd and Michael deliberately lingered at the bottom of the stairs while Cole asked Mr. Hagan to lock the roll of film in the office safe. She mentioned it to him as the manager came out from behind the desk and led them to the office.

"I doubt it means anything," he said. "You're the one who pointed out to me that we're all a little suspicious, remember? They're probably just impatient for the next 'clue' to turn up. Nobody's found one since we left the train."

Mr. Hagan opened the office door and stood aside for them to enter. They both saw the "promo mat'l" box at the same time, sitting smack in the middle of the desk blotter. While they waited for him to open the squat black floor safe behind the desk, Vicky managed to get a look at the mailing label. Sure enough, the box had been sent by the organization that sponsored the mystery weekends. She'd bet anything it contained at least the names of the actors, possibly even their publicity photos. Her eyes narrowed shrewdly as she tried to figure out how to get a look inside.

Chapter Eight

"You can't do it." Cole's low murmur couldn't have carried more than a few feet. "It would be cheating."

"It would not!" Vicky denied stoutly. Unlike Cole, she wasn't worried about being overheard. They were the only people on the stairs, or even in sight. "Cheating is when you break the rules. There's no rule that says I can't take a peek at what's in that box if I get the chance."

He gave her a stern, disapproving look. "It wouldn't be fair, and you know it."

"Says who?" she challenged. "How can you be sure that some of us weren't *meant* to see the box? We don't know how long it sat on the registration desk before we came along and noticed it. Mr. Hagan certainly wasn't trying to conceal it—it was sitting right out in the open."

They reached the top of the stairs. Cole stopped, pursed his lips and frowned down at his shoes, as if he were reluctant to concede that she might have a point.

"Besides," Vicky went on before he could think of another argument, "we're expected to follow up on whatever leads we're lucky enough to stumble across. That's the whole idea, isn't it? How else are we supposed to solve the crime—if and when it actually takes place, which I'm beginning to doubt will happen in my lifetime."

"You're rationalizing," Cole muttered. He placed a hand on the small of her back and started her down the hall with a gentle nudge. "It just seems unethical."

"Was it unethical of you to plant that pouch of pipe tobacco on the bar last night?" Vicky countered.

He came to an abrupt, startled halt. "You saw me?"

"Of course I saw you. How else would I have known? Obviously you don't see anything wrong with planting red herrings."

"Shh!" He cast an anxious glance down the hall. "That's hardly the same thing as breaking into the manager's office to sneak a look at something you know perfectly well you're not supposed to see."

Vicky closed her eyes and released an exasperated sigh. "Are you always such a stiff-necked old fuddy-duddy?"

His sandy brows pushed together over his nose. "I hardly think that objecting to the idea of breaking and entering qualifies me as a—"

"It was a rhetorical question," she interrupted with exaggerated patience. "And anyway, I never said anything about breaking and entering. I simply mentioned that *if* I happen to stroll by the office later, and *if* I happen to find the door unlocked, I might—*might*, mind you—go inside and take a look at whatever's in the box. Judging by your reaction to the idea, I guess it would be safe to assume that you wouldn't care to come along."

Cole glared at her as if she'd suggested he climb up on the roof, take off all his clothes and start yodeling. "No," he said emphatically, "I most certainly would not."

The boyishly exuberant Cole Madigan she'd spent the afternoon with had suddenly disappeared; in his place was the sober, slightly stuffy original. Oddly enough, Vicky found that she liked both models. Mischievousness made her goad him just a little more.

"Not even to be my lookout?" She heard his teeth come together with an audible click. "Guess not. Okay, relax; I won't mention it again."

"Is that supposed to set my mind at ease?"

He sounded so glum that Vicky relented. "You're a real spoilsport, do you know that? How about if I give you my word that I won't set foot in Mr. Hagan's office unless he's there. Would *that* set your mind at ease?"

A relieved smile instantly replaced his brooding expression. "Yes." His arm slipped around her waist as they started down the hall again. "Do you really think I'm a stiff-necked old fuddy-duddy?"

"Sometimes," she answered honestly.

"Then why did you give in?"

She shook her head with a rueful smile. "Damned if I know."

A surprised chuckle escaped him, and his arm tightened in a brief hug. Vicky expected him to release her when they reached his room. Instead, he passed right by it.

"I think we should keep a close eye on Paula from now on," he said as they approached the room the two women shared.

"I agree. She had plenty of opportunity to search my purse and camera bag."

"And possibly a motive for wanting to get rid of your film," Cole added. "Assuming she's involved with this Jeremiah person, she probably wouldn't want him to find out about Todd."

Vicky tugged Cole to a halt a few feet shy of her door. "Wait a minute; that's not right." There was a flaw in his reasoning. Todd had arrived late, just as the train was about to leave the station, and consequently she hadn't taken any pictures of him until later, when they were all in the bar car. But before she could remind Cole of that, he had pressed two fingers across her lips to silence her.

"What—?"

"Shh! Listen."

She quickly realized what he wanted her to listen to: a man and a woman—presumably Todd and Paula—were arguing inside the room. Cole's scruples evidently didn't extend to eavesdropping, Vicky thought as he inched closer to the door.

"Don't you think this is a tiny bit unethical?" she whispered.

He bent to murmur his reply in her ear. "The door isn't completely closed, and they're not making the slightest attempt to keep their voices down. They also know that most, if not all, of us are upstairs, getting dressed for dinner."

Vicky tried to ignore how close he was standing and how stimulating his warm breath felt against her skin. "You think they staged the argument?"

"It's possible. It could be part of the setup for the murder."

The corners of her mouth indented wryly. And he'd accused her of rationalizing! She would have given him a lecture on practicing what he preached, but in all honesty she was as eager to listen in on Paula and Todd's quarrel as he was. Toward that end, she sidled closer to the door. Just as she drew level with the frame, Cole snaked his arm around her from behind and hauled her up against his chest.

She could feel the agitated beat of his heart as he dragged her several feet back down the hall. "Not so close!" he protested in her ear. "Do you want them to see you?"

Vicky didn't answer. Her own pulse was far from steady, but her agitation had nothing to do with the fear of discovery. His arm exerted a warm, firm pressure under her breasts, while her derriere was pressed against the hard muscles of his thighs. She stood absolutely still, hoping that once they were a safe distance from the doorway, he would release her. He didn't. If anything, he seemed to crowd closer against her back, making it next to impossible for her to concentrate on what Paula and Todd were saying.

"You're getting all worked up over nothing, I tell you." That was Todd. He sounded annoyed, but there was also a hint of uncertainty in his voice. "There's no reason we can't continue to see each other when we get back to Chicago."

Paula made a frustrated noise. "You don't seem to realize what's at stake here. If he found out about you—"

"He wouldn't!"

"He would," Paula said with conviction. "Sooner or later, believe me, he would. And I don't even want to think about what would happen when he did." There was a pause before she spoke again. Her voice had suddenly become soft, coaxing. "Let's not fight about it. After all, it isn't as if I haven't been honest with you. I made it clear from the beginning that this couldn't possibly turn into a long-term relationship. I stand to lose too much—"

Todd cut her off, his voice low and harsh with anger. "Spare me, please. I can do without another recital of how much you stand to lose. You want it to be over with us— fine, it's over. But if you get back home and suddenly decide you want the kind of satisfaction that the old man's money and social connections can't give you, don't pick up the phone and expect me to come running."

Scarcely a second elapsed between the last word and the sound of quick, angry footsteps. Vicky stiffened as she realized that Todd was heading for the door. While she was frantically trying to think of what she would say when he opened it and found her and Cole lurking in the hall, Cole's other arm suddenly clamped around her rib cage.

Her feet left the floor, and almost before she could comprehend what was happening, he had covered the distance between her room and his. He set her down as abruptly as he'd picked her up, then spun her around, leaned back against the wall and pulled her between his legs. The next thing she knew, he was kissing her. Passionately.

Vicky made a sound that might have been a startled protest. Cole responded by deepening his kiss. One hand clasped the back of her head to hold her still. The other ran down her back to press her pelvis into his. The next sound to emerge from her throat was a soft moan.

When he lifted his head, her arms were around his neck, and she was resting against him. Vicky opened her eyes slowly, as if even so slight a movement required almost more strength than she possessed. She was excruciatingly aware that Cole must be able to read the desire in her eyes. It was all right, though, because when they were able to focus, she saw that the kiss had affected him just as powerfully. She tried to get her torpid brain to resume functioning.

"Todd?" She was mortified when the word emerged as a rasping croak.

Cole jerked his head toward the door beside them. "He went in there." His voice was even more hoarse than Vicky's. He swallowed, then cleared his throat. "At least I think he did. The door slammed shut a minute ago."

They seemed to simultaneously realize that they were still wrapped around each other. Vicky hastily withdrew her arms from his neck, but Cole wasn't as eager to release her as she was to be released. His embrace loosened by degrees before his arms finally fell to his sides. He was making sure she knew that he was letting her go reluctantly. If the circumstances had been different, she might have given in to temptation and lingered in his arms for another kiss, or two or three. But this wasn't the time or the place for a romantic interlude.

"We'd better get dressed for dinner." Her voice was still slightly husky, and her pulse hadn't yet returned to normal. Nor had Cole's. He might appear completely unruffled as he lounged against the wall and gazed at her with those cool blue eyes, but in the hollow at the base of his throat a tiny artery throbbed in quick time, betraying him.

"I'd rather get undressed," he murmured. Vicky's head snapped up, her eyes wide. The corner of his mouth lifted a fraction of an inch. "What's the matter? Didn't you know stiff-necked old fuddy-duddies have lascivious urges just like everybody else?''

"You learn something new every day," she quipped, then took a giant step backward, placing herself out of his reach, she hoped.

Cole clucked his tongue at her. "Now who's being a spoilsport?"

She laughed as she pivoted on one heel and started down the hall. "Sticks and stones..." she called out over her shoulder. "Meet you downstairs in half an hour."

Cole stayed where he was until she entered her room, a rueful smile hovering at the corners of his mouth. *That should teach you. Don't even try to play sexual games with her. All it'll get you is a bad case of frustration..*

She'd warned him that she didn't like to be pushed or manipulated. Well, that was fine. Or it would have been if only he weren't so aware that time was running out. He'd never been particularly aggressive, at least where women were concerned. He had never in his life "manipulated" a woman into bed. He wasn't sure he'd be able to if he tried. If a woman demonstrated reluctance—sincere reluctance, not the coyness women like Paula used to titillate and tease—he always respected her wishes and backed off.

He shoved his hands into his pockets and released a heavy sigh. But Vicky Rand was something totally new in his experience. She'd candidly admitted that she was attracted to him—had gone out of her way to tell him so, in fact—and then, in almost the same breath, she'd asked him not to take advantage of that fact for the rest of the weekend. Did she think he was some kind of machine, for heaven's sake?

She didn't exactly keep him at arm's length, but neither would she allow him to get close; not nearly as close as he'd like, anyway. She had employed a maddeningly frustrating but extremely effective strategy of advance and retreat— every time he advanced, she retreated. He snorted softly. Talk about being manipulative! She could give lessons.

Still, he had made some progress. She'd trusted him enough to tell him about her purse, which was definitely an encouraging sign. Then his suggestion that she give the film to Mr. Hagan to lock in the safe had earned him some Brownie points. And to add to the list, she'd agreed not to snoop around trying to find out what was in the box marked PROMO MAT'L.

A deep crease appeared between his brows. She'd given him several anxious moments over that. Maybe he should get word to Mr. Hagan to lock up the box, too, just to be safe. Removing his hands from his pockets, he glanced at his watch. If he didn't get a move on, there wouldn't be time to see to it before dinner. He started unbuttoning his shirt with his left hand and reached for the doorknob with his right.

IT HAD BEEN Paula's idea that the two of them go downstairs together. Say what you would about the woman, Vicky thought as they descended the staircase side by side, she certainly had a flare for the dramatic.

By the time they'd both showered, finished dressing and applying their makeup, everyone else had probably had a couple of before-dinner drinks in the lounge. The "half an hour" Vicky had carelessly flung at Cole had stretched to almost twice that as she'd waited for Paula to complete her elaborate toilette. Now he would no doubt think she was one of those dippy females who were never where they said they'd be on time.

What really irritated her was the knowledge that she could have made it downstairs in a half hour if she hadn't waited for Paula. And she wouldn't have waited except that she was afraid Paula would sulk for the rest of the evening if she went downstairs first and ruined their grand entrance.

Who could have predicted that they would wear almost identical outfits for dinner on Saturday night, the weekend's one semidressy occasion? They were each attired in a long, circular black skirt and a long-sleeved white blouse.

The skirts were exactly alike, and the blouses were similar enough to attract attention.

Vicky's was crepe de chine, styled like a man's shirt, with a row of tiny imitation pearl buttons down the front. Paula's blouse also buttoned down the front, but it was adorned with frilly ruffles in place of an ordinary collar. She couldn't possibly be wearing a bra under the blouse; the neckline plunged halfway to the waistband of her skirt, and the shimmery material was so thin that if there'd been any bands or straps beneath it, they'd have been clearly visible.

As the women reached the bottom of the staircase, the thought crossed Vicky's mind that any female who could wear a blouse like that in public without hunching her shoulders should never expect to be liked or respected by other women. But then any woman who *would* wear a blouse like that in public probably didn't give a hoot what other women thought of her.

They entered the lounge just as everyone else apparently decided to leave it for the dining room. *So much for our grand entrance,* Vicky thought as she watched Michael Espinoza follow his father and Bud Potts through the doorway connecting the two rooms.

"Half an hour, huh?" a deep voice murmured behind them. Both women turned and saw Cole perched on the arm of an overstuffed chair. He lifted his glass in salute as he rose, then deposited it on a handy table. "Ladies, I was just about to come upstairs and see if you'd both been done in."

Paula simpered and preened. "Oh, you. We girls need more time to put ourselves together than you do, that's all. Besides, we're worth waiting for, aren't we?"

Cole's gaze shifted from Paula to Vicky before he answered. "Definitely."

Although there had been no physical contact between them, Vicky felt as if he'd caressed her, intimately. In a way, he had—with his eyes and that single, softly spoken word. She was surprised to feel a flush of pleasure sweep over her body. How could he make all her capillaries dilate just by looking at her? She'd been in the same room with him for less than a minute, and already she was well on the way to being aroused.

The startled awareness in Vicky's eyes made Cole's heart give an excited little jump, but the surge of elation he felt was almost instantly dampened by frustration. Damn, why did these bursts of sexual electricity between them always occur when there were other people around? For a fleeting moment he wished he were a more impulsive person. If he were, he might have swept her up in his arms and carried her up the stairs, à la Rhett Butler, or at the very least hauled her against him and kissed her into a stupor.

He settled for offering her a smile and his arm. She returned the former and took possession of the latter, stepping in close as she did so. He could feel the soft curve of her breast through his sleeve and decided that maybe not being Rhett Butler wasn't so bad, after all.

He turned to offer his other arm to Paula but discovered that Todd had interrupted his siege of the inn's liquor supply to come forward and claim her. Cole and Vicky exchanged a relieved look when Paula placed her hand in the crook of Todd's elbow with a gracious little smile.

"Whew," Vicky said under her breath as they followed the other couple to the dining room. "I've been dreading that moment for the last hour. I was sure one of them would make a scene."

"Ditto," Cole agreed. "And the way Todd's been putting away the bourbon, I expected he'd be the one."

A worried expression flickered across her face. "He's been drinking heavily?"

"Like a fish, but fortunately he seems to be able to hold his liquor."

When they reached the dining room door, they saw that the other six members of the group were already seated at one large table. A second one had been set for four.

"Wonderful," Vicky muttered.

Cole placed his hand over hers and gave it an encouraging squeeze. "I don't think there'll be any trouble. It looks as if they've declared a truce."

If they had, it must have been the shortest one on record. Fifteen minutes later, the tension around the table could have been cut with a knife. Cole, of all people, was indirectly responsible. Searching for a way to get the conversation off to an amicable start, he'd made a casual remark about how similarly Vicky and Paula were dressed. If he'd left it at that, no doubt someone would have followed up with a comment about the weather, and the meal would have progressed fairly smoothly. Only he hadn't left it at that.

"It's amazing, isn't it, that two people can wear virtually the same clothes and yet look totally different in them."

It was immediately evident that both women had interpreted the remark in exactly the same way. It earned him a pleased smile from Paula, who obviously considered it a compliment, and a flat stare from Vicky, who just as obviously didn't.

She resisted the urge to ask him exactly what that crack was supposed to mean. Okay, so Paula had a peaches-and-cream complexion, a disgustingly perfect figure and a Betty Boop pout. She also seemed to have the intelligence of an avocado, not to mention—and Vicky would have bet a week's pay on this—dark roots. She reflected that some men's taste was all in their mouths.

Things quickly went from bad to worse. Paula evidently took Cole's comment as an invitation to flirt and thereafter devoted her attention exclusively to him. First Todd tried to get even by coming on to Vicky, but that only got him impatient looks and monosyllabic responses, since she was trying not to miss a single word Paula and Cole said to each other. Actually, Cole wasn't saying much. Mostly he was trying not to gape at Paula's chest and now and then sliding a quick, nervous glance across the table at Vicky.

Their food arrived, but none of them did it justice. Having been spurned by both women, Todd decided to sulk. While he was sulking, he consumed almost half of one of the two bottles of wine on the table, which did nothing to improve his mood. At that point, Paula decided to shift her attention from Cole to him. By then Todd was tight enough and angry enough to give her a dose of her own medicine. Blatantly ignoring her, he turned to Cole in the middle of one of her inane remarks to ask if he was ready for more wine.

From the corner of her eye, Vicky watched Paula's face turn a dull shade of brick red, which, she couldn't help noticing, clashed horribly with her hair. Glancing across the table, she intercepted another harried look from Cole. She returned it with a cool stare. If he hadn't spent the last ten minutes encouraging Paula, this sorry situation would never have developed.

The six people at the other table were carrying on a lively discussion and didn't seem aware of the storm brewing less than a dozen feet away as the animosity between Todd and Paula continued to escalate. Their subtle and sometimes not so subtle insults and innuendos grew increasingly malicious, until Vicky wondered nervously which of them would strike the first physical blow.

"It's amazing how childish grown men can be," Paula remarked as she cut a bite-size piece of prime rib. "They sulk and pout like babies whenever they don't get what they want. Personally, I've always thought it's a sign of insecurity."

Todd's smile could have cut granite. "I'm impressed, Paula," he murmured with apparent sincerity.

She glanced at him in surprise. "That I figured that out, you mean?"

"No, that you knew how to pronounce 'insecurity.'"

Vicky and Cole made a few futile attempts to initiate a normal conversation, then gave up and pretended to enjoy

their meal. Vicky had just stuck a forkful of green beans al-
mondine into her mouth when Todd apparently reached the
limit of his endurance. He stood up so quickly that his chair
went crashing over onto its back. There was immediate and
utter silence in the dining room as the six people at the other
table swiveled in their seats to see what on earth had happened.

"That's it," Todd muttered, staring at Paula with what
looked like disgust. "I've had it." His gaze darted to Vicky,
then Cole. "Please excuse me," he said with a tight smile.
"I seem to have developed a sudden case of indigestion."

Without another word, he dropped his napkin on the table and stalked out of the dining room. A few seconds later
the front door slammed.

Vicky swallowed her beans and reached for her wine-
glass, which gave her an excuse to avoid meeting Paula's or
Cole's eyes. She detested public scenes, and she held both of
them equally responsible for the one Todd had just created.

Bud Potts's puzzled voice ended the stunned silence.
"Good Lord, what was that all about?"

"Don't tell me a toupee turned up on Todd's plate," Gary
said, only half joking.

Cole cleared his throat in embarrassment. "No, nothing
like that. I think he, uh, took exception to something that
was said."

"A lovers' spat," Jayne concluded shrewdly. "Way to go,
Paula."

Paula glowered at her, then turned away with an insolent
toss of her head. Vicky curled her hands around the stem of
her glass to keep herself from slapping some sense into the
silly woman.

"He shouldn't be wandering around outside on his own,"
Fred Espinoza said with a frown.

Jayne agreed. "You're right, Fred. For all we know, they
might have staged a fight to give Todd an excuse to leave. He

could be setting up the murder at this very minute. Somebody ought to go after him and bring him back.''

Michael and Bud volunteered and hurried off to find Todd. After they'd gone, all eyes focused on Paula. She gave a disdainful sniff, collected her glass and the bottle of wine Todd had almost emptied and flounced into the lounge.

Vicky glanced at the other table to see if anyone intended to go after her. The more she thought about it, the more likely it seemed that Jayne—and Cole—might be on to something. He had suggested that the argument they'd overheard upstairs had been staged. What if he and Jayne were both right and both arguments were either elaborate red herrings or preludes to the murder? Either way, Paula's rather dramatic exit should ensure that someone would take the bait and follow her. Vicky figured that person would probably be Jayne. She was right.

Jayne abandoned her unfinished dinner and headed for the lounge, her mouth set in determination. Gary laid down his fork with a resigned shake of his head and went after her. Lyle and Fred hurried after Gary.

Cole turned to Vicky. ''Shall we join them?''

''Are you kidding?'' she replied. ''I wouldn't miss this for anything.''

They did miss Jayne's opening remark but arrived in time to see Paula pour more wine into her glass and to hear her tell Jayne to mind her own business. Jayne didn't seem inclined to do any such thing.

''Do you intend to continue this ridiculously juvenile behavior?'' she demanded impatiently. ''Even if it means spoiling what's left of the weekend for the rest of us?''

Paula's response was to throw the contents of her glass in Jayne's face. Vicky gasped. Cole muttered an astonished expletive. The other three men just stared, open mouthed and incredulous.

Jayne looked down at the saturated front of her beige silk dress and grimaced. "I guess that answers my question." She sounded more disgusted than angry. Vicky marveled at her composure as she calmly excused herself to go upstairs and change.

"That is one cool lady," Cole murmured to Vicky.

"You can say that again," she muttered. "I'd have decked the little bitch."

He tried to disguise his laugh as a cough, but he could see that Vicky hadn't been fooled. She was giving him the same chilly, narrow-eyed look he'd received every time he glanced at her during their short but memorable dinner. An ornery, mischief-making demon suddenly took possession of his tongue.

"You shouldn't squint. It causes wrinkles."

Vicky stared at him in stupefied silence, her eyes suddenly open as wide as possible. For a second or two she wavered between indignation and amusement. Amusement won out. Her lips curved in a reluctant smile.

"I wish you'd stop doing that."

Cole produced an expression of inquisitive innocence. "Doing what?"

"Throwing me off balance like that, as if you didn't know. You're the most unpredictable man I've ever met."

He looked startled, then pleased. "I am?"

Before Vicky could answer, the French doors opened and Bud Potts entered the room. He was alone. Everyone but Paula immediately rushed to his side to find out why. She glanced up at the commotion, then went back to sorting through the record collection in the far corner of the lounge. She seemed to have realized that for the time being it would be prudent to remain as inconspicuous as possible.

"Where's Michael?" Fred Espinoza demanded. He was obviously worried that his son had already become the murder victim.

Bud's shoulders slumped. "You mean he isn't here? I was hoping he'd already come back inside. We never did see Todd, and somehow we got separated." He shook his head dejectedly. "Damn it, anyway. I bet by now one of them's killed the other and done away with the body."

Fred clearly didn't care much for that idea. "That would be just like Michael," he muttered. "To let himself get killed and leave me to figure out who did it all by myself."

"Maybe a couple of us should go have a look around, see if we can find them," Cole suggested.

Lyle stepped forward with an eager grin. "I'm game if you are."

"No!" Vicky shook her head adamantly. "Absolutely not. Nobody else should leave the inn, or even this room, for that matter. What if one of them really is the killer?"

"If there's a killer running around loose out there, it isn't Michael," Fred interjected.

Cole ignored the interruption. "That's just the point, don't you see? If one of them is, he might well be stalking the other one . . . or using this time to set up any one of us. I think we should try to get them both back inside as quickly as possible."

He wouldn't be dissuaded, and Lyle was determined to go with him. Promising to stay together, they slipped out through the French doors. They hadn't been gone a full minute when Paula unexpectedly spoke up from the far corner.

"I'm sure it isn't necessary to point this out, but at the moment, Jayne, Todd, Michael, Lyle and Cole are all missing and unaccounted for." She turned and flashed an ingenuous smile. "That's half our little group. I wonder which of them will be coming back."

Chapter Nine

Fred spent the next fifteen minutes pacing back and forth between the French doors and the two tall windows at the front of the lounge, presumably watching for some sign that his son's "corpse" had been discovered.

Gary and Bud settled themselves in a couple of comfortable chairs to wait with barely contained impatience for whatever would happen next. Bud dealt with his nervous tension by filling his pipe from the pouch of tobacco Cole had planted on the train and puffing it to life. Gary fidgeted, drummed his fingers on the arms of his chair and periodically glanced at his watch.

If Paula shared their restlessness, she hid it well. She selected a few albums from the record collection and stacked them on the stereo turntable, then went to an alcove in which a small bar had been set up and fixed herself a Bloody Mary.

Vicky kept a watchful eye on all of them, but her mind was occupied with thoughts of Cole Madigan. Was he who and what he claimed to be, or an extremely gifted actor who had deliberately used the attraction she felt toward him to undermine her objectivity?

Had it been a mistake to trust him as much as she had? And what about that remark she'd heard Paula make when she and Cole had had their heads close together after lunch?

"Leave it to me," she'd said. Leave *what* to her? Had it been Paula and Cole whom Vicky had overheard outside the ladies' room that morning? If so, where and how did Todd fit in?

She was pondering that last question when Todd sauntered into the lounge from the dining room. He looked completely relaxed and at ease, smiling genially as he strolled over to the bar and poured himself a drink. Vicky considered suggesting that he'd imbibed enough alcohol for one night, but his hands were steady, and he wasn't staggering. She decided to mind her own business.

"Where the hell have you been?" Fred asked in a belligerent tone. "People have been out scouring the grounds for you ever since you took off."

Todd stared at him with surprise. "Really? Strange, I didn't see a soul, and I was always in sight of the inn. I walked around a while to cool off," he explained with a sheepish grin. "I apologize for that little scene at dinner. I realize I made an absolute ass of myself." His mouth quirking in a smile that looked slightly cynical, he presented Paula with a courtly little bow. "And a special apology to you, fair lady, for my unforgivably crass behavior."

Vicky silently revised her previous judgment. Despite appearances, he must be drunk. Or, she amended wryly, perhaps while he was outside cooling off, he had decided that the best way to get through what was left of the weekend would be to humor Paula.

Whatever the reason for his sudden change of attitude, it appeared to be working. Paula sank gracefully onto a sofa and patted the seat to indicate that he should join her. Her smile held the same overt sexual interest she'd displayed before their two quarrels, letting Todd and everyone else know that all was forgiven.

Fred eyed Todd suspiciously for a moment or two before he resumed pacing. Vicky suspected that he wasn't buying Todd's story—especially the part about not having seen anyone else while he was wandering around the grounds. Unfortunately, as Fred apparently realized, there was no way to know for sure whether he was lying.

Gary glanced at his watch again, then rose from his chair. "Jayne's had more than enough time to change," he muttered. "I'm going up to see what's keeping her."

He was back downstairs in under three minutes. "She's gone," he announced flatly.

Bud jerked forward in his chair, the stem of his pipe clamped between his teeth. "What do you mean, she's gone?"

"I mean she's gone," Gary snapped. "G-o-n-e, gone. As in vanished, disappeared, flown the coop."

"Damn," Fred said in disgust. "First Michael, now Jayne."

Everyone looked at Todd. He held up both hands as if to ward off an attack. "Hey, wait a minute! I don't know where she is. I told you, I didn't see anybody from the time I left until I came back inside. You said there were people out scouring the grounds for me," he reminded Fred. "I assumed Jayne was one of them."

Paula wound her arm around his and cooed, "I believe you."

"Your loyalty would be touching," Gary told her sharply, "if it weren't for the fact that less than an hour ago the two of you were at each other's throats."

Paula's mouth formed a resentful pout. "I fail to see how our little tiff could possibly have anything to do with whatever's happened to Jayne...if anything *has* happened to her. Hasn't it occurred to the rest of you that maybe *she's* the murderer and that at this very minute she might be doing away with poor Michael?"

"Guess again, Paula," a smoky female voice drawled.

Six heads swung toward the arch leading to the lobby as Jayne entered the lounge on the arm of an obviously living, breathing Michael Espinoza. She'd changed into a stylish pair of rust flannel slacks and a gold turtleneck sweater. The effect she created was the kind of casual elegance most women would give their eyeteeth to be able to achieve. The patterned scarf she'd folded and tied around her head to hold her hair off her face looked like raw silk.

Gary and Fred spoke at the same time. "Where the hell have you been?"

Jayne slid an amused glance at Michael. "Ladies first," he murmured with a grin.

"Well, after I changed my clothes, I decided to look out our bedroom window and see if anything suspicious was happening on the lawn. Sure enough, there was Michael, skulking around the corner of the building." Jayne shrugged. "I figured he might have killed Todd or Bud, or maybe both of them, so I ran downstairs and slipped out the back door. I planned to sneak up behind him and catch him disposing of a body, or the murder weapon or something."

At that point Michael picked up the story. "Except by the time she got outside, I'd decided to give up and come back in. I never did see Todd, and somehow Bud and I had gotten separated. I figured the sensible thing to do was check to see if either or both of them had turned up yet, then get some reinforcements if they hadn't. I'd just turned around to head for the nearest door—which happened to be the same one Jayne had decided to use. We came creeping around the corner at the same time and scared each other half out of our wits."

"End of story," Jayne said. "I'm afraid neither of us saw or heard anything interesting, unless you count the bullfrog glee club warming up down at the pond."

"Did anything exciting happen while we were gone?" Michael asked hopefully.

His father answered just as the French doors opened and Lyle and Cole reentered the room. "Not a damned thing."

Fred sounded disappointed and a little put out. Vicky knew how he felt. It was something of a letdown to have everyone once more present and accounted for. Still, she had a hunch that something significant had happened during the last half hour or so. For approximately half that time—as Paula had pointed out—five of the ten members of the group had been out of the room, supposedly roaming the grounds, looking for one another. It seemed highly unlikely that none of them had so much as caught a glimpse of any of the others.

"Are you thinking what I'm thinking?" Cole murmured as he came to stand beside her. She gave him a questioning look. "Someone just had a perfect opportunity to see to some last-minute details," he said softly. "Who was gone the longest?"

Vicky thought for a moment. "I'd say it was a toss-up between Todd and Jayne. He beat her back by about five minutes."

"But Jayne had to go upstairs, change clothes and come back down," he pointed out. "That must have taken—what would you say, ten minutes or so?"

"Probably. Which means that she was gone approximately the same amount of time as you and Lyle."

His mouth thinned in impatience. "We were together every second. If you don't believe me, go ask Lyle."

"That won't be necessary," Vicky murmured. "I believe you." Which was half true. He and Lyle might have stuck to each other like glue the entire time they were outside, but that didn't rule out the possibility that Cole was one of the actors. For that matter, Lyle and Bud could be, too. Maybe Bud had deliberately lost Michael so he could slip away to take care of his part of the preparations for the murder. When he'd returned alone, it could have been the signal for Lyle and Cole to leave and finish setting things up....

"I can hear you thinking," Cole said dryly. "It's a shame you don't put that overactive imagination to better use. Have you ever considered writing fiction—for instance, murder mysteries?"

"No," she said in a repressive tone. "I haven't."

"Mmm, on second thought I guess it's not such a hot idea at that. You'd probably make all the characters psychopathic killers and forget to include a victim."

Vicky's cheeks felt hot. "I'm only trying to consider all the possibilities."

"Right. Well, when you figure out whether I'm one of the good guys or one of the bad guys, let me know. I'll be mingling with all the other suspects, trying to pick up something in the way of a clue."

Vicky's teeth worried her lower lip as she watched him walk away. He'd sounded fed up just now, as if he had very nearly reached the limit of his patience where she was concerned. She tried to tell herself that didn't bother her in the least. It shouldn't have, but it did. She didn't want Cole Madigan to be fed up with her. When he looked at her, she didn't want to see irritation or impatience in those impossibly blue eyes. When he spoke to her, she didn't want to hear annoyance in his voice.

Face it, Victoria, she told herself glumly. *You're smitten with the man. Your precious objectivity was shot to hell the first time he kissed you.*

There was no use trying to deny it. She'd been attracted to him on a purely physical level the instant she'd set eyes on him. What red-blooded heterosexual female wouldn't be? And if the attraction had remained purely physical, she could have dealt with it in her usual no-nonsense style.

Only it hadn't remained purely physical. At some point during the last twenty-four hours, she had actually started to like him. What was more, she sensed that if she wasn't careful, the liking could easily develop into a full-blown infatuation—for a man who could be merely playing a part; a man who might have deliberately set out to lead her around in circles while his fellow actors got on with staging the phony murder.

PAULA AND TODD SWAYED together in a dimly lit corner, not so much dancing as stimulating each other's libidos; in the background, Johnny Mathis crooned about chestnut trees and wishing wells. The Espinozas were playing something called back-alley bridge with Bud and Lyle, and the Kaysers had retired to the love seat, where they were engaged in a low, intense conversation. Vicky wondered if their talk had anything to do with the sudden vanishing act Jayne had pulled earlier and/or the fact that when she'd reappeared, it had been on the arm of Michael Espinoza.

Vicky had placed herself on a sofa in the northeast corner of the lounge; from there she could keep an eye on everyone else while she brought her notes up to date. At least that had been her intention. So far she'd added less than one complete line of new squiggles to the notebook, and the only person she'd been keeping an eye on was Cole Madigan.

He'd spent the past hour avoiding her. He hadn't been obvious about it; he was too well-mannered to snub her openly. Still, every time she'd tried to approach him, he had managed to find a way to evade her. Now he was kibitzing the card game, his right hand in the pocket of his slacks as he monitored the play from behind Fred's chair. Fred didn't seem to mind either his presence or his frequent questions, which Vicky knew would have driven her to distraction. But to be honest, he only had to be in the same room with her to do that.

Cole lifted his head suddenly and looked across the table, across the lounge, straight into her eyes. Vicky's fingers clenched, and the fine-line ballpoint she held created an indecipherable mark on the notepaper. Cole slowly withdrew his hand from his pocket, hesitated a moment, then started toward her. Vicky tried to swallow and found that her mouth and throat had suddenly gone dry.

"Mind if I join you?" he asked.

"Of course not." It was ridiculous to feel so flustered, she told herself. She'd been trying to talk to him for more than an hour, hadn't she? Well, now was her chance.

He sat down beside her, close beside her—so close that the sleeve of his sport coat brushed the sleeve of her blouse. Vicky couldn't have moved away if she'd wanted to; she was already sitting at the end of the sofa, right up against the arm. Cole casually stretched his legs in front of him, crossing them at the ankles.

"Well, have you decided?"

The softly spoken question caught her by surprise. "Have I decided what?"

"Whether I'm one of the good guys or one of the bad guys."

Had she? She hesitated, unconsciously biting her lower lip.

Cole leaned back and folded his arms over his chest. "You've got five seconds to make up your mind."

Vicky gave a startled jerk. "Now wait just a minute!"

"Four...three..."

"That's not fair! You can't expect—"

"Two..."

"All right!" she blurted. "You're one of the good guys." Cole's mouth started to curve in a pleased smile. "I think." His smile evaporated. Before he could say anything or get up and leave, Vicky asked, "Will you answer some questions for me?"

He observed her in stoic silence for a moment and then moved his head in a barely perceptible nod. "Three."

"Three," she repeated flatly. "You're a regular chatterbox tonight, aren't you? All right, question number one: Did you plant the toupee on my plate last night?"

"No. By the way, for every answer I give you, I expect one in return. Next question."

Vicky's suspicions flared up. "You didn't?"

"Do you have a hearing problem, or was that question number two?" He sounded slightly bored. "If I answer the same question twice, it counts as two answers."

Vicky stared at him in exasperation. "Could you be twins?" she muttered, then hastily held up a hand. "Don't count that. I was just thinking out loud." Cole's lashes lowered to screen his eyes, but not before she saw the amused gleam in them. "All right," she said brusquely. "Question number two: When I left your compartment this morning, you were sound asleep. Yet when I came back less than fifteen minutes later, you'd already dressed, made your bed and gone to the dining car. The obvious conclusion is that you were in an awfully big hurry. I'd like to know why."

Cole swiveled to face her. The amusement was gone from his eyes. Now they were watchful, intent. "Why do you ask?"

Vicky was tempted to ask if that was his first question. But if she did, and if he said yes, she'd have to tell him about the conversation she'd overheard that morning. She had almost decided to tell him, anyway, but first she wanted to hear where he claimed to have been—and with whom— while she was in the ladies' room.

"You're being evasive." She held his eyes as she said it. "Which is only going to make me more suspicious."

For a moment she thought he would refuse to give her any kind of answer. The corners of his mouth turned down, and something like irritation flickered in his eyes. But then he sighed as if in resignation and lifted his left arm to the back of the sofa. Vicky knew without looking that his fingers were within millimeters of her neck. She tried to blot the knowledge from her mind.

"I've never been any good at fencing with words," he said. "I'll stop if you will."

"You're on. You go first. You still haven't answered my last question," she reminded him.

"All right," he muttered with obvious reluctance. "First, I wasn't really asleep when you left the compartment."

Vicky's eyes widened in surprise, then began to glow with a slow-burning anger. Anticipating her, Cole quickly leaned forward, clamping his right hand on the arm of the sofa. She sucked in her stomach in reaction. Unfortunately, it wasn't possible to retract her breasts, as well. His arm pressed against them intimately.

"Don't do that...crowd me like that," she protested.

Cole's jaw firmed stubbornly. His arm remained in place. "You were getting ready to jump up and stomp off in a fit of indignant outrage or something," he accused. She glared at him, but he pretended not to notice and plunged ahead. He spoke softly, but his voice held a hint of challenge.

"As I said, I wasn't asleep when you got up this morning. I just let you think I was. I was not only wide awake; I spent several very pleasurable minutes shamelessly ogling you while you paraded around in your skimpy little nightshirt."

Vicky's mouth fell open. She couldn't decide whether she was more angry or mortified. She refused to even consider the possibility that she was more pleased than anything else. "Why, that's...that's..."

"Licentious?" he offered helpfully. "Lecherous? Lewd?"

"Yes!" she snapped. "Not to mention—"

"Exciting?" he suggested with a wicked grin.

Color bloomed in her cheeks. "Absolutely not." And that had to be one of the three biggest lies she'd ever told in her life.

"I suppose you expect me to apologize. Well, I'm not going to. You look beautiful in the morning, with no makeup and your hair curling around your face. I'd have told you so, but I didn't know what kind of mood you were in, and I was afraid you might throw your suitcase at me."

Vicky's gaze dropped to her lap; her fingers were fiddling nervously with her pen. Lord, did he have any idea how he was affecting her? "You, uh . . ." Her voice was little more than a croak. She paused to clear her throat, then mumbled, "You thought I was beautiful?"

"Breathtaking," Cole said fervently.

"My hair looks like a bird's nest in the morning."

"No."

He said it so decisively that she looked up—straight into a pair of blue eyes that had begun to darken with desire. *Bad move,* she thought giddily.

"It's glorious." His gaze moved to her hair, his voice dropping to a husky murmur. "I wanted to reach up and touch it, find out if it feels as soft as it looks . . . wind it around my fingers."

As he spoke the last few words, his right hand lifted from the arm of the sofa. Vicky sat frozen in breathless anticipation, unable to tear her gaze from his. His eyes had turned a smoky blue-gray, and he was breathing shallowly through slightly parted lips. His hand halted less than an inch from its objective, his fingers almost, but not quite, touching her hair.

"Michael, you idiot, that was my ace you just trumped!"

Fred's indignant complaint was loud enough to break the spell. Vicky stiffened, though whether the reaction was caused by self-consciousness or resentment, she couldn't have said. Cole looked as if he'd just been rudely awakened from a sound sleep. He blinked, then apparently noticed that his hand was poised to seize a fistful of her hair. He snatched it back, at the same time shifting to put several inches of space between them. They each inhaled a deep, calming breath.

"I don't suppose you brought along a hat," he murmured wryly.

Surprised, Vicky jerked her head. "No, I never wear hats."

"Not even in the winter?" He was staring at her hair again.

Squelching a smile, she shook her head with enough force to emancipate a few bouncy curls. "Earmuffs."

His lips curved in an unbelievably sexy smile. "I bet you look adorable in earmuffs."

"Cute as a button," Vicky confirmed with a straight face. "So…as soon as I left the compartment, you threw on your clothes and rushed off to the dining car, no doubt hoping to catch Jayne and Paula in their peignoirs and get in a little more ogling during breakfast. How am I doing so far?"

Cole settled back against the cushions and calmly re-folded his arms over his chest. "You're not even close."

She gave him a skeptical look. "Says you. You've already admitted to being a lewd, licentious lecher."

"I give you my solemn word, I haven't had a single lech-erous thought about anyone but you since approximately five-fifteen yesterday afternoon."

Vicky hoped the little thrill of pleasure she felt didn't show on her face. "Hah! Then that must have been your twin drooling all over Paula at dinner."

A slow smile spread over his face, baring two rows of perfectly aligned white teeth and making his eyes crinkle at the corners. "You were jealous!"

He sounded so pleased that Vicky had to purse her lips to keep them from stretching into a smile as wide as his. "Don't be ridiculous." Flicking an invisible speck of dirt from her blouse, she added primly, "I was disgusted."

He leaned sideways to murmur low in her ear, "You were *jealous*! Admit it."

She turned her head so that they were nose to nose. "Was that your first question?"

"If I said yes, would you answer it honestly?"

"Of course." She paused for a beat, then smiled and added, "As soon as I get the two answers you still owe me."

A pleased expression entered Cole's eyes as he straight-ened. "Just as I expected. There's a devious, conniving mind lurking under that glorious hair."

Vicky inclined her head graciously. "I'll take that as a compliment. Now will you please get on with it."

"Very well." He got comfortable by drawing one bent knee onto the sofa and resting his arm along the back. The position had the added advantage of allowing him to look into her eyes while he spoke.

"You wanted to know why I left the compartment in such a hurry this morning. There's a simple explanation. I'd arranged to meet the Kaysers for breakfast. After you left, it suddenly occurred to me that if I wasn't in the dining car when they got there, they might come back to collect me and run into you. Or notice your camera bag or something and realize you'd spent the night in my compartment."

Vicky gaped at him, wondering if she'd misunderstood. "Are you telling me you cleared out in such a rush because you were trying to protect my reputation?"

"Well, I thought you'd prefer that no one found out." He sounded a bit defensive to Vicky. "I mean, if it got back to your editors that you'd spent the night with one of the men in the group—" He broke off with an uneasy shrug. "It just seemed best not to take any chances."

Vicky shook her head in amazement. "Cole, that was very thoughtful of you. I don't know what to say."

His smile was tinged with relief. "You don't have to say anything, as long as you're suitably ashamed for whatever you were thinking." He didn't squander one of his questions by asking exactly what it was she'd been thinking. He assumed that sooner or later he would find out. "That's two down and one to go. What's the third question?"

Vicky tapped the point of her pen against the open notebook, trying to decide which of a half-dozen questions to ask.

"Well?" Cole prodded impatiently. "Come on; I'd like to get to my questions sometime tonight."

"Just a minute," she murmured. "I'm thinking."

"Maybe I can hurry things up a little. Let's see; you already know that I sleep in the buff." Vicky wisely chose to ignore that remark. "What else could you possibly be curious about?" he mused aloud. She didn't enlighten him, so he took a few wild stabs. "I'm not married, engaged or otherwise committed, I don't have any communicable diseases, and I get along well with all animals and most children." She slanted him a wry glance and didn't comment. "I also call my mother at least once a week," he added with an appealing grin.

Her pen stopped tapping. "That's all very interesting, but what can you tell me about a woman named Erica?"

Cole instantly sobered. "Erica? That's the name I saw in your notebook, next to 'net exp.' I planned to use one of my questions to find out who she is and why she's mentioned in your notes."

"That would have been two questions," Vicky pointed out.

One corner of his mouth twitched upward. "I was hoping you wouldn't notice."

"My devious, conniving mind notices everything. Am I to take it, then, that you don't know anything about Erica?"

Cole shook his head. "Absolutely nothing. I give you my word. Is she important . . . a clue or something?"

Vicky told him about the conversation she'd overheard that morning, not leaving anything out. "But it was impossible to identify their voices, and they didn't call each other by name," she concluded with a disappointed sigh.

Cole's expression was thoughtful. "When I got to the dining room, Paula and Todd were already there. Jayne and Gary arrived a couple of minutes later, just ahead of you."

"So it could have been either couple I heard outside the ladies' room," Vicky said in disgust. "Well, rats, I don't know any more now than I did before."

"Wrong," Cole corrected. "You know I'm not the actor you heard mention Erica's name—that is, assuming you believe me for a change."

She waved her hand in a magnanimous gesture. "I've decided to give you the benefit of the doubt."

"I'm overwhelmed. Okay, my turn. Question one: While I was outside with Lyle, you didn't happen to stroll by the office and take a peek inside that box, did you?"

Vicky drew back in offense. "I told you I wouldn't."

"Well, you didn't actually promise. You said, 'How about if I give you my word,' et cetera. And knowing your devious, conniving mind . . ."

"Cross my heart, I didn't go anywhere near the office. In fact, I didn't leave this room. Honestly, I don't understand you," she said with a sorrowful shake of her head. "Why did you agree to be partners if you don't trust me?"

Wry amusement flickered in Cole's eyes, but before he could reply, there was an excited disturbance at the card table. Apparently Bud had reached into his coat pocket for his tobacco and discovered a small foil packet.

"Finally, another clue!" Vicky exclaimed. She jumped up and went to see what it was.

Cole followed, but with less enthusiasm. *Great,* he thought. *Another clue. Just when I've started to make a little headway with her.*

"What is it?" Michael asked as Bud turned the small packet around in his hand.

Bud extended his arm and squinted. "Darned if I know."

"Give it here," Lyle commanded, reaching across the table. "You know you need your bifocals to read anything smaller than a K-mart sign."

Bud handed him the packet. Lyle and Fred bent over it as if they were two spies examining a top-secret coded message. "It's a package of hair coloring," Fred said triumphantly. "Burnished mahogany."

"Mahogany?" Bud muttered with a frown. "That's a hardwood. Who'd want hair the color of a chest of drawers, for heaven's sake?"

The activity around the table attracted the Kaysers' attention. "What's going on?" Gary asked as they hurried over.

Lyle held up the packet while Bud explained how he'd happened to find it. "Somebody must have slipped it into my pocket while we were all milling around earlier...right after Lyle and Cole came back inside."

"The question is Who?" Michael remarked.

"And Why?" his father added. "How do we tell if this is an honest-to-goodness clue or just another dumb red herring?"

"I can answer that, Fred," Jayne murmured. Everyone looked at her in question. "It's just another dumb red herring. I know, because it belongs to me."

Chapter Ten

Jayne reached up to remove the folded scarf she was wearing as a headband and revealed a patch of violent green hair.

"Apparently the wine Paula doused me with earlier caused some sort of chemical reaction," she explained. "I guess I should have known better than to use a cheap temporary rinse, but I wanted to see how I liked being a redhead before I committed myself to a permanent dye job, and this weekend seemed like a good time to try out a new color." She grimaced.

"I didn't figure the new color would be spinach-green, though. By the time I got upstairs, it had already started to turn. I opened my makeup case to get the spare pack of rinse I'd brought along, but it was missing. I figured it would show up sooner or later."

"Well, it's obvious that there are only three people who could have taken it," Gary claimed. "It had to have been either Todd, Bud or Michael."

The mention of his name finally snared Todd's interest. He came over to see what was going on, pulling Paula with him. "What am I being accused of now?"

Bud and Michael had already started making denials, so he didn't get an immediate answer.

"Just a minute, Gary," Michael said. "I don't know anything about your wife's hair dye."

"Actually, it's only a rinse," Jayne put in. No one paid her any attention, least of all Michael.

"I was outside looking for Todd when it was taken—*if* it was taken. In case any of you have forgotten, Jayne was the one who suggested that somebody ought to go after him and bring him back. Who's to say she wasn't setting Bud and me up?"

Jayne rolled her eyes and muttered. "That's the most asinine thing I've heard all weekend."

"Very good point, Michael," Bud said stoutly. "Now that I think of it, it *was* Jayne's idea for us to go after Todd."

"Back up a minute," Todd said in confusion. "What was that about hair dye?"

"Rinse," Jayne snapped. "It's a rinse, not a dye, dammit."

Paula stepped close to Todd's side and glared at Jayne like a mother protecting her young. "There's no need to swear." Jayne just stared at her in disgust.

"Good Lord," Todd murmured. "There's a big green spot in the middle of your head."

"And there's a big empty spot in the middle of yours," Jayne retorted acidly. "I need a drink." She draped the scarf around her neck and headed for the bar.

Cole's elbow nudged Vicky's ribs to get her attention, but she ignored him and kept making furious scribbles in her notebook.

Bud decided to get in his two cents' worth while he had the chance. "I don't see how you figure I could be the culprit, Gary. I was outside, too, remember? Besides which, I'm the one somebody planted the stupid dye on."

"Rinse!" Jayne snarled from the bar alcove.

Todd looked completely bewildered. "Let me get this straight. Jayne was dying her hair green and somebody sneaked in and swiped the package of dye she was using. Is that right?"

Everyone looked at him as if convinced he didn't have a brain in his head. Cole's elbow gave Vicky's ribs another, more forceful poke. She stopped scribbling long enough to scowl at him. He nodded toward the French doors to indicate that he wanted her to come outside. She gave an impatient shake of her head and continued taking notes. Jayne strolled back to the table. She was carrying a highball glass three-quarters filled with amber liquid.

Gary cleared everything up for Todd, then turned to Bud. "Just because you were the one who 'found' it doesn't put you in the clear. You could have taken it and kept it hidden in your pocket until now."

"Damn right he could have," Jayne concurred.

Paula pursed her lips in disapproval. "I asked you a minute ago not to swear."

Jayne smiled and swirled the liquor in her glass. "I wonder what effect straight scotch would have on *your* hair," she murmured pleasantly. "One more word and we're all going to find out."

An angry flush stained Paula's face, but she had sense enough to hold her tongue.

Cole's patience suddenly ran out. The point of Vicky's pen slid off the page as he grasped her arm and started pulling her toward the French doors. The rest of the group was so busy flinging accusations and insults at one another that no one noticed they were leaving.

"What are you doing?" she demanded. "We could miss an important clue!"

"This will only take a minute." He opened the doors with his free hand and hustled her out onto the veranda, then along it several feet toward the front of the inn.

Beyond the edge of the veranda, the lawn, trees and shrubs were bathed in eerie silver-white moonlight. But under the sloped roof it was dark—so dark that if Cole's hair had been any less blond, he could have melted into the shadows next to the building and become virtually invisible.

A shiver scampered down Vicky's spine. She instinctively put her back to the wall, hugging her arms. "It's cold out here. Hurry up and tell me why you dragged me out like that and then let's get back inside."

Cole's eyes gleamed as he gazed at her. Then his teeth flashed in a sudden, wolfish grin. Vicky stared up at him in shocked comprehension, her eyes like saucers, as his hands lifted and slowly closed around her throat.

"Damn," she muttered in self-disgust. "I should have seen it coming."

"Yes, you should have," he agreed. His thumbs pressed up beneath her chin, tilting her head back. "I warned you about allowing yourself to be lured away from the group."

"I could scream."

His thumbs stroked gently back and forth, administering both a caress and a warning. "I bet I could stop you."

"Oh, hell." She closed her eyes in resignation. "All right, you win. Just get it over with."

A husky chuckle whispered past his lips an instant before they closed softly on hers. For a second or two Vicky was too stunned to realize that his hands had moved to cradle her jaw. He sipped delicately at her mouth, coaxing her lips to relax, to part and finally to cling. By the time his tongue made its first tentative approach, her arms had found their way inside his coat and wrapped themselves around his chest.

Cole's mouth lifted from hers a fraction of an inch. "What's this?" He sounded amused. "I thought you wanted me to just get it over with."

Vicky reluctantly opened her eyes. Speech was an effort she didn't want to make, but she forced herself. "I thought you were going to—"

"Strangle you," Cole finished for her. "I probably should." His right hand returned to her throat, but his touch was so gentle she knew he was only teasing.

"I'm sorry," she murmured huskily.

His thumb began tracing a lazy spiral down her neck, moving lower with each loop, finally stopping when it reached the base of her throat, where an artery was throbbing much faster than it should have been. He smiled into her eyes. "Prove it."

Vicky knew she should refuse or at the very least make a token protest. She did neither. Stretching up, she captured his smiling mouth with an eagerness that startled them both. Cole's lips parted on a gasp, allowing her to push her tongue past his teeth.

When her tongue entered his mouth, Cole felt his entire body clench in response. Nothing that had happened between them had prepared him for her sudden display of aggressiveness. He was completely disarmed, unsure how to react. He tried to remember his original reason for bringing her outside as his fingers slipped into her luxuriant hair and his mouth opened over hers.

He kissed her hungrily, but his hands stayed above her shoulders. They tangled in her hair, his fingers moving over her scalp in a slow, erotic massage that made her weak with longing. Vicky moved against him in deliberate provocation, but he didn't seem to get the message.

"Cole?" she gasped between kisses. "I know you have a thing about ... my hair ... but the rest of me could do with a little atten—"

His head jerked up as if she'd bitten him. "Hair! Of course—*hair*!"

She stared at him dazedly. "Hair?"

He nodded. "Hair." Pulling her arms from around him, he moved to lean back against the wall at her side. His breathing sounded labored, so she decided it would be safe to assume he hadn't stopped kissing her because he found her totally repugnant.

"Well?" she prodded. "If it's not asking too much, I'd like a more complete explanation than just 'hair.'"

He exhaled a soft laugh. "Sorry. I was just catching my breath. You did such a good job of distracting me that I forgot what I brought you out here to tell you."

"Which was?" she said dryly.

"Last night, didn't Bud say that he and Lyle were hairdressers?"

"I think what he said was that they were co-owners of a beauty salon. What about it?"

Cole turned toward her, casually resting his shoulder against the wall. "Well, wouldn't someone who owns a beauty salon know a package of hair coloring when he sees it?"

Vicky abruptly forgot about her irritation. "You'd think so, wouldn't you?"

"Yet Bud didn't. Neither did Lyle, for that matter. It was Fred who figured out what it was by reading the label. Obviously they lied about what they do for a living."

"I have a feeling that isn't the only deception the little devils have perpetrated," Vicky muttered. "I'm fairly certain they've been pulling everybody's leg about their…shall we say, personal relationship."

"You don't think they're gay?" Cole asked in surprise.

"Let me put it this way. I'd be willing to bet that their sexual preferences are pretty much the same as yours."

"And we've already established that I'm attracted to females." He leaned closer. "Especially females with big brown cocker spaniel eyes—"

"I beg your pardon."

"—and masses of soft curly brown hair."

"You make me sound like a lapdog."

She caught a flash of white as he smiled. "Not at all, though I certainly wouldn't object if you wanted to curl up on my lap."

"How generous of you." Vicky made her tone neutral, trying not to dwell on how tempting the offer sounded. "Don't you think we'd better go back inside?"

"In a minute." The pads of his fingers brushed her cheek, his touch so light she almost managed to convince herself she'd imagined it. "As soon as you answer my second question."

Which, Vicky was sure, would have something to do with the way she'd reacted to the attention he'd given Paula at dinner.

"Oh, God, my notebook!" she gasped in alarm. "I must have dropped it. Can you see it?" Not giving him time to answer, she sank down on her hands and knees and began to grope along the floorboards.

"What—! Your notebook? Vicky, for heaven's sake, get up from there. You'll ruin your clothes."

"Don't you understand? I have to find it." She injected a hint of desperation into her voice. "I won't be able to write my article without it. You're not standing on it, are you?"

Cole muttered something she didn't quite catch under his breath, and then suddenly he was on his knees beside her, cautiously patting his palms against the veranda floor. Quite by accident, her searching fingers located the missing stenographer's book. She grinned and swept it under the voluminous folds of her skirt.

"Have you found it yet?" she asked.

"No," he said. "And this floor feels filthy. I'd think you'd take better care of your notes, considering what an important element of your work they are. How did you manage to drop it, anyway?"

Vicky struggled to keep laughter out of her voice. "I think it happened when you were kissing me."

Cole's patting halted for a second. "Oh. Well, in that case, I—Ow! Damn it!"

"What's wrong?"

"Splinters," he said succinctly. "Look, this is ridiculous. We'll never find it in the dark. Let's go inside and see if we can round up a flashlight."

Vicky collected the notebook, then gathered her skirt up in her hands. "You're probably right," she agreed as she rose to her feet. "You stay here and keep looking. I'll be right back."

Something in her voice must have tipped him off. He came off the floor like a released spring, reaching out to hook an arm around her waist before she could move away. His free hand slid down the sleeve of her blouse to where her fingers clutched the notebook.

"Well, well, what have we here?"

Vicky tensed, not sure how he was going to react. "I really did drop it," she said quickly. "Honest. When I thought you were going to strangle me," she added as extra insurance.

"And were you really going to go inside and leave me out here, crawling around on the floor in the dark and collecting a bunch of splinters?" Cole countered.

"I'm sorry about your hand." She knew she'd overdone the sympathy when she saw his lips twitch. "Does it hurt?"

"Like hell."

"Aw, poor baby." Vicky dropped the notebook again, deliberately this time, to grasp his hand and lift it to her mouth. She placed a gentle kiss on his palm. "Is that better?"

"Not really. The splinters are in the other hand."

He let her remove his arm from her waist but immediately replaced it with the other one. Vicky cradled his injured hand in both of hers to carry it to her lips. She heard his breathing falter as her mouth moved softly against his skin.

"Does that hurt?" she asked, knowing perfectly well that his reaction had nothing to do with pain.

"Not . . . exactly."

Her tongue darted out to stab at the center of his palm, and then her teeth grazed the heel of his thumb. Cole inhaled sharply. "Funny," he said in a strained voice, "I never knew the hand was an erogenous zone."

"You didn't?" Vicky murmured as she guided his hand to her waist. "And I thought you were some kind of genius."

"Yes. I mean, I am," he confirmed in a distracted mutter. "But I suppose I've lived a pretty sheltered life by most people's standards." A trace of humor entered his voice as both arms closed around her. "Shut up in a dull old laboratory with all those test tubes and Bunsen burners, I mean."

Vicky circled his neck with her arms and leaned into his chest. "Not much action in the old lab, huh?"

"None, as a matter of fact," he said with a wistful sigh. "Unless you count watching the white rats breed."

Her rich, throaty chuckle was cut off as his open mouth closed warmly on hers. He let her taste the fire inside him, but he also made sure she knew that he had it under control. When he eased his mouth from hers, Vicky didn't pull away. In fact, she nestled closer, rubbing her face against his throat.

"You're different tonight," she said softly.

His arms contracted in a brief hug. "I decided I'd better try to earn some points for finesse," he said with wry honesty. "To make up for last night."

His candor left her momentarily speechless with surprise. When she didn't immediately respond, Cole felt a twinge of anxiety. "Well? How am I doing?"

Vicky lifted her head. She was smiling. "So far, not half bad." She gave him a quick, light kiss, then eased out of his embrace. "We really ought to go back inside. We may already have missed something important."

"All right," Cole said reluctantly. After stooping to retrieve her notebook, he slipped his arm around her waist and led her back to the French doors.

Vicky waited until she'd stepped across the threshold before she spoke again.

"By the way, you know that question you didn't get to ask me? The answer is yes, just a tiny bit."

Glancing over her shoulder, she saw him frown in confusion for a moment before comprehension dawned. She hurried on into the lounge before he could grab her and drag her back outside. From the look in his eyes, she suspected he was contemplating doing exactly that, and they'd already spent too much time away from the rest of the group.

"Well, it's about time," Lyle said as Cole stepped inside and pulled the doors together. "We were about to organize a search party."

"No cause for alarm," Vicky assured him. "We were just conducting a short strategy session out on the veranda."

Jayne gave them both an amused once-over. "Oh, is that what they call it nowadays? Goodness, what is that on your skirt?"

Vicky glanced down and grimaced. "Offhand, I'd say it's dirt."

"I bet they've been out digging a grave," Fred remarked from his chair.

"No," Cole murmured dryly. "Just crawling around on the floor looking for Vicky's notebook." There was a devilish gleam in his eyes as he handed it to her. "Try to hang on to it from now on, all right?"

"I'll do my best," she replied demurely.

While he brushed at his knees, she glanced around the room. Paula and Todd were still in the corner, but they were no longer dancing. In fact, if Vicky was any judge of body language, they were at each other's throats again.

"Oh, no," she muttered. "Don't tell me we're in for a repeat performance."

"It's already started," Jayne said in disgust. "You missed the opening fireworks. If Paula doesn't end up being the one who gets iced, there's no justice in the world."

"You shouldn't have spoken her name aloud, darling," Gary said. "You've summoned her forth."

Jayne uttered a shockingly vulgar swear word as Paula started across the room in their direction. "Excuse me, please," she said, turning toward the bar. "If I have to put up with much more of dear Paula's shenanigans, I may wind up killing her myself."

Jayne needn't have worried. This time Paula's sights were fixed on Cole. She breezed past Vicky and Gary as if they had suddenly turned invisible and proceeded to wrap herself around Cole's arm.

Cole looked like a man who'd unexpectedly found himself squeezed between a rock and a hard place—flustered, slightly alarmed, but determined not to panic. Vicky decided she would give him precisely one minute to think of a tactful way to rid himself of Paula. While she silently counted off the seconds, Todd stalked past on his way to the French doors.

"I need some air," he said in passing. "I'll be right outside on the porch."

When Vicky reached the thirty-second mark, Paula's melon-tipped fingers began climbing the front of Cole's shirt. He hastily captured her hand, then couldn't seem to decide what to do with it. Eventually he put it back on his sleeve and gave it a couple of awkward pats. Vicky resisted the urge to gnash her teeth. As she approached the count of fifty, Paula said something that made his dimple flash. Vicky stopped counting and went to join Jayne at the bar.

"Men!" she remarked pithily as she slapped her notebook down on the Formica counter and reached for an open bottle of bourbon.

Jayne lifted her glass in agreement. "You can say that again. Unreliable finks, every one."

Vicky frowned at her. "What are you complaining about? Gary obviously adores you."

Jayne shrugged. "Guess I'm just in an agreeable mood."

They were laughing when Cole walked over. His face wore an uncertain expression. "Vicky?"

"Get away from me."

"Now look, I didn't—"

"Why don't you go compare notes with Todd, you unreliable fink?"

Jayne spluttered over her drink. "Uh, excuse me, I think I hear my husband calling me."

"I didn't ask her to come over, you know," Cole said defensively.

Vicky waved a hand in dismissal. "You don't owe me any explanations. It's nothing to me if you want to make a fool of yourself over that...that..."

"Floozy?" he supplied with a grin. "You really *are* jealous, aren't you?"

"Nonsense," she said haughtily. "My sense of propriety is offended, that's all."

"Do you know, this is the first time a woman's ever displayed jealousy because of me. I think I could get to like it."

Vicky gave him a hard, level look and took a drink of her bourbon. "What did she mean by 'Leave it to me'?" she asked flatly.

Cole blinked. "Who? What?"

"In the bar car after lunch, when you and Paula were whispering sweet nothings in each other's ears, I heard her say, 'Leave it to me.' What did she mean—leave what to her?"

He flushed guiltily. "Oh, that."

"Yes, that." Vicky's voice oozed sarcasm. "I want to know exactly what she meant."

He studied the toes of his shoes. "In the first place, nobody was whispering sweet nothings in anybody's ear. I, er, asked her if she thought she could keep Todd occupied for the rest of the weekend." He shrugged and shifted from one foot to the other. "I suppose you could say I was trying to eliminate the competition. She gave me one of her cat-that-ate-the-canary smiles and said, 'Leave it to me.' I didn't realize you heard."

When he lifted his head, a complacent smile was playing around the corners of Vicky's mouth. "If I were the vindictive sort, I could really rub your nose in it," she said mildly as she set her glass on the bar and collected her notebook. "You do realize that?"

He nodded solemnly. "Oh, yeah. Aren't you going to finish your drink?"

Vicky shook her head. "At the rates they charge for these weekends, you wouldn't think they'd have to water down the booze, but that bourbon's definitely been diluted with something."

Cole's eyes narrowed at the word "bourbon." He turned to lift the almost empty bottle from which she'd poured, sniffing at it suspiciously. Next he sampled the liquor in her glass.

"See what I mean?" Vicky said. "If you mixed it with something, you might not be able to tell, but when you drink it straight like that, you can tell it's been watered down."

"Has all the liquor been tampered with, do you think, or is it just the bourbon?"

Vicky shrugged. "I've only had the bourbon. But Jayne was drinking scotch, and she didn't say anything. Why? Is it some kind of clue?"

"Possibly. Todd was drinking bourbon before dinner."

"More than likely from this bottle," Vicky added eagerly. "It was more than three-quarters empty before I poured from it. Do you think it was left here deliberately, as some kind of prop or something?"

"I wouldn't be surprised." He hesitated, scanning the array of bottles lined up along the bar.

"You're not thinking of sampling everything, are you?" she asked anxiously.

Cole grinned. "Not on your life. But I'd like to get my hands on the bottle of wine Todd was swilling from at dinner. It would be interesting to see whether it was actually grape juice."

Vicky's eyes lit with excitement. "Paula took the bottle in here, remember? Maybe it's still lying around somewhere. Let's separate and look for it."

"All right," Cole agreed. "But try not to be too obvious." She gave him a slightly insulted look but didn't reply. "You take the south half of the room, and I'll take the north half."

While they were covertly searching for the wine bottle, Paula zeroed in on Cole again. He didn't exactly beat her off with a stick, but by refusing to stand still, he managed to prevent her from taking possession of his arm or any other part of his anatomy. Vicky watched with barely restrained delight as he made a complicated series of zigs and zags that succeeded in placing various pieces of furniture between him and Paula. She finally gave up and walked off in a huff. Cole caught Vicky's eye and pantomimed wiping sweat from his brow. She shook her head at him and went back to looking for the wine bottle. Moments later, she spotted it lying on the floor beside one of the armchairs just as Paula announced in a petulant tone that she was bored silly with waiting for something to happen and would be upstairs in her room if and when anything did.

"Good riddance," Michael uttered under his breath as she swept out of the lounge.

"Amen," Jayne drawled. "But she's right about the waiting being tedious. I brought along a book to read just in case things got boring. I think I'll go up and get it."

After Jayne left, Bud rose from his chair. "Well, folks, it promises to be a long night. I don't know about the rest of you, but I didn't get to finish my dinner. I think I'll go see if I can scrounge up some kind of snack in the kitchen."

"Good idea, Bud," Fred Espinoza remarked. "I'll go with you. Maybe we can put together some sandwiches or something."

When they'd gone, only five members of the group remained in the lounge: Vicky, Cole, Gary, Lyle and Michael. They all exchanged expectant looks.

"Do you get the feeling that things are building to some kind of climax?" Michael asked. Gary and Lyle nodded eagerly. Gary even rubbed his palms together in anticipation. He was grinning from ear to ear.

The French doors suddenly opened, and Todd reentered the lounge. He stopped, a startled, slightly wary expression on his face as five heads swiveled toward him in unison.

"You know, hanging out with you guys could give a person a severe case of paranoia," he said as he closed the doors. "I notice that Miss Congeniality is no longer present. I don't guess there's any chance somebody knocked her off while I was out?"

"'Fraid not," Lyle answered dryly. "She's retired to her room until something exciting happens."

Todd's relief was obvious. "You're all witnesses to this," he said as he crossed to the bar and reached for a glass. "I'm making a solemn vow. Never again will I let a strange woman pick me up on a train ."

Cole and Vicky exchanged a sharp glance when he lifted the bottle of diluted bourbon and emptied what was left of it into his glass. While she had Cole's attention, Vicky inclined her head slightly to indicate the wine bottle lying at her feet. He casually made his way over to her, but before either of them could think of a way to collect the bottle without drawing attention to themselves, Bud and Fred returned, bearing trays of sandwiches, cups and a coffeepot.

Their appearance provided the necessary distraction. While Gary, Michael and Todd were busy pushing two coffee tables together to hold the trays, Vicky let her notebook slip out of her hand. When she bent to retrieve it, she managed to grasp the neck of the bottle, as well, then concealed it in the folds of her skirt as she edged behind a sofa. A minute later she came back around the sofa and deposited the bottle in plain view on an end table.

"The damn thing's empty," she told Cole in disgust. "Bone-dry. Paula must have thrown the last of it at Jayne."

"Did she drink any of it first?"

"I don't think so. She'd just poured it into her glass when Jayne asked her if she intended to continue her childish behavior."

Since for the moment there didn't seem to be anything else they could do, they wandered over to join the others. Vicky dropped her notebook onto a chair so she'd have both hands free, then selected a ham sandwich. When she turned toward the other tray for a cup of coffee, she discovered that Todd had already filled several cups.

"Cream or sugar?" he asked with a smile.

"A little cream, thanks."

He seemed to be in much better spirits. Even allowing for the fact that Paula wasn't around to torment him, Vicky couldn't quite accept the abrupt change in his disposition. He didn't appear to be tipsy. Whether or not the wine he'd consumed at dinner was really wine, she didn't think half a bottle would have caused such a sudden mood swing; and if the watered-down bourbon had made him tight, it should have been evident long before now. Yet there was an almost feverish gleam in his eyes, and he was smiling like a crooked politician on election eve—from the teeth out.

He was smiling that politician's smile as he leaned forward to hand her a brimming cup of coffee, which he released at the same time that Vicky reached out to take it from him. She instinctively backed up a step, just in time to avoid being scalded.

"Oh, God, I'm sorry!" Todd cried in remorse. "I thought you had it."

Fred exclaimed in concern. So did Lyle. Cole dropped his sandwich on the floor and whirled toward her. "Did it burn you?"

"No, I'm all right," Vicky assured them. "My skirt may never be the same, though."

"Just be grateful it's floor-length," Gary told her.

"Believe me, I am."

Cole's expression was grim as he reached into his coat pocket for his handkerchief. Dropping to one knee in front of her, he began to dab at her skirt. Vicky opened her mouth to tell him not to bother. Then she noticed the piece of paper that was lying on the floor beside him.

"Here, what's this?" Bud snatched up the paper and squinted at it furiously.

Lyle plucked it out of his hand. "'One o'clock, under the sycamore tree,'" he read aloud.

Vicky glared at Cole. "Now wait a minute," he protested. "I know what you're thinking, but I did *not* arrange to meet Paula or anyone else under a sycamore tree at one o'clock."

"Of course you didn't," Todd said with a smirk.

Cole scowled at him as he rose to his feet. "Damn it, I don't even know what a sycamore tree looks like!"

"Right," Todd agreed. He was still smirking. "I believe you. Still, better you than me."

Cole turned back to Vicky. "I swear to you, I have no idea where that note came from or who wrote it."

"Sure looked like it came out of your pocket," Fred remarked. "Along with your handkerchief."

"All right, maybe it did, but anybody could have planted it there."

Bud spoke up in a firm voice. "I couldn't have. I haven't been close enough to you all night to put my hand in your pocket."

"Neither have I," Michael declared.

"Anyway," Lyle put in, "this looks like a woman's handwriting."

Cole leaned over his shoulder to peer at the note. "It's not Vicky's. Hers isn't that neat."

"Thanks," she muttered. No one paid her any mind.

"Well, if any of you are thinking Jayne might have written it, you're way off base," Gary told them. "She isn't even a mystery fan. She only came along this weekend to please me."

The claim drew seven skeptical glances. Bud consulted his watch, then looked up with a grin. "There's a simple enough way to find out who wrote the note. It is now precisely twelve minutes before one. I suggest we go find this sycamore tree and see who shows up under it."

Chapter Eleven

Todd immediately started organizing a search of the grounds, claiming he was sure the note was an important clue. "Whoever planted it may plan to commit the murder at one o'clock under the sycamore tree."

The Espinozas, Bud, Lyle and Gary gave Todd's idea their enthusiastic support. Evidently none of them detected the error in his logic. If everyone stayed inside the inn, the would-be murderer would be hard pressed to come up with a victim. Vicky said as much to Cole, while the other six divided into teams and discussed the best way to conduct the search.

"I know," he replied with a grin. "but this is the most excitement they've had since we left the train. Let's not spoil it. Besides, a murder is *supposed* to be committed this weekend, remember? It wouldn't be sporting to deliberately prevent the actors from doing their jobs."

Todd and Michael went off in search of some flashlights. Meanwhile, Bud and Lyle decided to stick together, because, as Lyle put it, "You won't be able to see your nose in front of your face, and if you went with somebody else, you'd probably get lost and end up playing the part of the corpse."

Since Michael had apparently cast his lot with Todd, Fred paired up with Gary, who seemed to have forgotten Jayne completely. Vicky asked if he didn't want to go upstairs and invite her along, or at least let her know he was leaving.

"I'm sure she wouldn't want to come," he said with a dismissive shrug. "She's probably got her nose stuck in a book. Besides, if everything works out, we should all be back inside in fifteen minutes or so."

Cole made it clear that he expected to be teamed with Vicky and, furthermore, that he expected her to stay close to his side. She wasn't altogether comfortable with that arrangement—the note had fallen out of his pocket, after all—but she decided she'd probably be at equal risk with any of the others. And, if she was with him, at least she would know where he was and what he was doing.

Realizing that her long skirt would only hamper her, Vicky asked him to wait while she ran up to her room to change. She met Jayne on the stairs. Jayne was carrying a paperback novel. A white angora sweater was draped over her shoulders, and she'd retied the scarf around her head to cover the green spot.

"Where's the fire?" she asked.

Vicky sent her down to look for Gary, saying that they'd found what could be a major clue and that he would explain.

When she reached her room, she was surprised to discover Paula in it, sprawled on the bed, idly flipping through a copy of *Vogue*. She had assumed not only that Paula had written the note but that by now the woman had slipped outside to wait for her intended victim under a sycamore tree. But if Paula was still inside and Jayne was still inside, then for whom was everyone supposed to search the grounds?

There wasn't time to figure it out. Cole was waiting downstairs, no doubt impatiently, and Vicky suspected that by the time she joined him, some of the others might have already taken off. She yanked the tail of her blouse free and hurried across the room to the chest of drawers. After she'd tossed a faded pair of jeans and a navy-blue sweatshirt onto the bed, Paula sat up, her magazine forgotten. "What's going on?"

Vicky shed her skirt and blouse and started tugging on the jeans as she gave the other woman a condensed report of what had happened. "So we're all going out to see if we can find this sycamore tree." She pulled the sweatshirt over her head, then glanced around impatiently. "Damn, where are my other shoes?"

"I put them in the closet. You say it was Todd's idea to go outside and look for this tree?" Paula sounded surprised.

Vicky retrieved her flats from the closet and slipped them on. "That's right. He's really fired up about it; seems to think the note is a clue that'll lead us straight to the scene of the murder. He and Michael even divided the property into sections for the different teams. Personally, I think the whole thing's simply another red herring, but I'm going along just in case I'm wrong.

"Besides," she added with a wry laugh, "even if it *is* a red herring, I don't care to stay behind and risk having one of them sneak back to knock me off while everybody else is outside."

Paula heard her out with a pensive frown. She seemed more subdued than she'd been all weekend. For once the expression in her eyes was thoughtful, almost meditative. Vicky couldn't help thinking that it was a pity Paula felt she had to play the flirt to gain attention. In a sudden flash of insight, she sensed that beneath the expertly applied make-up and practiced pout, there lived an intelligent, sensitive woman. Too bad Paula took such pains to keep her hidden.

"You've got a point there," Paula murmured. "About staying behind when everyone else goes outside, I mean. I think I'll come along, too."

Vicky tried to convince her to take a wrap, but Paula insisted she was warm-blooded and wouldn't need one. Since

Vicky had already stayed upstairs longer than she'd intended, she didn't argue.

There was no one in the lounge. Vicky's doubts about Cole immediately resurfaced. He had promised to wait for her.

"Where is everybody?" Paula asked. She sounded anxious, slightly alarmed.

"They must have left. We can try to catch up with them, if you don't mind going out on our own. They can't have been gone long." Even as she made the suggestion, Vicky was thinking that Paula was hardly dressed for tramping around the grounds in the dark. Her long skirt would have been hindrance enough, without those high-heeled sandals.

Paula's teeth worried her lower lip. She seemed to be having difficulty making up her mind. Vicky had just about decided to tell her to go back upstairs and barricade herself in the room when Cole entered the lounge from the veranda.

"Well, it's about time," he said irritably. "Come on; let's get going. The others have a five-minute head start on us."

Vicky ignored the peremptory command. "Where have you been?"

"Out on the veranda, trying to keep track of everybody else while I waited for you. Where did you think I'd been, hanging out under a sycamore tree? I told you, I don't even know what one looks like. Hello, Paula."

"Hello." Vicky did a double take at the total lack of interest in Paula's voice. Cole might have been her grandmother for all the enthusiasm she displayed. "Is Todd gone already? I'd hoped to catch him before he left."

Vicky rolled her eyes in disbelief. Talk about blowing hot and cold. Paula couldn't seriously think Todd would want her tagging along with him after the way she'd been behaving.

"Sorry," Cole told her. "He and Michael were the first ones out of here." Turning back to Vicky, he added, "They found two flashlights in the pantry next to the kitchen. They took one and gave the other to Bud and Lyle, and the four of them took off as if they were on a scavenger hunt or something. Fred had a penlight on his key chain. He and Gary decided they'd make do with it.''

"What about us?" Vicky asked.

His mouth curved sexily. "I'm afraid we'll have to make do with moonlight.''

Conscious of Paula's watching them, Vicky let her eyes tell him how nice that sounded. "Did Jayne make it downstairs in time to catch Gary?''

"Yes, she got here just as he and Fred were leaving. She went with them." Cole looked slightly uncomfortable as his gaze slid from Vicky to Paula and back again. "We really ought to get a move on. Will you be coming with us, Paula?''

Though he'd asked politely, Vicky noticed the lack of feeling in his voice. She suspected Paula had noticed it, too. If so, the woman didn't give any indication.

"Yes," she said firmly. "I think I will. Where are we supposed to look?''

They had been assigned the northwest section of the grounds, including the area surrounding the garage. Vicky suggested that rather than follow the veranda around the inn, they could save a little time by using the French doors in the reading room. Paula hurried across the lobby ahead of them.

"Did you invite her along?" Cole's question sounded almost like an accusation.

"What do you think?" Vicky replied.

"Well, couldn't you have talked her out of coming?" he demanded. "Considering how much trouble she's already caused—"

Vicky gave him a jab with her elbow to shush him as they entered the reading room. Paula was waiting for them by the French doors.

"Come on, you two," she called impatiently. "If we don't hurry, we'll miss out on all the fun."

"We're right behind you," Vicky said.

"Shouldn't she be wearing some kind of wrap?" Cole asked as they followed Paula out onto the veranda.

"She's warm-blooded."

"I don't doubt that for a minute, but I still think she should have put on a sweater or something."

"I told her that, Cole. She wouldn't listen. If you're so concerned about her, you can always give her your jacket."

He thought she was being sarcastic. "I'm not concerned about her," he muttered under his breath. "Not the way you're implying, anyway."

"I wasn't implying anything, for heaven's sake," Vicky said in exasperation. "What's wrong with you?"

"You want to know what's wrong with me?" he said as they descended the veranda steps. "I'll be happy to tell you what's wrong with me."

Paula stopped and frowned at them. "Listen, you two, this is hardly the time for a lovers' quarrel."

"Mind your own business," Cole told her tersely.

Vicky added a firm "And we're not lovers."

Cole turned and scowled down into her face. "*That's* what's wrong with me."

Vicky couldn't believe he'd said that. She didn't know whether to laugh or throw her arms around him. She settled for shaking her head and walking off toward the garage, leaving Cole and Paula to follow.

"Hey, slow down," Paula complained. "This isn't a race, for crying out loud."

Vicky halted, then counted to ten, slowly. There was no pleasing the woman. "I thought you were afraid we'd miss out on all the fun," she said when Paula came tottering up on her ridiculously high heels. She was clutching fistfuls of her skirt to hold it off the ground.

Cole stepped in front of them and planted his hands on his hips. "Let's just stop for a minute and consider the situation. Has it occurred to either of you that at this moment every single member of the group is out scouring the grounds for a sycamore tree?"

Paula looked at him as if he'd suddenly started raving in a foreign language. "What do you mean, has it occurred to us? Of course it's occurred to us. Why do you think we're here?" Turning to Vicky, she muttered, "I thought he was supposed to be smart."

Vicky smiled at Cole's offended expression. "I think the point he's making is that we're *all* out looking for the sycamore tree, presumably because we expect the murder to be committed under it. There's nobody left to be the murderer . . . or the victim, either, for that matter."

"Exactly," Cole said. "I suspect the note was just a means of sending everyone on a wild-goose chase. What do you say we go back inside and wait? The others will eventually either reach the same conclusion or give up and come back in when they don't find anything."

His suggestion was so reasonable, so logical, so clearly the only sensible thing to do, that he didn't for a moment expect either of them to disagree.

"Are you crazy?" Paula shrilled. She sounded as if she considered it a definite possibility. "I'm just starting to enjoy myself. Why should I go back and sit in that stuffy old lounge while everybody else is out having fun?"

"Fun?" Cole echoed incredulously. "You call traipsing around the countryside in the middle of the night without so much as a flashlight fun?"

"Well, it sure beats sitting around indoors, doing nothing," Paula countered with a defiant lift of her chin.

Cole looked to Vicky for support. He got an apologetic shrug instead. "I'm here to get a story, remember? I need to be where the action is. But you don't have to stay with us,

Cole. You're free to go back inside, if that's what you want.''

"Women!" he exclaimed with a combination of exasperation and disgust. "I'll never understand them if I live to be a hundred!"

"Let's start by checking out that clump of trees over by the garage," Paula suggested.

Vicky nodded eagerly. "Good idea. Are you coming, Cole?"

"Most unreasonable, illogical creatures on the face of the earth," he grunted as he fell in behind them. "This is probably a stupid question, but do either of you have any idea what a sycamore tree looks like?"

"Nope," Vicky replied cheerfully. "Not the foggiest. How about you, Paula?"

"Well, I think they're tall."

Cole glanced around at the towering black shapes surrounding the inn. "That should make it easy."

Either his sarcasm went right over Paula's head, or she chose to ignore it. "And I seem to remember that they have broad leaves."

"Big help," Cole grumbled under his breath. "I can't even make out the branches, much less the leaves."

"Will you stop grousing?" Vicky said over her shoulder. "Not ten minutes ago you were complaining because I took so long to change clothes. You couldn't wait to get outside." She repeated his words in a fretful singsong. "'The others have a five-minute head start.'"

"I did not whine!" he told her indignantly. "I've never whined in my life. Ouch! Damn it, anyway!"

Vicky instantly stopped and spun around, instinctively reaching out to him. Her hand closed on his arm. "What is it?"

"I stubbed my toe on something. This is absurd. We can't even see where we're going. Why won't you be reasonable and come back to the inn?"

"Vicky told you you don't have to stay with us," Paula reminded him. "If you really don't want to be here, go on back. We won't mind, honest."

"He wouldn't do that, Paula," Vicky murmured. Her fingers crept up his sleeve until they reached his neck. "He'd never leave two women alone in a potentially dangerous situation." Her voice was soft, affectionately indulgent.

"Damn right," Cole said soberly. "If I did something like that, they'd probably kick me out of the SSNOFD."

"The SSNOFD?" Vicky repeated.

"The Society of Stiff-Necked Old Fuddy-Duddies."

She laughed and patted his cheek. "Well, I certainly don't want your expulsion from the SSNOFD on my conscience."

"Does that mean you'll go back to the inn?" he asked hopefully.

"No, it means we'll help you maintain your membership in good standing by pretending that we need you to come along and protect us. Right, Paula?"

"If you say so. Personally, I think you're both a little strange. There isn't really a Society of Stiff-Necked Old Fuddy-Duddies, is there?"

"Of course there is," Vicky said. She clasped Cole's hand as they started forward again. "Cole's a charter member."

When they reached the three trees growing at the corner of the garage, they discovered that all of them were maples.

"Don't say a word," Vicky warned Cole. "There are still lots of possibilities."

"All right," he said with a defeated sigh. "I give up. We'll stay out all night and check every tree, bush and shrub on the property if that'll make you happy. Just point me in the direction you want to go."

Vicky paused to glance around. There were three or four trees at the front of the inn and a whole row of them lining the opposite side of the drive. It might well take the rest of the night to check all of them.

She turned to look in the opposite direction, toward the rear of the building. Paula was standing a few feet to her left, waiting patiently, apparently content to let Vicky decide what their next move would be. Her white blouse shimmered in the moonlight, making her easy to keep track of as long as she didn't stray more than three or four yards away. Cole's silver-gold hair made him equally easy to spot even without a light.

"We could split up," Vicky suggested tentatively.

Cole vetoed the idea at once. "Absolutely not."

"But we could cover three times as much territory in the same amount of time that way," she argued.

"I said no. It's out of the question. Subject closed, all right?"

Vicky folded her arms in a gesture of stubborn defiance. "No, it's not all right. Give me one good reason why we shouldn't split up and each check out two or three trees, then regroup and start over."

"I'll give you two good reasons," he said calmly. "First, in case you've forgotten, Paula is the only one of us who thinks she *might* be able to identify a sycamore tree if she happened to stumble across one in the dark. Second, if we split up, the murderer could pick us off one by one, at his or her convenience. If you want a third reason—"

"No, that's all right," Vicky muttered.

"So where do we look next?" Paula asked. "There are lots of trees out back. Oh, look, there's a light! Some of the others must already be looking over that way. Why don't we go see if they've found the right tree?"

Vicky was willing to go along with the idea, if only because it meant she could postpone deciding where they should search next. Cole's suggestion was beginning to sound like the best course of action, after all, though she was loath to admit it. She hadn't realized how many trees the property contained or what an impossible task locating the lone sycamore among them would be without any kind of light to guide them.

Cole cautioned them to stay close together as they set off across the lawn. The light, which was little more than a faint yellowish glow, seemed to originate near the pond. It dipped and bobbed in an erratic pattern, moving left several feet and then right for approximately the same distance before suddenly swinging back to the left again.

"Somebody's going over the same section of ground," Vicky murmured. "Retracing his steps . . . as if he's pacing back and forth."

Cole agreed. "It certainly looks that way, doesn't it?"

Paula shouldered her way between them. "Do you think he's waiting for somebody . . . like maybe his victim?" she asked in an excited whisper.

"Or his accomplice," Vicky added. Though she tried hard not to be, she was every bit as excited as Paula, and it came through in her voice. She reminded herself that she was a reporter covering a story, that she wasn't supposed to get personally involved or carried away by any of this silliness. It was only make-believe, after all, an elaborate play staged for the amusement of a bunch of upper-middle-class mystery buffs.

"Let's sneak up on him," she suggested with a fiendish grin.

"Terrific idea!" Paula said in approval. "We could circle around behind him. . . ."

"And hide in the bushes."

"There aren't any bushes down by the pond," Cole pointed out. "Besides, you're forgetting how steep the banks are, not to mention slippery. We'd probably end up falling in."

"There you go being a spoilsport again," Vicky told him crossly. "You don't have any spirit of adventure."

"I teamed up with you, didn't I?" he countered. "All right, we'll get as close as we can, see if we can identify whoever it is. But I insist that we don't get any closer to the pond than the gravel path. I have no desire to end the evening, looking like the creature from the black lagoon.''

Vicky led the single-file procession as they crept across the lawn, keeping to the shadows beneath the trees as much as possible. Cole stayed right behind her, close enough to grab her baggy sweatshirt if she showed any inclination to disregard his instructions. Paula brought up the rear, her skirt bunched around her hips. Vicky glanced back once to make sure she was keeping up.

"Don't worry about me," Paula whispered. "I'm right behind you."

When they reached one of the paths that Vicky and Cole knew would eventually lead to the one circling the pond, they followed it to a fork, where Vicky halted. Cole was so close behind her that she could feel his breath on the back of her neck.

"I don't see the light anymore, do you?" she whispered.

"No, but I think it was off to the right."

She nodded. "Okay. Stick with me, partner."

"Like Sears and Roebuck," he murmured in her ear.

She'd taken one step in the direction he'd indicated when a sound like an exploding firecracker suddenly fractured the silence. It was immediately followed by a scream

"What—!"

"Gunshot," Cole said curtly. Before Vicky could react, he grabbed hold of her hand and took off for the narrow end of the pond at a dead run.

Vicky stumbled down the path at Cole's side, praying she wouldn't trip over anything in the dark. By taking two steps to his one, she was barely managing to keep up with him; but what about Paula? She glanced back over her shoulder to check on the other woman.

"Cole!" she panted in alarm. "Cole, stop! Paula's gone."

He didn't even slow down. "Don't worry; she'll catch up with us."

"No." Vicky tried to tug her hand free. "Either stop and listen to me or let me go!"

He didn't let her go, but he did stop. "All right," he said impatiently. "What's so important that it can't wait until we find out who fired that shot?"

"I told you, Paula's gone."

"And I told you that she'll catch up. If she hadn't worn those crazy shoes and a long skirt in the first place, she wouldn't be having so much trouble—"

"She's not behind us!" Vicky snapped in exasperation. "At all! Get the picture?" She took a moment to catch her breath and control her temper. "She must have taken the other path back there at the fork. If she was within fifteen feet of us, we'd be able to see her. Her blouse practically glows in the dark."

"Is that Vicky Rand up there?" a voice called from the darkness below them.

Cole whirled toward the pond. "Who is it?"

"Bud Potts. Stay where you are. I'll come to you."

The beam of his flashlight preceded Bud up the bank. He was breathing heavily by the time he reached the path.

"What were you doing down there?" Cole asked suspiciously. "I thought you and Lyle were supposed to take the southwest section."

Bud nodded. "We were, and we did. All we found were maples, elms, a few birches and a couple of pin oaks. Not a sycamore in sight. We thought we saw a light down this way, so we came to see if whoever it was had had any better luck."

"And had they?" Vicky asked.

"Couldn't say. We never found anybody. I saw what I thought was a likely-looking tree and went to check it out— I swear, it couldn't have been more than ten feet away—and when I went back to tell Lyle it was just another silver maple, he was gone. I've been pacing back and forth down there for the last ten minutes." He aimed the flashlight down the slope to indicate where he'd been.

"My night vision's so lousy I knew I'd never be able to find him even with a flashlight, but I hoped that sooner or later he'd see the light moving back and forth and realize it was me. And then I heard that shot...." He heaved a sigh. "If old Puddin' Head's gone and got himself killed, he'll probably claim it was my fault for wandering off to check that tree."

Vicky had to squelch a grin at "Puddin' Head." If these two were putting everybody on, they were certainly doing it with panache.

"If the shot was meant for Lyle, there must be a woman with him," she said. "That was definitely a female scream I heard right after it."

Bud's brows drew together in confusion. "But you're the only woman who came outdoors. Paula and Jayne are still upstairs; at least they were when we left."

"Not anymore," Cole told him. "Jayne is with Gary and Fred, and Paula was with us until a minute or so ago."

"When she apparently decided to take off on her own," Vicky added. "To try and find Todd, I suspect."

Bud groaned. "You mean round three is about to commence?"

"Only if she finds him," Cole drawled. "If he's smart, he'll hide out somewhere until she gets tired of looking. She seems to have a very short attention span. Could you tell which direction the shot and the scream came from?"

Bud thought both had come from the southern end of the pond, though he pointed out that the water and the trees surrounding it might have distorted the sounds, making them seem to originate from one direction when in fact they'd come from somewhere else.

The three of them followed the path until it curved to the east and the ground started to fall away toward the pond. The sleeve of Jayne's white sweater alerted them to the fact that she was cowering behind the trunk of a huge oak tree a few feet from the path. Once they'd spotted her, they quickly realized that Gary was with her. Fred Espinoza was hiding behind the elm next door. They heard Fred before they saw him.

"Who goes there?" he demanded as they approached.

Bud drew up in surprise. "Did he really say, 'Who goes there'?" he asked Vicky under his breath. "Good heavens, he must think he's in an old John Wayne movie. Next he'll be asking for the secret password." She pressed her lips together to contain a giggle. "It's us, you idiot," Bud responded gruffly. "Why on earth are you skulking behind that tree?"

"Who's 'us'?" Fred returned suspiciously. "Identify yourselves."

"What did I tell you," Bud muttered. "He does think he's in an old John Wayne movie."

Vicky hoped she'd be able to remember all this when she started putting together her article. "Fred, it's me, Vicky. Cole and Bud are with me. What's going on?"

"Vicky!" Jayne cried in relief. "Thank goodness." She came out from behind the oak. "You won't believe what happened!"

"Wait a minute," Bud said. "Don't you want to know the secret password?"

Vicky told him to behave himself. "Did you guys hear a noise like a gunshot a few minutes ago?"

"Did we *hear* it?" Jayne repeated shrilly. "We didn't just hear it, we were the targets!"

Chapter Twelve

"Are you saying someone deliberately shot at you?" Cole asked sharply. "For real?"

"That's exactly what I'm saying," Jayne confirmed. "Tell him, Gary."

"She's right," Gary said as he went to Jayne's side and slipped an arm around her waist. "We spotted a light down by the pond and started out to investigate. When we got to this point on the path, somebody took a shot at us. I know it sounds incredible, but it's true. Some lunatic really did fire a gun at us!"

"We believe you," Vicky said. "All three of us heard the shot and then a scream."

Jayne pressed closer to Gary's side. "They probably heard me in the next county. I've never been so terrified in my life."

Bud attempted to reassure her. "Whoever fired the shot was most likely using a starter's pistol, or maybe a blank. I expect is was just one of the actors doing his bit to add a touch of realism."

"It was a little *too* realistic as far as I'm concerned," Jayne said grimly. "I'd swear I heard the bullet whiz past my ear."

Bud smiled and patted her arm. "I imagine it was just a mosquito. This is the time of year for them, and that pond's probably a breeding ground."

Jayne conceded that he could be right, on both counts, but declared that she'd had more than enough excitement for one night and was calling it quits. "I'd rather be indoors curled up with a good book, anyway. I think I'll take a nice long bath and wash my hair . . . see if I can get it back to its normal mousy brown," she added with a wry smile. "I really don't think the patchwork look suits me."

Gary offered to go back inside with her, but she refused. "Don't be silly, darling. You know you're having the time of your life."

The rear door of the inn was only about twenty-five feet away. The five of them escorted her to it, then waited until she was safely inside before discussing what their next move should be. Cole suggested that since the pond seemed to be attracting so much activity, they should split up and circle it to see who or what they could find. One o'clock had come and gone, so there didn't seem to be much point in continuing to search for a sycamore tree, but Paula and Lyle were still missing. While no one came right out and said so, Vicky suspected they were all assuming that one of them would turn out to be the murder victim.

Fred and Gary took the path nearest the inn, while Cole, Vicky and Bud continued on around to the far side of the pond. They agreed to meet at the fork where Cole and Vicky had been standing when they heard the shot.

Bud turned the flashlight over to Cole, who walked a couple of feet ahead. He swung the beam from side to side as they slowly made their way along the narrow path. By the time they were halfway around the pond, they still hadn't found any bodies—or anything that seemed at all out of place, for that matter.

"Maybe I should go take a look a little closer to the water," Cole suggested.

"If you do, watch your step," Bud advised. "The ground down there's slicker than cat—uh, excrement on a linoleum floor. I almost fell in when I went to check that tree."

"What an interesting figure of speech, Bud," Vicky murmured. "I don't believe I've ever heard that one before." Turning to Cole, she said firmly, "If you go, I'm going with you."

She could make out enough of his face in the glow from the flashlight to know that he was about to give her an argument. "We shouldn't split up," she said quickly. "As you pointed out not long ago, that would make it possible for the murderer to pick us off one by one, at his or her convenience."

"You really get a kick out of throwing my words back in my face, don't you?" he said in a resigned tone. "Oh, all right, but for heaven's sake be careful. Are you coming, too, Bud?"

"No, I think I'll just hide behind this tree until you get back."

Cole took a firm grip on Vicky's arm, and they started making their way gingerly down the bank. They hadn't gone more than five or six feet when they heard the second shot.

"Judas Priest!" Bud yelled. "Did one of you just get killed?"

"No," Vicky answered as she and Cole scrambled back onto the path. "We're both okay. Where did that one come from?"

"North, I think," Cole said.

Bud disagreed. "No, west, toward the inn."

"Well, maybe a little west of north."

"How are we supposed to know where to look when you can't even agree on a direction?" Vicky complained.

"It's like I said before," Bud told her. "The sound bounces back from the trees and the water, so it's hard to tell exactly where it came from. But I still say that this time it came from due west."

"Well, we can't go due west," Cole said. "We'd walk right into the pond."

"Good point," Bud conceded. "Okay, let's just keep going the way we were headed."

Vicky muttered something about being teamed up with two of the Marx brothers.

"You know," Bud speculated as they hurried along the path, "we only have Fred's and the Kaysers' word for it that somebody shot at them. It's possible one of them fired both shots."

Vicky glanced at him sharply. "I hadn't even thought of that!"

"Fred and Gary should have been almost directly across the pond from us when we heard the second shot," Cole mused. "Which means that if Bud's right and it did come from due west, one of them could have fired it."

"But if one of them did, then all three of them must be actors," Vicky pointed out. "And if Fred's an actor, Michael must be, too. But Michael teamed up with Todd. Why would he have done that?"

Cole shrugged. "Maybe to throw suspicion off himself, or because Todd was the intended victim all along. Speaking of Michael and Todd, it just occurred to me that they're the only members of the group we haven't seen or even heard of since we came out. Don't you think that's a little strange?"

"Not if one of them's the killer," Bud said. "Right now I'd be happy just to find Lyle . . . alive and in one piece."

At the point where the path started to curve back toward the inn, someone called out to them from up ahead. They stopped, and Cole instinctively stepped in front of Vicky. She appreciated his gallantry, but at the same time she wished his shoulders weren't quite so broad. She stood on tiptoe to peer over the left one.

"Who is it?" Cole called back to whoever had hailed them.

"Todd." The gravel crunched under his feet as he ran to meet them. He staggered to a halt several feet away and leaned forward, bracing his hands on his knees for a few seconds while he caught his breath.

"Whew, am I glad to see you guys," he said, panting. "I lost Michael about ten minutes ago, and he has our light. I've been stumbling around in the dark trying to find him. Then I heard two gunshots. At least I think that's what they were. I don't mind telling you, I started to get a little nervous after that."

"Where were you when you heard the shots?" Cole asked.

"I was still pretty close to the inn when I heard the first one. Michael and I were already headed down this way, but we split up for a couple of minutes, figuring we'd be able to cover more ground. I'd just realized that I couldn't see his light anymore when I heard the shot. I decided to come on down to the pond, hoping to meet up with him again somewhere along the way. Only I didn't. And then I heard the second shot. It sounded a lot closer than the first one. That's when I started to worry."

"You're not the only one," Bud muttered. "I think we're all beginning to feel a little edgy. When I signed up for this weekend, I sure didn't expect some nut to be taking potshots at us in the middle of the night."

"Amen to that," Todd agreed fervently. "This is a little more excitement than I'd bargained for. By the way, I thought you and Lyle were together. Don't tell me you've lost your partner, too."

"I'm afraid so," Bud said heavily.

Vicky was growing impatient with all this conversation, which wasn't accomplishing a single thing as far as she could tell. She pushed at Cole's shoulder to move him out of the way. "We're wasting time standing here talking," she said as she stepped between him and Bud. "Whoever fired those shots could be halfway to Indianapolis by now."

Todd stared at her as if she'd suddenly appeared before him in a puff of smoke. "Vicky!" he blurted in surprise. "I didn't see you standing there."

"Cole was shielding me with his body," she told him. "In case you were a mad killer."

Todd's soft laugh sounded forced. Under the circumstances, she supposed it had been a tactless thing to say. For all they knew, some maniac might be loose on the grounds, firing real bullets out of a real gun—definitely not the kind of thing one should joke about.

The four of them continued on around the pond, retracing the route Todd had just taken from the inn. Cole and Vicky led the small procession, since Cole was carrying the only flashlight, with Bud and Todd following close behind. They slowed their pace as the path began to slope downward at the northern end of the pond. A few minutes later Todd spotted something lying beneath one of the trees at the edge of the water.

His startled exclamation made Vicky jump in alarm. For a moment she thought he'd seen someone lurking in the deep shadows under the trees, or possibly the barrel of a gun as the moonlight glinted off it. But then he grabbed Cole by an arm and started dragging him down the bank toward the pond, babbling something about "she must have slipped and fallen in."

Bud came up to stand beside Vicky. "She?" he said in a puzzled voice. "Who is he talking about?"

"I have no idea, but I'm certainly going to find out. Come on."

As Vicky skidded down the bank, it occurred to her that the "she" to whom Todd had referred could only be one person. She waited until she'd managed to dig her heels into the soft, spongy earth and bring herself to a halt, then asked anxiously, "Is it Paula?"

"Yes," Cole answered tersely. "Stay there. Bud, come give us a hand."

Vicky wasn't the least bit tempted to disregard his curt instruction. She stood rooted to the spot as Bud lumbered past her in the dark. There was a brief interval of silence, then a series of sloshing sounds. Someone was wading into the pond. Vicky hugged her arms, suddenly chilled to the bone. The only possible reason anyone would have for entering that stagnant, scum-covered water would be to retrieve something from it.

"Hey, what's going on down there?"

The booming voice came from directly above her. Vicky started violently. She would have screamed if her heart hadn't been blocking her throat.

"Who...who is that?" she called when she could breathe again.

"Gary and Fred. We've got Lyle and Michael with us. Vicky, is that you?"

She closed her eyes as a weakening wave of relief swept through her. "Yes, it's me."

"What the devil's going on? You're not down there by yourself, are you?" The anxious concern in Gary's voice was enormously comforting. Vicky felt the strength begin to return to her limbs.

"No, Cole's here. And Bud and Todd. Gary, I think you'd better come down here. Something's happened."

The quaver in her voice must have told them that the something that had happened wasn't anything good. All four men came scrambling and sliding down the bank.

"Are you all right?" Gary asked when he reached her.

Vicky nodded. "I'm fine. It's Paula."

"Paula!" Michael and Lyle cried at the same time.

"How did she get out here?" Fred chimed in. "The last I knew, she was up in her room, sulking and being bored."

"She came out with Cole and me," Vicky explained. "But then she slipped away from us and apparently ended up down here."

"Has she been hurt?" Lyle asked.

"I don't know. Todd saw her from the path. He said she must have slipped and fallen into the pond. The three of them are over there now, checking."

"Where?" Fred demanded. "Under that tree?"

"Yes. Cole told me to stay back. I don't think he wanted me to see what they'd found." Her voice started to wobble again, just a little, on the last few words.

Lyle grasped her hand and gave it a comforting squeeze. "Why don't the rest of you go find out what's happening? I'll stay here with Vicky."

Her fingers curled around his large, square hand in gratitude as the other men trooped off toward the dim yellow glow of Bud's flashlight. A minute later someone said, "Oh, my God," in a shaken voice. Vicky's grip became a vise, but Lyle didn't complain. Another minute passed, and then another, before one of the two lights began moving toward them.

Todd appeared first. Michael was right behind him. Cole brought up the rear. When he got close enough for Vicky to make out his golden hair, she released Lyle's hand and hurried forward to meet him. They both slowed, then stopped less than two feet apart. Vicky took one shocked look at him—his dripping clothes, the grim set of his mouth, the large dark spot on the front of his sport coat—and knew what he was going to say before he spoke.

"She's dead."

Vicky felt as if her blood had suddenly turned to icewater. She heard Lyle mutter something savage and profane, but the words sounded mild compared to the obscenity that had just fallen from Cole's lips.

"This is for real, isn't it?" she heard herself say in a strange voice. "It isn't the phony murder we've all been waiting for."

Cole shook his head. "I wish to God it was."

"How?" she asked in a voice thick with dread.

He gave the answer she'd both feared and expected. "She was shot." He hesitated briefly, as if he didn't want to add the rest. "In the back."

"God Almighty," Lyle whispered in horror.

"That's not all." Cole inclined his head toward the spot where he and Todd had discovered Paula's body. "That tree we found her under—Bud says it's a sycamore."

FRED WANTED TO TAKE Paula's body back to the inn, but Cole and Gary pointed out that the police would probably prefer they didn't.

"Lord knows what kind of evidence we've already destroyed," Bud added. "All of us tramping around down here, I mean . . . if there were any footprints, we've obliterated them."

"Well, we didn't do it deliberately," Todd retorted with a touch of defensiveness. He was obviously upset about what had happened. "How were we to know Paula had been murdered?" His voice shook slightly, and he took off up the path in a hurry.

Todd's reaction was a harbinger of the anxiety that soon set in. By the time the others had reached the inn most of them were casting furtive glances at one another, then quickly averting their eyes when the one being observed turned in their direction. The suspicion they'd displayed at the beginning of the weekend was nothing like the paranoia that affected them now.

One of them had been murdered in cold blood, and they all knew that the killer was still among them. He or she—no one was exempt from suspicion—might be the person who had sat across the dinner table last night, played a friendly game of cards or discussed the commodities market.

That in itself was sobering and frightening enough. But the worst fear, the one that caused a chill to creep along the spine of each and every one of them at some point during the next few hours, was that the murderer wasn't finished, that he or she might strike again, as senselessly as before. Hadn't someone, presumably the same person who'd killed Paula, fired a shot at Fred and the Kaysers *before* she was shot in the back? What if they were dealing with some kind of psychopath, someone so deranged that his or her behavior was utterly impossible to predict?

The first order of business was to wake Mr. Hagan and ask him to phone the police. It took several minutes to make him understand that the disheveled mob crowded into the hall outside his apartment had come to report a real murder, not one of the make-believe kind he was accustomed to.

After Mr. Hagan had been notified, Gary announced that he was going upstairs to tell Jayne what had happened. Noticing the suspicious looks he received from several of the others, Vicky volunteered to go with him. They found Jayne in her pajamas and robe, drying her hair at the dressing table. She was understandably shocked and shaken by the news.

"My God," she whispered. "It could have been one of us, Gary...you or me or Fred. If the first shot hadn't missed, one of us might be lying dead out there instead of Paula."

"Or along with Paula," Gary said grimly. "Until someone comes up with a motive for her murder, we have to consider the possibility that the murderer didn't have one— that he's just totally insane. If that's the case, even if he had hit one of us, he still might have strolled down to the other end of the pond and killed Paula."

Jayne finished drying her hair and then went downstairs with them. The green patch was still visible but not as noticeable as it had been now that she'd washed the auburn rinse out of her hair. They met Cole in the lobby. He was headed for the stairs. Jayne gasped and clamped a hand over her mouth when she saw him.

He glanced down at himself, his mouth twisting in a bitter parody of a smile. "I was going to wait to take a shower until after the police arrived, but Mr. Hagan says they might not be here for half an hour or more. I'll be back as soon as I've cleaned up and changed."

As he passed Vicky, she reached out to brush her fingers across the back of his hand. He paused long enough to give her a wan smile, then continued on to the stairs.

"He pulled her out of the pond," Gary said to Jayne. "At first they thought she'd fallen in and drowned. Cole carried her onto the bank to start administering CPR. That's how her blood got all over the front of his jacket."

Vicky shivered as she followed the Kaysers to the lounge. She hadn't known the details. On the way back to the inn Cole had been grimly silent. Now she understood why. Discovering the circumstances of Paula's death had been horrible for all of them, but it must have been a hundred times worse for Cole—and for Todd, she thought with a rush of compassion. He must feel terrible, knowing that the last words he and Paula said to each other had been spoken in anger.

The atmosphere in the lounge was tense. Todd stood hunched over the bar, his back to everyone, drinking steadily. Bud was the only person without a glass in his hand. He sat in one of the overstuffed chairs, calmly puffing on his pipe and frowning at a point that seemed to be equidistant between the end of his nose and the nearest wall. There had been frequent references to his poor vision, but Vicky hadn't seen him wear a pair of glasses all weekend.

She, Jayne and Gary entered the room just as Fred was commenting that Lyle couldn't verify his whereabouts at the time Paul was shot.

"Looks like it's started," Gary murmured under his breath. "Before this night's over, we're all liable to be at each other's throats."

To Lyle's credit, he remained calm in the face of Fred's provocation. "I've already explained that Bud and I had gotten separated and I'd been trying to find him. When I heard you and Gary coming along the path, I came to meet you. I asked you both if you'd seen Bud. You told me that he was with Cole and Vicky and that you were going to meet the three of them near the north end of the pond. I'll be glad to go over the whole thing again for the police when they get here, but I'll be damned if I'm going to repeat it for you to pick apart. I didn't kill her. I'll admit that a couple of times I was tempted to turn her over my knee, but I did not kill her!" He paused to take a long drink from his glass. "And that's the last time I intend to say it, at least to any of you."

"That's tellin' him," Bud approved from his chair. "Hell, Fred, I could have told you Lyle wouldn't hurt a fly. He gets squeamish when he has to squash a cockroach or a spider. It all goes back to Korea."

"That's enough, Bud," Lyle said wearily. His friend ignored him.

"He saw enough killing to last three lifetimes. When he came back, the first thing he did was give away all his hunting gear—rifles and shotguns, even the knives. Said he'd never touch another killing tool, and he never has."

There was dead silence in the room for several seconds, during which Vicky walked over to the chair on which she'd dropped her notebook. Much as she hated the idea, she knew she should be getting everything down on paper. That was her job, after all, the reason she was here. As she unclipped her pen, Bud spoke again. His tone was deceptively casual.

"You know," he said around the stem of his pipe, "Lyle isn't the only one who can't provide a witness to his whereabouts at the instant Paula was killed. Michael and Todd were wandering around on their own about then, too. How would you like it if one of us started pointing a finger at your son, Fred?''

Fred glanced at Michael. ''I wouldn't,'' he admitted quietly.

''Are you suggesting that I killed her?'' Michael jumped out of his chair, his face flushed with anger. ''I've told you that I wasn't anywhere near the pond where she was shot! I was still up by the inn, looking for Todd. Just because nobody saw me doesn't mean I'm the murderer, for God's sake.''

''Of course it doesn't,'' Bud agreed mildly. ''That's my point. Calm down, Michael. Nobody's accusing you of anything.''

But Michael wasn't so easily appeased. ''It sure sounded like it!''

''Shut up and sit down, Michael,'' his father said wearily. ''All Bud is saying is that unless and until somebody confesses, we have no way of knowing who killed Paula. Even if we think we know, there were no witnesses, so we can't prove anything.''

''The gun would have the murderer's fingerprints on it, wouldn't it?'' Jayne asked.

Todd spoke for the first time since he'd returned to the inn. His voice was fraught with bitter cynicism. ''Maybe. Except it's probably buried in a foot of mud at the bottom of the pond.''

''What makes you think that?'' Gary demanded.

Todd shrugged and went to stare out one of the front windows. ''I just figure that whoever shot her would want to get rid of it, and the fastest and most convenient way would have been to throw it into the pond.''

''If it's there, the police should be able to retrieve it, don't you think?'' Fred said in a hopeful tone.

Cole entered the lounge as Fred finished speaking. He'd showered, changed into light gray slacks and a white crewneck sweater and replaced his ruined wing tips with the loafers he'd been wearing on Friday. His hair was still damp. "I presume you're talking about the gun," he said as he crossed the room to take the chair beside Vicky's.

"Yes," Jayne answered. "Todd thinks the murderer may have thrown it in the pond, and Fred was just saying that if he did, the police ought to be able to recover it."

"What do you think, Cole?" Gary asked. "If it's there and they do manage to dredge it up, would they be able to get a viable set of prints from it?"

"It's possible, I suppose. It would depend on the make of the gun, the composition of the grip, the alkali content of the water and how long it had been submerged—any number of things. But I don't think they'll find the gun in the pond."

Todd had turned from the window to listen to Cole's answer. "Why not?" he asked.

"It's too obvious," Cole said. "Isn't that the first place you'd look for it?"

"But if it isn't in the pond, where would it be?" Lyle wondered.

Cole hesitated before answering. He was reluctant to contribute to the suspicion and mistrust that already existed, but if he didn't say it, sooner or later someone else would. He leaned forward, resting his arms on his thighs, his hands clasped between them, and glanced around the room.

"The murderer could still have it, or he could've hidden it someplace where it would be easy for him to get to."

The statement had approximately the same effect as if Cole had pulled the gun from beneath the cushion of his chair and pointed it at each of them in turn. Their expressions reflected first shock, then horrified comprehension, as what he'd said sank in.

"I don't think he actually has it on him," Cole added in a soft but confident tone. "That would be stupid, and whoever murdered Paula isn't stupid. If he were, he'd have done something to give himself away by now.''

''Is that supposed to be reassuring?'' Jayne demanded shakily. ''If I have to be confined to a house in the middle of nowhere with a murderer, I think I'd be more comfortable knowing he's a little on the dumb side.''

Cole shook his head firmly. ''No, you wouldn't. Stupid people do stupid things—desperate, irrational things—when they're threatened or their backs are to the wall. I'd much rather know that the enemy possesses a shrewd, cunning mind and probably higher-than-average intelligence.''

Vicky understood what he was saying. ''That kind of person wouldn't do or say anything to give himself away,'' she murmured. ''If he knew no one had seen him commit the crime and there was no evidence to implicate him, he'd probably just play it cool . . . be patient and wait out the investigation.''

''And try not to draw unnecessary attention to himself in the meantime,'' Cole added.

Bud expelled a short bark of laughter. ''Now the accusations should really start flying! Nobody will want to look as if he's deliberately trying *not* to draw attention to himself.''

The remark coaxed a reluctant smile from Cole as he leaned back in his chair. ''You may have a point, Bud, but I for one don't intend to accuse anyone of murder until I'm a hundred percent sure I have the right person.''

Vicky wondered if anyone else had noticed that he hadn't said, ''*Unless* I'm a hundred percent sure.'' He'd said ''until.'' Yes, she decided; at least one other person would have noticed. Cole had just let the murderer know that sooner or later he intended to discover the person's identity. It didn't occur to her to wonder whether he could. She just hoped he knew what he was doing by throwing out such a direct challenge.

Something outside drew Todd back to the window. "At the risk of drawing unnecessary attention to myself," he said dryly, "I think I should tell everyone that we have company. The cops are here."

Chapter Thirteen

The first law enforcement officers to arrive were the county sheriff and one of his deputies. They were soon joined by several Indiana state troopers. The sheriff, the deputy and all but one of the troopers were examining the scene of the murder when two plainclothes detectives, also from the state police force, arrived. It quickly became obvious to the people in the lounge that the detectives were in charge. One of them introduced himself as Lieutenant Abernathy and addressed the group as a whole. He didn't waste time on preliminaries.

"Sergeant Farrell and I will want to question each of you separately. We'll get to that in a few minutes, but first there's another matter you may be able to help us with."

The lieutenant was a large man, well over six feet tall, with curly light brown hair and pudgy cheeks. He stood with his feet braced apart, one hand jingling the change in his pocket as he spoke to them in a soft, matter-of-fact tone. Nothing about him—not about his demeanor, his relaxed posture or the pitch of his voice—prepared them for what he had to say.

That afternoon the body of another murder victim had been discovered in the baggage car of the commuter train to which the mystery-train cars had been attached. The victim was a female Caucasian, estimated age between twenty-five and thirty, five feet six inches tall, with brown hair and green eyes. It had been determined that she was killed before the train left Chicago, but so far the police hadn't been able to identify her.

"Didn't she have a purse?" Jayne asked.

Lieutenant Abernathy shook his head. "No purse, no wallet, no identification of any kind."

Bud removed his pipe from his mouth long enough to ask, "Do you think she was killed in the process of being robbed?"

Abernathy pursed his lips and rocked back on his heels. "I might, if she'd been shot or stabbed—she was strangled, by the way; did I mention that?—and if her body hadn't been crammed into a steamer trunk in the baggage car of a train. Your typical robbery-murder victim is usually found in a dark alley or a parking lot—someplace like that. What it all boils down to is that we have a series of coincidences that are just a little too coincidental for me to swallow." He ticked the points off on his fingers as he enumerated them.

"One, we believe our Jane Doe was killed shortly before the train left the station. Two, all of you were passengers on a special section of that train. Three, we now suddenly find ourselves with a second murder victim, who also just happened to be aboard that very same train.

Gary Kayser asked the question that was on everyone's mind. "Are you saying that you think one of us might have killed the woman who was found in the baggage car?"

"At the moment, there are no suspects in that case," Abernathy answered quietly. Vicky reflected that he should be working for the federal government; he had answered the question without actually answering it.

"I'd like to pass her picture around. If any of you remember seeing her at the station, let Sergeant Farrell or me know. We're especially interested in finding out if she was with anybody." He turned to the other detective and held out his hand. Sergeant Farrell withdrew an eight-by-ten black-and-white glossy from a plain manila envelope and gave it to him.

"I'd better warn you that this was taken by the medical examiner," the lieutenant said as he handed the photo to Fred. "Sorry, but it's the only picture we have of her. Please examine it carefully. Now, who'd like to be the first to get the questioning over with?"

"Whew!" Vicky said under her breath after Gary and Jayne had left with the two detectives. "I have the feeling not much gets by him."

"He seems to know his business," Cole agreed.

Michael walked over to hand him the picture, grimacing as Cole took it from him. "It's pretty gruesome," he warned. "You can see the bruises on her neck."

"Did you recognize her?" Vicky asked.

Michael shook his head. "I'm happy to say I've never seen her before in my life. Neither has Dad."

He went back to rejoin his father, and Vicky moved over to perch on the arm of Cole's chair. This wasn't the first time she'd seen a photograph of a corpse, but still she winced slightly.

"She looks vaguely familiar," Vicky said after a moment.

"She should," Cole murmured. "It's the woman whose picture you were taking at the station, when I stepped in front of you."

"What? Are you sure?" She bent her head to scrutinize the photo.

Cole slipped his arm around her and pulled her closer, placing his mouth beside her ear. "Shh, keep your voice down," he cautioned under his breath. "It's entirely possible that someone in the group did kill her."

Vicky stiffened. "Oh, my God. Do you really think—"

"At this point I think our motto should be 'Better safe than sorry.'" He gave her an encouraging squeeze. "When Abernathy and Farrell finish questioning the Kaysers, we'll ask to be next. That way we can tell them what we know without any of the others overhearing."

"All right," Vicky agreed. "They'll probably want the film, won't they?"

"Mmm, I should think so."

"I'm glad you thought of having Mr. Hagan lock it up in the safe."

"So am I. Don't be nervous."

Vicky tried on a smile that didn't quite fit. "What makes you think I'm nervous?"

"Well, for one thing your fingernails are shredding my pants."

She glanced down, then quickly pulled her hand away from his thigh. "Sorry. I guess I am a little nervous. What should we do now—until Gary and Jayne come back, I mean?"

"Behave as if nothing unusual has happened, I think. You go back to where you were sitting, and I'll take the picture over to Bud."

Vicky turned to him, her eyes huge and darkened by anxiety. "Do I have to go back over there?"

He had to conquer the urge to draw her down onto his lap and wrap his arms around her. "I think you should," he said.

"All right." As she started to slide off the arm of his chair, Cole reached out to capture her hand and give it a brief, hard squeeze.

"Trust me," he said softly.

Her fingers returned the pressure of his. "I do."

His eyes lit with pleasure. He held her hand a moment longer, then released it and got up to take the photograph to Bud.

Jayne and Gary had left the lounge at a quarter past two. They returned about twenty minutes later. When they appeared in the doorway, Vicky and Cole rose simultaneously to take their places.

"Boy, you're a couple of eager beavers," Todd remarked from the sofa where he was lounging.

Cole shook his head with a tired smile. "We just want to get it over with."

"It's not too bad," Jayne said. "Sergeant Farrell took me into the kitchen, and Lieutenant Abernathy questioned Gary in the dining room. Mainly they wanted us to go over everything that happened after we left the inn."

"In detail," Gary added dryly. "Several times."

Jayne leaned close to Vicky to whisper, "I think they wanted to see if our stories would change. It was just like one of those police shows on television. Sergeant Farrell kept asking the same questions over and over, and Gary says Lieutenant Abernathy did the same thing with him."

But once the detectives heard what Cole and Vicky had to tell them, the couple was taken to the dining room, and the questioning about the events of that night was condensed to a brisk ten-minute session.

"We'll come back to this later," Lieutenant Abernathy said as he made a few scribbled notes. "Right now I want to concentrate on why your purse and camera bag were searched and what might be on this film other than the picture of our Jane Doe. Try to remember all the pictures you took and what was in each of them. Not just the people but any stuff you might have picked up in the background or the surrounding area—that kind of thing."

"What good will that do?" Vicky asked with a frown.

The detective shrugged his massive shoulders. "It could be that you accidentally got something on film . . . for instance, Jane Doe talking to the person who killed her. It's a long shot, but I have a hunch—" He broke off and turned to Sergeant Farrell. "Joe, go ask Mr. Hagan to meet us in his office, then pick one of the troopers to run that film to the lab as soon as we get it out of the safe."

The sergeant was headed for the door before Abernathy had finished speaking. "I'll get Nolan to do it. He can take the bullet in at the same time."

"Bullet?" Vicky repeated in a faint voice. "You already took the bullet out of..." She trailed off without finishing.

"Lord, no!" Abernathy said quickly. "That's the coroner's job. One of the men found a slug embedded in a tree out back. The Kaysers claim somebody took a shot at them not long before Ms. Danvers was killed. We're ninety-nine percent sure this bullet is the one that was fired at them and that it came from the same gun that killed Ms. Danvers, but we'll have to run it through ballistics to be positive."

When they reached Mr. Hagan's office, he was already there, wringing his hands and muttering to himself as he paced from one side of the small, square room to the other. He quickly acquainted them with the reason for his distress.

"I've managed this place for more than thirteen years, and never, not *once*, has anything like this happened. I told them. I told them they'd regret letting those mystery-weekend people rent the inn, but would they listen? Oh, no. First there's a murder on the property, and now look." He flung an arm toward the desk in agitation.

"The box!" Vicky exclaimed as she spotted it. She hurried over to the desk, picked up a pencil and pried back one of the torn box flaps. "It's been ripped open."

"I'm not talking about the box!" Mr. Hagan said indignantly. "My desk! My beautiful, handcrafted rosewood desk has been vandalized, damaged beyond repair."

Lieutenant Abernathy squeezed past him to walk around the desk. He lifted a piece of the splintered wood and held it up for Cole and Vicky to see. "Somebody sure did a number on it, all right. Looks like he used a crowbar. Was this box inside the desk?"

"Yes, in the lower right-hand drawer."

Abernathy frowned. "You didn't have the film locked up in there, too, did you?"

Mr. Hagan looked insulted. "Of course not. Valuables belonging to guests are always locked in the safe." He sounded as if he hardly considered that a roll of film qualified as a "valuable."

"And before you ask," he added defensively, "it hasn't been opened. Somebody may have tried, but you couldn't get that safe open with a stick of dynamite. It's as solid as the Rock of Gibraltar."

The lieutenant heard him out patiently. "That's very reassuring, Mr. Hagan. It's too bad about your desk, but I'm sure we'll be able to apprehend the person who damaged it. Now, I'd appreciate it if you'd open the safe for us. The film you locked up for Miss Rand could be an important clue in a murder investigation."

"Well, why didn't you say so in the first place?" the manager muttered. He knelt in front of the squat black floor safe and had the door open in seconds. "Here," he said, handing the roll of film to the lieutenant. "There's your clue. Though I'd think you'd be more concerned about finding the gun that somebody ripped my desk apart to get."

"Gun?" Abernathy repeated sharply. "There was a gun in the desk?"

"That's right. A pearl-handled thirty-eight revolver. It's quite valuable, a collector's item."

Trooper Nolan was dispatched with the roll of film and the bullet, and the remaining officers were given a description of Mr. Hagan's pearl-handled .38, which had been securely locked in the top drawer of his desk before he and Mrs. Hagan had retired for the night.

Vicky waited until the lieutenant had finished with Mr. Hagan, then asked him about the "promo mat'l" box. He claimed he hadn't opened it. His instructions were to open the box in the morning, when the mystery-weekend participants were ready to leave for the return trip to Chicago.

Until then, he was to keep the box under lock and key. Under no circumstances was he to allow any of them access to it.

"I knew it!" she exclaimed a few minutes later to Cole. "Something in that box identified the actors. Why else would he have to keep it under lock and key until we were ready to leave? Darn it, Cole, if I hadn't listened to you, I could have found out who they are. Now somebody's beaten me to it and taken the list or whatever was in there, and it's all your fault."

Lieutenant Abernathy had finished questioning them—for the time being, anyway—and they were standing in the hall between the dining room and the office. The lieutenant had given short shrift to the box, declaring that it had nothing to do with the murder investigation currently under way and therefore wasn't worth discussing. Evidently Cole agreed with him.

"For heaven's sake, Vicky," he said impatiently. "Two people have been murdered in the last thirty-six hours, we may very well be suspects in one crime, if not both, and all you can think about is that dumb box."

The lieutenant stuck his head out the dining room door. "Hey, if you two want to duke it out, that's fine by me, but go do it someplace else, okay? I'm trying to conduct an investigation here."

Vicky clasped Cole's hand and started leading him down the hall, toward the front of the inn.

"I'd really rather not go back to the lounge," he murmured. He sounded exhausted, wiped out. She lifted his arm and draped it around her shoulders, then completed the link by wrapping her arm around his waist.

"How about the reading room? I don't think there's anybody in there."

The room was vacant, though someone—possibly the Kaysers—had occupied it recently. The wide-screen television had been left on, the volume turned down low. The screen and one reading lamp provided the only illumination. Vicky led Cole to a plush sectional upholstered in oyster velvet and pushed him down onto it.

"I like the furniture in here a lot better than the stuff in the lounge," she said as she sat beside him and bent over to remove his loafers.

"Mmm, it sure beats that love seat by a country mile. Are you undressing me?"

"No, just trying to make you comfortable."

"Oh. Is there any chance I could talk you into undressing me?"

Vicky sank into a cushy corner and grasped his arm, then gave it a gentle tug. He fell against her willingly, his head coming to rest on her shoulder. His arms circled her just beneath her breasts, and he snuggled closer.

"Maybe some other time," she replied as she stroked his temple. "Are you okay...emotionally, I mean? You know, after finding Paula and dragging her out of the pond.... Are you okay?"

He sat up and moved one hand to the back of her head, sliding his fingers into her hair. "You're sweet," he murmured huskily as his lips closed on hers, tenderly, too briefly. "And I'm okay. Still a little shaken—sort of punch-drunk, I guess. But okay. How about you?"

She closed her eyes and rested her forehead against his. "I'm not sure how to put it. I know it's irrational of me, but I feel . . . guilty."

"I know," he murmured.

She pulled back to look at him. "You, too?"

"We're probably not the only ones. I imagine the others are feeling the same way. None of us had a very high opinion of Paula. At some point we all said or at least thought some pretty harsh things about her."

Vicky nodded solemnly. "But I wouldn't have believed any of us despised her enough to kill her. God, I still have trouble believing it really happened."

"I know," Cole said again. His voice was rough, and he rubbed his cheek against hers in distress. Vicky wrapped both arms around him and held him tight.

Neither of them spoke for several minutes. They just held onto each other, both drawing comfort from their closeness. Finally, Cole exhaled a long, cleansing sigh and moved to alter their positions so that they sat with their backs against the end unit of the sectional, their legs stretched out side by side.

"My arm was going to sleep," he explained. Vicky was glad to see that his grin was almost back to normal.

"Cole?" she asked tentatively. "Why were you so determined that I shouldn't look in the box?"

She felt him tense for a moment, but he relaxed again almost immediately.

"I guess there's no harm in telling you now. My brother is on the board of the organization that puts these mystery weekends together. Every once in a while they arrange for someone to come along and check that everything's running smoothly—to see if the service on the train and at the inn are top quality, if the actors are giving the participants their money's worth, and so on. I drew the job this weekend."

The admission clearly astonished her. "So you only came along as some kind of...company spy? And all that stuff about wanting to be Travis McGee and live on a houseboat in Florida was just a bunch of hooey?" The disappointment she felt came through in her voice, and she sat up abruptly. "Does that mean you knew who the actors were all along?"

Cole calmly pulled her back against his side. "I have no idea who the actors are. I wasn't given any more information than the rest of you were. And what I said about wanting to be Travis McGee isn't hooey. I've always been a big MacDonald fan, John D."

"A few days ago, Bob—that's my brother—called and asked if I'd be willing to take his place this weekend. He and his wife had planned to come, but they're both doctors, and both of them had patients in intensive care and didn't think they should leave town for a few days. At least that's what he told me. I suspect he may have used the mystery weekend as a sneaky way to get me to take a break from my work. He knows I haven't taken a vacation in three years.

"Anyway, Bob made all the arrangements for me while I finished the tests I've been conducting for NASA. The plane from Phoenix was late getting in, so I had to come to the train station directly from the airport. There wasn't even time to stop by my apartment. Then I had to get hold of Bob at the last minute to find out exactly what it was he expected of me."

"Which explains the attaché case and the phone call you made at the station," Vicky murmured. "I'm sorry I doubted your story." She decided there was no reason to tell him that she'd gone through his attaché case on the train.

"You doubted everyone's story," he replied with a smile. "You never take anything at face value. You're always questioning, probing, digging for more information."

Vicky shrugged. "You have to be inquisitive to be a good reporter."

He nodded solemnly. "And observant, and imaginative. Let's see if we can put those qualities to work for us. I've been thinking . . . about who could have killed Paula."

"And have you reached any conclusions?"

His shoulders moved in a restless shrug. "So far I've been concentrating on narrowing down the possibilities."

"Using the process of elimination, you mean? I've been doing the same thing off and on ever since we came back to the inn. Bud was with us, so we know he didn't do it. And we saw Jayne enter the inn by the back door."

"But could she have come back out, shot Paula and made it inside again before the rest of us?"

Vicky shook her head. "I don't see how. When Gary and I went up to their room to get her, she'd just got out of the tub. She was drying her hair. And before you claim she could have run in just ahead of us, thrown on her pajamas and stuck her head under the faucet, let me add that she'd been there long enough to wash out the auburn rinse. Her hair was back to its 'normal mousy brown.' There was only a very small patch of green left, and it was a lot lighter than it had been before."

"All right, that's two down and five to go. How about Lyle?"

"No." Vicky said it with such conviction that Cole looked at her in surprise. "Didn't you notice how he reacted when you told us Paula was dead? He wasn't just shocked, Cole; he was angry—angry that someone would dare to take another person's life. Then, while you were upstairs changing, Bud said something that explained his reaction." She repeated what Bud had told Fred about Lyle's reaction to his experiences in Korea. "And I believe what Bud said. He wasn't making it up. I'd bet my last cent on it."

"Okay, I'll trust your judgment. So far we've eliminated Bud, Jayne and now Lyle. That leaves Michael, Fred, Gary and Todd."

"I don't think Gary did it," Vicky said. She gave him an appealing look. "Do you?"

Cole shook his head with a slightly apologetic smile. "You're talking about intuition, which I don't happen to put much stock in."

"But . . ." she coaxed.

He sighed. "But no, somehow I can't see Gary shooting a woman in the back."

"Well, that narrows it down to the Espinozas and Todd."

"But if we're going to rule out Gary—which I'm not convinced we ought to do, based on nothing more than intuition—we also have to rule out Fred. He and Gary were together when Paula was shot, remember."

Vicky slumped in dejection. "All those police shows make it look so easy. I have a terrible feeling we're overlooking something really important, something that would give us an entirely different perspective. Someone shot at Jayne," she murmured, more to herself than to Cole, "and missed. And then he shot at Paula; only that time he didn't miss."

"What makes you say that?" Cole asked sharply.

She gave him an odd look. "Because she's dead."

He shook his head in impatience. "No, not that part. Why did you say someone shot at Jayne? Why Jayne? Why not Fred or Gary?"

Vicky waved a hand in a gesture that said the answer should be perfectly obvious. "They were both women, and we've agreed that the killer has to have been one of the men."

The logic of that completely escaped Cole, but it didn't matter, because he'd locked onto something else. "Move," he said abruptly. "Let me up."

Vicky wondered if she'd missed something he'd said. "What?"

"Let me up. I need to pace." He pulled his arm out from under her, then climbed over her as she just lay there staring at him in confusion.

"Jayne and Paula, Jayne and Paula," he chanted as he paced up and down beside the sectional.

"Cole? Are you all right?" Vicky asked anxiously.

"Hmm? Yes, fine." Unconsciously, he started snapping his fingers. "Jayne and Paula. Red hair. No, that can't be it." He noticed that Vicky was looking at him as if she thought something had gone seriously wrong with his mental processes. "It's all right. I do this when I have to work out something tricky. Don't pay any attention to me."

Vicky folded her legs Indian style and sat back to wait out this strange ritual. Don't pay any attention to him? Didn't he realize what an incredible sight he made, pacing back and forth like that and muttering to himself?

"Jayne and Paula. Different heights, different builds. Damn, it's got to be there. Come on, come on. Jayne and Paula."

One of the state troopers started to pass the door, then spotted Cole and halted, his brow furrowed under the brim of his campaign hat.

"Nothing to worry about," Vicky told him with a nervous smile. "He always does this when he's trying to work out something tricky."

The policeman shook his head as if to say, "It takes all kinds," then moved on.

"Cole!" she whispered fiercely. "There's a cop outside who at this very minute is probably calling the guys with the butterfly nets to come and get you."

"Don't distract me," he muttered as he reached the end of the sectional and pivoted. "Not hair, not height, not physical build. Clothes. Slacks and skirt. White sweater and white—Oh, my God!"

Vicky untangled her legs and sprang off the sectional. "Cole! What is it?"

He didn't even hear her. His mind was racing, sorting and analyzing information with furious precision, eventually arriving at the only possible conclusion. It had been there all along, right in front of his eyes. Damn, he felt stupid, moronic, slower than a slug.

Vicky was beginning to be really worried. His eyes looked glazed, and he'd gone pale. "Cole Madigan, if you don't answer me, I'm going to punch you right in the dimple!"

"What?" He blinked as if he were emerging from a trance. "Vicky. Oh, Lord, Vicky, I've got it."

"Sit down and tell me," she urged, drawing him back onto the sectional with her. He surprised her by immediately wrapping both arms around her in a tight embrace. "Cole! What is it? What's wrong? You're scaring me."

He didn't want to scare her. It was enough that the realization that had just hit him like a lightning bolt had terrified him half out of his mind. He sat back but kept one arm around her, holding her close.

"It's all right," he lied, somehow managing to keep the fear out of his voice. "I'm sorry I scared you. There's nothing to be afraid of." Another lie, monstrous.

"Well, then, tell me."

He inhaled a deep breath, striving for calm, struggling to create logic and order from the chaos in his mind. He wasn't accustomed to fear or confusion. They threw everything out of kilter, made him feel disoriented, unable to function.

"All right." He drew another deep breath and felt his pulse begin to return to normal. "I'll take it one step at a time, in reverse."

"In reverse?" Vicky repeated blankly.

"It'll be easier to understand that way. First, until we told Bud, you and I were the only two people who knew Paula had come outside last night."

Vicky gasped. "Wait a minute, I think I've already figured out step two. If Bud was the only person we told and he was with us from then on, then that must mean—"

"That the murderer never intended to kill Paula."

"But . . ." Vicky began, then floundered. "Was it just a random killing, then?"

"No. Back up a little. Before Paula was shot, someone fired at Jayne. But he couldn't have been after Jayne, either, because only four people knew she was outside—Gary, Fred, you and I."

Vicky felt a chill sweep up her spine. "And Gary and Fred were with her when the first shot was fired."

"Right." Cole hugged Vicky a little closer. "Now, stop and think. What did Jayne and Paula have in common?"

She remembered what he'd said a minute ago, just before he'd seemed to go into that trancelike state. "Jayne was wearing a white sweater, and Paula had on a white blouse . . . is that it?"

"Yes, that's it. And what would you have been wearing if you hadn't run upstairs at the last minute to change?"

The breath became suspended in Vicky's lungs as she finally comprehended what he'd been leading her to. The pieces all fell into place at the same time, with a resounding crash that echoed inside her head.

"Oh," she whispered, groping for his hand and clutching it fiercely. "Oh, Cole. My God. It was me. He wasn't after Jayne or Paula. He was trying to kill me!"

Chapter Fourteen

Vicky was stunned, horrified by the realization. "He didn't even know they were outside. He was shooting at Jayne's white sweater and Paula's blouse. God, he killed her because she was wearing a white blouse! If she'd only thrown on a sweater, like I asked her too—"

"Stop. Vicky, sweetheart, don't. It wasn't your fault."

She didn't realize she was crying until he pushed a snowy white handkerchief into her hand. She sniffed and gulped, then sniffed some more, until she finally had herself fairly well under control.

"All right now?" Cole asked with gentle concern.

She nodded, lifting her head to give him a slightly watery smile. "I'm okay. Cole, we have to figure out who it is."

He stared at her mutely, an expression very much like awe in his eyes. "You're incredible, do you know that? We just discovered that someone is trying to kill you. You cry a few tears, dry your eyes and then say, calm as you please, 'Cole, we have to figure out who it is.' Aren't you afraid? Aren't you worried that he might try again? *I'm* sure as hell worried about that!"

"He isn't likely to try anything while we're here at the inn, with policemen swarming all over the place," she pointed out. "But after we leave...yes, frankly, I'm scared to death that if we don't figure out who he is so Abernathy can arrest him and put him behind bars, he might come after me again. And the worst thing is, I don't even know why! That's why we have to find out who he is and why he's after me, now, before he has a chance to get away.''

''I have a feeling the reason has something to do with that film you shot at the railroad station,'' Cole murmured. ''You remembered to tell Abernathy about the woman's purse, didn't you?''

''Yes, I described it in detail.'' She hesitated, frowning in concentration. ''Cole, just suppose for a minute that the same person killed both women. Could he be after me because he thinks I saw something I shouldn't have back at the station?''

''Abernathy seemed to think that might be the reason someone tried to get the film...because you'd inadvertently taken a picture of him doing something incriminating, or at least suspicious. The logical assumption is that the person who's trying to kill you is the same person who searched your purse and your camera bag.''

''Okay, let's take it a step further. Assuming that this person killed both Abernathy's Jane Doe and Paula—thinking she was me—let's also assume that Jane Doe was Paula's missing sister.''

Cole's eyes widened in astonishment. ''What? How on earth did you arrive at that conclusion?''

''It isn't a conclusion...yet,'' Vicky said absently. ''I'm sort of working this out as I go.''

''No kidding.'' There was a hint of amusement in his voice.

She went on as if he hadn't spoken. ''Let's go back to Friday afternoon. Paula claimed that her sister was supposed to have come with her this weekend but had to cancel at the last minute.''

''And Todd handed her a note confirming that fact in front of both of us.''

Vicky made an impatient, dismissive gesture. "But neither of us actually read the note, so we can't know for sure what it said. Where was I? Oh, now I remember. On Saturday morning I overheard two of the actors, a man and a woman, discussing a third actor named Erica. The woman was complaining because Erica had canceled out of the trip at the last minute."

"But you said you didn't recognize the woman's voice," Cole pointed out. "And Paula's voice was distinctive enough for you to have recognized it."

Vicky nodded. "Yes, the voice she normally used was certainly distinctive. But then so was everything else about her—her clothes, the way she walked, even her mannerisms. She was almost a caricature."

Cole's eyes narrowed. "What are you getting at?"

"Be patient for just a few more minutes," she urged. "I'm coming to the part you may have trouble keeping up with. If Erica was Paula's 'sister,' Paula had to have been one of the actors."

Baffled, Cole shook his head. "I'm not just having trouble keeping up, you've lost me completely."

"Okay, I'll back up for a bit. A third woman, supposedly Paula's sister, was to have been assigned to the compartment with Paula and me on the train. Ours was larger than the others, remember?" He nodded, so she assumed he was with her so far and went on. "Whether or not Paula and the woman who didn't show up were truly sisters, obviously they knew each other. And if they weren't sisters, for some reason they were planning to pretend that they were for the weekend. Still with me?"

"I think I'm beginning to see the light. It's fascinating to observe how your mind works."

Vicky slashed him a wry glance. "I suspect that might have been an insult, but I'll let it pass for now. All right— while we've established that Paula and the no-show knew each other, there's nothing to indicate that Jayne knew her or that she was expecting anyone else to join the group. In fact, at dinner on Friday she remarked that Paula had told her about the sister. That conversation had to have taken place after we all got on the train, because Paula was waiting for her sister to show up and didn't go aboard until the last minute."

Cole grinned at her. "You're really good at this."

"Thank you," she said modestly. "Now we're coming down to the wire. The man and woman I heard on the train Saturday morning were actors. The woman had to have been either Paula or Jayne. But of the two of them, Paula was the only one who'd been expecting another party to come on the trip—her 'sister,' who must have been the Erica I heard them talking about."

"Brilliant!" Cole exclaimed. He sounded sincere. "So Paula and Erica—Abernathy's Jane Doe—were both actors. But who was the man you heard talking to Paula on the train? A few minutes ago we'd whittled the list of suspects for Paula's murder down to Fred, Michael and Todd."

Vicky made another dismissive gesture. "Scratch Fred. You're forgetting he was with Gary."

"Oh, right. So the actor had to have been either Michael or Todd."

"It was Todd," she said with conviction.

"How can you be so sure?"

She gave him a slightly patronizing smile. "Who handed Paula the note at the station—the one that was supposedly a message from her sister?"

"I'd forgotten all about that," Cole admitted sheepishly.

"Paula stuck the note in her purse. I hope it's still there. I'd bet anything that if Abernathy sent one of his men up to get it, it would say something like 'Erica isn't coming. Improvise.'"

Cole shook his head in admiration. Then he suddenly sobered. "But if Todd is the third actor, we don't have any kind of evidence—even circumstantial—that he killed either woman. And even if we could prove that he killed Paula by mistake, thinking she was you, we still need a motive for Erica's murder.''

''I know,'' Vicky said with a sigh. ''We'll just have to hope there's some kind of solid evidence on the film. I have a hunch that the missing lizard purse is important, too. It may provide a motive...if they ever find it. Otherwise, why would he have taken it?''

''Maybe he just wanted to make it harder to identify her body.''

''But he must have realized that she would be identified, sooner or later, so taking her purse would only buy him a little time—a few hours at most. I have a gut feeling that there's a tie-in with Paula somewhere. If Paula had found out that Erica was murdered at the station, maybe she'd have automatically suspected Todd. Maybe that's why he needed to buy some time.''

Cole's forehead creased in a puzzled frown. ''I don't follow you. Why would Paula have suspected him of murdering Erica?''

''That's the sixty-four-thousand-dollar question. What if Todd was involved with Paula and seeing Erica on the side...?''

''A love triangle?''

''It wouldn't be the first time jealousy was the motive for murder.'' Vicky was about to suggest that they report their conclusions to Lieutenant Abernathy, but something she heard on television made her jump up and rush over to the set.

''Where are you going?'' Before Cole had finished the question, Vicky was on her knees in front of the control panel.

''Damn, where's the volume control for this thing?''

He came over to show her, raising the volume so that the female reporter's voice could be heard clearly.

"This is a Chicago channel, isn't it?" Vicky asked. There was a barely subdued excitement in her voice.

"Yes. It's the twenty-four-hour news channel that went on the air a few months ago. What is it? What did you hear?"

Vicky waved a hand at him to be quiet. "Shh, I'm not sure, but I think she said that guy behind her was Jeremiah something or other."

The reporter was talking about the distinguished-looking older man whose picture was projected on a screen behind her desk. She identified him as Jeremiah Fowler, formerly vice-president of the special-projects division of one of the largest cable networks, who had just accepted the post of general manager and programming director for a group of Chicago-based television and radio stations.

Then the news channel aired a taped segment from a press conference that had been held earlier that day, during which Fowler explained that he'd decided to make the move primarily because he wanted to spend more time with his wife. He claimed to be excited about the new position and looking forward to working in the Chicago area. When the camera cut back to the anchorwoman in the studio, Vicky gasped. A different picture was now displayed on the screen behind her.

"Mrs. Fowler, the former Paula Danvers, is a Chicago-area actress who has been involved in several local stage productions during the past few years. She was out of town and unavailable for comment about her husband's career move. Fowler will assume his new duties..."

The reporter's voice droned on, but Cole and Vicky were no longer listening. They remained kneeling on the floor in front of the set, staring at each other as they assimilated what they'd just seen and heard.

"'All my love, Jeremiah,'" Cole quoted softly.

"I had it backward," Vicky said. "He wasn't involved with Paula and seeing Erica on the side—he was involved with Erica and having an affair with Paula. And Erica probably found out . . ."

"And threatened to go to Paula's husband . . ."

"So he killed her."

"But we can't prove it, dammit!"

"We don't have to," Vicky said as she scrambled to her feet. "That's Abernathy's job. Come on; let's go tell him."

IN RETROSPECT, it was easy to spot the many small things that had all but gone unnoticed, or at least failed to rouse anyone's suspicion: Vicky's near miss on the train platform, when Todd had conveniently managed to let her camera fall beneath the wheels. Todd's numerous and often lengthy absences, several of which Paula had probably helped him arrange—no doubt as part of the script she thought they were following. Cole's "accident" with the van, when Todd had obviously wanted to get at the film in Vicky's camera bag. And the argument between Todd and Paula that Cole and Vicky had overheard upstairs and that had sounded so convincingly realistic. Having spoken to her husband earlier, Paula had apparently decided to end her affair with Todd, and Todd hadn't taken the news well. That particular quarrel hadn't been staged.

"You know what they say about hindsight," Lieutenant Abernathy remarked after listening to Cole and Vicky rake themselves over the coals for not having figured everything out sooner. "It's always twenty-twenty. Judging by what I've heard from you and the others, I don't think anyone could have anticipated what happened here, and you can't prevent what you can't anticipate. Stop beating yourselves up for not being mind readers or fortune-tellers."

"But some things happened as recently as a few hours ago," Vicky protested. "For instance, it was Todd who suggested—no, *insisted*—that we all go out and search for a sycamore tree. He organized everything, even divided the grounds into sections."

"So he'd know where to look for you," Cole put in. "Except none of us stayed in the section we'd been assigned to, and that threw him off. He shot at Jayne, thinking she was you. Then, a little later, he saw Paula at the opposite end of the pond, wearing that black skirt and white blouse that were so much like yours."

"He must have thought he was seeing double," Abernathy remarked dryly.

Vicky gave a dispirited sigh. "I still think we should have smelled something fishy."

Abernathy slid off the counter where he'd been sitting. He had suggested they talk in the kitchen, since the dining room was right next door to the lounge.

"Hey, you two have done the biggest part of my work for me. Give yourselves a little credit, for Pete's sake. Thanks to you, we should have this case wrapped up in a nice tidy bundle and ready to hand over to the prosecutor's office before another twenty-four hours are up."

"Has the lab finished developing Vicky's film yet?" Cole asked.

"Yeah, Nolan called just before you two dropped your latest bombshell on me. He should be here soon with the pictures. Keep your fingers crossed that they'll somehow connect our friend Hamilton to the Jane Doe murder. I'd better get back to the dining room. We still have three people to question, including Hamilton."

"You're going to question him the same as everybody else?" Vicky asked in surprise.

The lieutenant nodded. "You bet. At this point I don't want to do anything that might tip him off that we're on to him. If we're lucky, he just might say something during questioning to give himself away."

As they entered the hall, one of the troopers walked up to Abernathy and handed him a small plastic bag. A piece of paper with a couple of lines of handwriting was sealed inside.

"Is this the note from her purse?" the lieutenant asked.

"Yes, sir."

Abernathy read the brief notation and handed it to Cole.

"Well? What does it say?" Vicky demanded impatiently.

Cole grinned as he passed the plastic bag back to Abernathy. "'Erica isn't coming. Improvise.'"

"We're lucky she kept it," the officer said. "She might just as easily have thrown it away." He gave the bag back to the trooper along with a couple of brief instructions.

As the man started toward the front of the inn, Vicky suddenly thought of something that might be important. "Wait. Call him back."

The lieutenant looked mildly amused by the terse command, but he did as she asked.

"I just remembered," Vicky said when the trooper had returned. "There's another note. The one that said, 'One o'clock, under the sycamore tree.' Lyle has it, I think. At least, he was the one who read it."

"That would be Lyle Skelton," Abernathy said to the trooper. "One of the construction workers…the one in the gray tweed coat. See if he still has the note."

Cole and Vicky exchanged an astonished look. "Construction workers?" Cole said after the man had gone off to find Lyle.

Abernathy nodded. "I guess by rights they should be called businessmen, since they co-own a small remodeling and home-improvement company, but that was how they referred to themselves."

"Son of a gun," Cole murmured.

Vicky grinned and said, "Told you so."

When the lieutenant had returned to the dining room to resume his questioning, they went to the lounge to see what, if anything, was happening. They passed the trooper and Lyle at the door just as Lyle reached inside his sport coat for

the note about the sycamore tree. The Kaysers were nowhere to be seen.

"Where are Jayne and Gary?" Vicky asked. She was
careful not to glance in Todd's direction. Just being in the
same room with him gave her the willies, and she was afraid
that if she looked directly at him, he would somehow be able
to see everything she knew, as if her face were a billboard on
which was plastered the message *Todd Hamilton is a cold-
blooded killer*.

Fred answered her question. "Across the lobby, watching *Murder on the Orient Express*. While you two were
talking to the police, they found the videotapes Todd told us
about. Jayne had never seen that movie, and she said she
was still too wound up to sleep, anyway."

Bud rose from his chair and stretched. "Well, I'm sure as
hell not. It's time I hit the sack." He gave Vicky an affec-
tionate smile as he passed her on the way to the door.
"Come on Lyle. You're too old to be keeping such god-
awful hours too."

The trooper politely stood aside to allow the two of them
to precede him into the lobby.

"You know, I was just thinking," Bud remarked to the
young man as he followed them out. "The last time I stayed
up almost twenty-four hours, I wound up in jail for being
drunk and disorderly, or some such ridiculous thing. Anything like that ever happen to you?"

"No, sir," the trooper replied with a grin.

Sergeant Farrell appeared in the doorway to the dining
room and asked for Mr. Hamilton and Mr. Fred Espinoza.
He sent Todd in to Abernathy, and he and Fred headed for
the kitchen.

When they'd gone, Michael plopped down on one of the
sofas with a muttered oath. "Damn, I wish they hadn't left
me till last. I hate this infernal waiting, the way the whole
thing's dragging on and on. How much longer is it going to
take, for crying out loud?"

"They're just trying to be thorough," Cole told him. Glancing at his watch, he added, "And it's only been about two and a half hours since we found Paula's body. It just seems longer because we're all under so much strain. If it's the waiting that bothers you, why don't you go watch the movie with Gary and Jayne? At least it would keep your mind occupied."

Michael decided that it wasn't such a bad idea. He got up from the sofa and headed across the lobby to join the Kaysers. Cole glanced around the room with a wry half smile. Vicky thought she knew what he was thinking. She wrapped her arms around his chest and hugged him. "Don't you want to sit down?"

"Actually, I'd rather lie down, but all the sofas are too hard, too short or too lumpy to accommodate two people."

"We'll work something out, Goldilocks," Vicky murmured. She took his hand and led him to one of the big overstuffed armchairs, then pushed him down in it and squeezed herself in beside him. "See? What'd I tell you?"

"This one's just right," he said with a straight face.

Vicky smiled and wriggled closer to him, working her left arm beneath his back so she could hold him the way he was holding her. They were both silent for several minutes, simply enjoying the holding and the being held. After a while, Vicky released a long, sighing breath.

"It looks like Abernathy has everything almost wrapped up, doesn't it? Of course, I'd feel better if we could come up with some concrete evidence, something that would make it possible for him to nail Todd for at least one of the murders. But it looks as if they'll have enough to charge him with suspicion, at least."

Cole sensed that she was still afraid Todd might come after her if for some reason the police couldn't make the charges stick. He pressed a soft kiss on the top of her head. "I'm sure that when those pictures arrive, the cops will be able to charge Todd with more than just suspicion. He went to some pretty desperate lengths trying to make sure that film would never be developed. Whatever's on it must be awfully damned incriminating.''

''Or whatever he *thinks* is on it. I'm not getting my hopes up. It's possible there won't be anything in any of the pictures that will connect Todd to the Jane Doe murder—which, face it, is what we've been counting on. And so far there's not a shred of solid evidence that would justify charging him with Paula's murder. No witnesses, no weapon, nothing. If only we could come up with *something*!'' she said in frustration.

''I have this awful feeling that there's something else we've missed or overlooked—something that happened while everyone was outside looking for the sycamore tree—but for the life of me I can't figure out what it is.''

Cole tucked her head under his chin and began to massage her shoulders, using his strong fingers to knead the tension from them. ''Something that happened while we were all outside,'' he repeated.

''Mmm,'' Vicky murmured drowsily. Exhaustion, both physical and emotional, and the firm but gentle ministrations of his hands combined forces to sap her strength and energy. She felt herself slipping slowly and inexorably toward dreamland. She didn't want to go to sleep, not while Todd Hamilton was under the same roof. She stirred restlessly.

Cole's warm breath caressed her ear as he whispered a tender reassurance. ''Shh, it's all right. I'm here. Sleep for a while if you want.''

''Can't,'' she mumbled. ''Have to figure out what we missed.''

His lips brushed against her temple. ''I'll work on it while you rest.''

She burrowed into his arms, nestling closer to his warmth. As she dropped off to sleep, a contented smile hovered at the corners of her mouth.

Twenty minutes later, Cole's hands were shaking her awake. "Vicky? Vicky, honey, wake up!"

She muttered an incoherent protest, but he only shook her harder. "Stop that," she told him irritably. "Leave me alone."

"Come on, sweetheart; you have to wake up. It's important."

The urgency in his voice finally got through to her, and she reluctantly dragged herself off his chest. "It'd better be," she warned as she raked a hand through her tousled hair.

"It is. You know that something we'd missed that you couldn't think of?"

Vicky sat up, suddenly wide awake. "You figured it out? Is it really important, or did you just wake me up because your arm had gone to sleep again?"

There was an excited glitter in his eyes that she'd never seen before. "It's important, all right." The excitement was in his voice, too. "It ought to put Todd Hamilton behind bars for the rest of his natural life."

Chapter Fifteen

When Cole had finished telling her, Vicky was at least as agitated as he was, and even more eager to take this new information to Lieutenant Abernathy. Unfortunately, the detective was still questioning Todd in the dining room. For most of the next half hour they took turns watching the hands on Cole's watch creep toward 4:30 A.M. Finally they heard Fred and Sergeant Farrell approaching the door.

They'd had plenty of time while clock watching to make their plans. Vicky stayed where she was, curled up in the chair, her feet tucked under her, while Cole went to speak to the sergeant. If Fred showed any signs of trying to eavesdrop, she was supposed to distract him until Cole had passed on the message for Abernathy. The lieutenant had cautioned them against confiding in any of the other members of the group.

But as it happened, they needn't have been concerned that Fred would try to eavesdrop. He asked Vicky where Michael was, then said he was beat and intended to go to bed and sleep for twelve hours or until the police decided they could all go home, whichever came first. Vicky wished him pleasant dreams and then watched the sergeant cross the lobby to get Michael.

"Farrell says we should wait for Abernathy in the kitchen," Cole said when he came back to her. "He'll join us as soon as he's finished with Todd."

Vicky held out her hand for him to pull her up out of the chair. "Maybe we should stop in across the way and tell everybody we're going up to bed," she suggested. "Then when Todd comes out and we're not around, he won't get suspicious."

"Good idea," Cole approved. But after they'd said their good-nights—which technically should have been good mornings—and passed through the lobby, he drew her to a halt at the foot of the stairs. "Are you sure you want to do this? I can handle it from here on, and I'd feel better knowing you were up in your room, with one of Abernathy's men standing guard in the hall outside."

Vicky stretched up to kiss him on the mouth. "You're sweet to worry, but I'm sure. I want to do it—for Paula, but also for myself. Wait here. I'll be right back."

She was downstairs again in two minutes. Her hands were empty. "Where is it?" Cole asked.

"Here." She patted a small bulge under her sweatshirt. "I didn't want to carry it in case we run into Todd before we get out of the building, so I tied it around my waist."

They'd been waiting in the kitchen for ten minutes when Lieutenant Abernathy arrived. One of the troopers was with him.

"Hamilton's worried," the detective announced. "Close to the edge, I think. For a few minutes it was very tense in there, but just when I thought he might crack, he pulled it all back together again." Abernathy shook his head in frustration. "That is one cool customer. I deliberately mentioned the pictures to Joe before I started questioning Hamilton—asked if Nolan had made it back from the lab with them—and the guy didn't even bat an eyelash."

"The pictures aren't here yet?" Cole asked anxiously. "He should have been back an hour ago."

Abernathy sighed and rubbed his hand over his mop of curls. "Yeah, but Nolan had a flat tire. He decided to go ahead and change it rather than radio for somebody else to come and get the pictures, but when he opened his trunk, the damn spare was flat, too. Another cruiser's on the way to pick up the pictures and bring a new spare tire. Nolan's captain is driving the other cruiser," Abernathy added with a slightly malicious grin. "I'd love to be there to hear what he has to say about two flats on the same vehicle in the same night."

"Surely he can't blame Nolan because his tires went flat," Vicky said indignantly.

"You'd better believe it. A trooper is personally responsible for the maintenance of his cruiser, and that includes the rubber." Dismissing the unfortunate Nolan from his mind, Abernathy turned to Cole, suddenly all business. "Joe tells me you may have some kind of evidence that Hamilton killed Mrs. Fowler. Where is it?"

"Outside," Cole said. "Under the sycamore tree at the northern end of the pond."

Abernathy frowned. "The spot where you found her body?"

"That's right. We'll give you all the evidence you need, Lieutenant, but we have to hurry. It'll be light out very soon."

Lieutenant Abernathy looked a bit skeptical but decided to give them the benefit of the doubt. "Lead on," he said, extending his arm toward the door.

"First we'd better get a couple of flashlights," Vicky said. The lieutenant borrowed them from two of the troopers, then selected one of the senior officers to go along.

Cole and Vicky had agreed that in order to do this right, they should retrace the route they'd taken the night before, after they'd separated from Gary and Fred and started around the pond with Bud. They left the inn by the back door, then took the path to the right that circled the pond.

"Is it really necessary to hike all the way around the pond?" Abernathy asked as he followed them down the incline at the southern end. He leaned backward and held his arms out for balance on the way down, then leaned forward, puffing slightly as the path rose again on the other side.

"Yes," Vicky told him firmly. "It's really necessary."

"Hang in there, Lieutenant," Cole encouraged. "I promise it'll be worth it. We want to make sure there's no question in your mind about the validity of this evidence."

"At this rate, I may not live to see it," Abernathy replied between huffs and puffs as he trudged up the slope behind them. The officer who'd accompanied them gave him a boost from behind and received a glare for his trouble.

Cole used the flashlight he was carrying to point out the approximate spot where they'd been when they heard the second shot—the one that had killed Paula. A little farther on, he and Vicky stopped abruptly.

"This is pretty close to where Todd came running up to us, wouldn't you say?" Cole asked.

Vicky glanced around. "Close enough. Now?"

He hesitated. "This isn't necessary. You don't have to do it."

Abernathy stepped closer when he heard the misgiving in Cole's voice. "Do what? What's she going to do?"

"I'm going to give you the evidence you need to send Todd Hamilton to prison for life," Vicky told him. Her voice was clear and firm. She turned to Cole and flung an arm around his neck. "Stop worrying. The place is crawling with cops, right, Lieutenant?"

"Like flies on a dung heap," he confirmed. "I wish I knew what the devil was going on here."

"Patience, Lieutenant. It won't be much longer." Vicky gave Cole a quick kiss, then switched on the flashlight Abernathy had provided. "Give me three minutes." She was already walking away from them as she said it.

"Two," Cole called after her. "Two minutes, Vicky; that's all you get."

"Three!" she yelled back over her shoulder as she removed her rolled-up white blouse from under her sweatshirt.

Cole waited two and a half minutes before he continued leading Lieutenant Abernathy and the trooper around the pond. She was lucky to get that much time. He'd wanted to run after her the second she disappeared into the darkness. As it was, he knew he was walking too fast. He made himself slow down, then thought the hell with it and speeded up again. He stopped just short of the spot where Todd had grabbed his arm and started dragging him down the bank. He switched off the flashlight, then walked around behind Abernathy, turning him so that he was facing the place where they'd discovered Paula's body.

"I assume there's a point to all this," the lieutenant said dryly.

"Yes, there's a point. What do you see?"

Abernathy frowned. "What do I see?" He sounded as if his patience was beginning to wear thin. "I see some trees and a little bit of sky. That's about it. What am I supposed to see?"

"How about over there?" Cole asked, stretching his arm out so that his index finger pointed directly at the base of the sycamore tree. "Anything?"

"Nothing. Mr. Madigan, I've been up all night."

"So have I," Cole said bluntly. "So has Vicky." He turned the flashlight back on and aimed the beam where his finger had been pointing. "How about now?"

Abernathy let out a long-suffering sigh. "Now I see the leaves of a tree."

"Below us," Cole said.

"That's right. Below us. Jensen, do you also see the leaves of the tree below us?"

"Yes, sir," the trooper replied soberly. "I do."

"Happy, Mr. Madigan? We both see the leaves of the tree below us."

Cole gave the lieutenant a tight-lipped glance and walked forward a few feet. Abernathy shook his head and followed. Jensen brought up the rear.

"One more time, Lieutenant." Neither of the policemen could have missed the sudden tension in Cole's voice. He directed the beam of the flashlight down toward the pond. "Still see nothing but leaves?"

"That's it . . . just leaves."

Not bothering to raise his voice, Cole called, "Vicky?"

"Yo!" came the instant response from almost directly below them.

"Tell the lieutenant where you are."

"I'm lying on the ground under the sycamore tree, right at the edge of the pond."

"And?" Cole prompted.

"And? Oh—and I'm wearing a long-sleeved white blouse. Which, I might add, cost me a bundle and isn't going to be fit to mop the floor with after this. Hurry it up, will you, Cole? I want to go inside and take a bath."

"All right, sweetheart, just another couple of minutes." Keeping to the path, he led the policeman on around the northern end of the pond. They could see the northeast corner of the inn between the trees. When they reached the top of the incline, Cole stopped and turned around, facing back in the direction they'd just come.

"Okay, Vicky, you can stand up now."

As the three men watched, a wraithlike figure rose from the ground beneath the sycamore tree and hovered eerily. The specter waved its arms at them.

"I'll be damned," Lieutenant Abernathy murmured.

"Were we right?" Vicky called out. "Can you see me from that side?"

"We can see you, Miss Rand. Well enough to put a thirty-eight slug through you."

Vicky gave an excited whoop and started scrambling up the bank. Cole went to meet her and help her up the last few feet. As soon as they were back on the path, she threw her arms around his neck for an exuberant hug.

"So he shot her from here," Abernathy said. "And the place we stopped at a few minutes ago?"

"That was where Todd claimed to have spotted Paula's body," Cole answered. "As we just proved, he couldn't possibly have seen her from there. We couldn't just now, and I was shining a flashlight down from the path."

"Todd didn't have a flashlight," Vicky pointed out.

Abernathy nodded slowly. "He couldn't have seen her body, yet he led you straight to it."

"Which was a stupid mistake on his part," Cole said. "He could only have known she was there if he was the one who'd shot her."

"You see," Vicky explained, "the branches on that side of the tree droop more. In fact, they hang right out over the water. Also, I think the ground's a little higher over there."

Cole draped an arm around her shoulders and pulled her against his side. "Well, Lieutenant, do you think you've got enough now to charge Todd with murder?"

"More than enough. Congratulations, both of you. That was a fine piece of work. Now, what say we get back inside? Miss Rand can take her bath while I arrest Hamilton for the murder of Paula Danvers Fowler."

As they started up the steps to the veranda, all hell broke loose inside the inn. A woman screamed. Someone shouted, "Look out; he's got a gun!" A second later two shots rang out.

"What the—!" Abernathy and Jensen simultaneously drew their weapons. Abernathy jerked his head toward the ornamental shrubbery at the base of the veranda. "You two get down and stay out of the way."

Cole didn't wait to be told twice. He yanked Vicky off the steps and pushed her down into a flower bed, then threw himself on top of her.

Above them, Abernathy started yelling through the back door. "Joe! Templeton! Bultmeier! Lansing! Will somebody answer me, dammit!" Lowering his voice, he instructed Jensen to slip around to the front and see if he could find out what the hell had happened.

Vicky squirmed beneath Cole, who was spread-eagled on top of her. "I can't breathe!"

He shifted his weight to one side but kept a leg and an arm thrown over her. "Stay down."

"I have every intention of staying down, believe me," she said in a shaky voice. "Is it Todd? Has he got a gun? Who screamed?"

He placed a hand over her mouth. "Shh, I'm trying to listen. There's somebody at the dining room window. I think it's one of the cops."

"Nolan, is that you?" Abernathy barked.

"Yes, sir."

"When did you get back?"

"Just a few minutes ago, sir."

"Would you kindly tell me what the hell is going on in there?"

"It's Hamilton, sir. He apparently had the murder weapon hidden in the lounge—in an empty ice bucket, we think. When he saw me delivering the photographs to Sergeant Farrell, he flipped out. He's taken Mrs. Kayser hostage and has a set of keys the manager says belong to one of the vans out in the garage. He says he's leaving and if anybody tries to stop him, he'll kill Mrs. Kayser."

"Omigod," Vicky whispered. "He's got Jayne." Her fingernails made dents in Cole's back. He didn't notice.

"We heard shots," Lieutenant Abernathy said. "Are there people down?"

"Sergeant Farrell was hit in the right thigh, but I don't think it's serious. He managed to get into the manager's office after Hamilton shot him. He says the bullet only tore some muscle and that he's all right."

"He damn well better be," Abernathy said grimly. "All right, where is Hamilton now?"

"In the lobby."

Abernathy swore under his breath. "So he can see straight down the hall, right?"

"Yes, sir."

"Dammit, why couldn't he have picked one of the corner rooms, where we'd at least have him confined?"

"It wouldn't have made any difference," Vicky told him. "You can get out onto the veranda from all the public rooms."

"She's right, Lieutenant," Nolan said.

Abernathy pinched the bridge of his nose between his thumb and forefinger. "The phone's in the office, isn't it?"

"Yes, sir."

"Can you talk to Joe without Hamilton hearing you?"

"No, I can't, sir."

"All right, then, slip out and use the radio in one of the cruisers. Notify the post that an armed murder suspect and his female hostage may be leaving here shortly in a van." He turned to Cole and Vicky. "Quick, give me a description of the vans."

"Late-model Chevys," Cole said. "Brown and tan."

"Did you get that, Nolan?"

"Yes, sir." The trooper repeated Cole's description.

"All right, get a move on."

"Are you going to let Todd leave with her?" Vicky asked.

"I may have to," the lieutenant said heavily. "I won't push him. He's already killed two women. The due bill wouldn't be any higher for three."

There was some kind of commotion from the front of the building. Vicky recognized Todd's voice shouting at someone—presumably one of the troopers—to stay away or he'd kill her.

"Oh, God, he's left the inn," she murmured. "He's taking Jayne to the garage." She felt Cole easing away from her, but by the time it dawned on her what he meant to do, it was too late to grab him and pull him back. "Cole!" she whispered fiercely. "No!"

She scrambled to her feet and followed him as far as the corner of the veranda, then watched in breathless terror as he darted from tree to tree, zigzagging his way across the lawn toward the garage.

She realized what he had in mind when Todd backed into view. He had Jayne clamped against him with one arm around her waist, while he held the barrel of Mr. Hagan's pearl-handled .38 pressed against her ribs. He must have thought the policemen inside the inn were his only threat. Obviously it hadn't occurred to him that anyone might be behind him.

But Cole was. Waiting silently in the shadows beneath one of the maples at the corner of the garage. He knew he had to time his move exactly. If he was off by a fraction of a second, Jayne might be Todd's next victim. He held himself back when he wanted to lunge forward. *Wait. It has to be smooth. Smooth and fast, like a scorpion's sting.*

Vicky held her breath as she watched Todd drag Jayne across the lawn, drawing even closer to the corner of the garage. Cole was there, waiting. What would he do? Did he have a plan, or was he just hoping Todd would give him some kind of opening? There was a blur of movement as a shadow seemed to separate itself from the trees and rush out to meet Todd and Jayne. Vicky sucked in a jagged chunk of air.

Cole didn't allow himself to hesitate or reconsider once he'd set his body in motion. The element of surprise was all he had going for him; he couldn't afford to lose it. His right hand punched up under Todd's elbow from below. Using his arm as a lever, he forced Todd's hand and the gun in it away from Jayne's body. Jayne's reflexes were blessedly quick. He'd prayed they would be. She instantly became one hundred and fifteen pounds of dead weight against Todd's other arm, pulling him off balance for the second or two Cole needed.

"Go!" he yelled as he used both hands to shove the gun up over Todd's head. Todd's finger belatedly squeezed the trigger, but Jayne had already wrenched herself away from him and was staggering behind one of the trees.

"Freeze!"

"Freeze!"

"Freeze!"

"Freeze!"

Cole looked around and found himself facing a semicircle of state troopers, all with their guns drawn and pointed, it would appear, straight at him. Half his mouth twitched in a nervous smile as he edged away from Todd. He hadn't planned to take Mr. Hagan's .38 with him, but Todd shoved it at him and promptly thrust his arms straight up in the air. His eyes were wild with panic.

"Don't shoot! For God's sake, don't shoot!"

"You have the right to remain silent," one of the troopers began as he came forward to handcuff Todd.

Cole held the gun out in front of him by the barrel and was immensely relieved when Lieutenant Abernathy stepped forward to take it from him. At that point the rest of the troopers returned their weapons to their holsters and led Todd away.

Jayne stuck her head out from behind the tree. "Is it safe to come out now?" Then she spotted Gary racing across the lawn and decided not to wait for an answer. They made a very romantic picture as they ran to meet each other.

Vicky hurried over in time to hear Abernathy remark gruffly, "Nice work, Mr. Madigan. Even if it was a damn stupid thing to do. You could have got both yourself and Mrs. Kayser killed, you know.''

Cole hardly noticed what the lieutenant was saying. He'd seen Vicky approaching, and his face was wreathed in a happy, just-plain-glad-to-be-alive smile. ''Thank you,'' he said to Abernathy, turning to Vicky and sweeping her up in a huge bear hug.

''You crazy fool!'' she cried. ''He's right, you know. You scared me half to death. I almost died of heart failure.''

''You!'' Cole said with a shaky laugh. ''When I looked around and saw all those guns pointed at me, *I* nearly died of heart failure.''

She let her head fall back and smiled up at him. ''Oh, but it was such a brave thing to do. I'm so proud of you.''

Of course, then he had to kiss her. When they came up for air, Lieutenant Abernathy was standing a couple of feet away, his hands clasped behind his back, watching them with an indulgent smile.

''Don't mind me,'' he said. ''I can wait.'' Cole and Vicky drew apart in embarrassment. The lieutenant grinned. ''What say we go inside and have a look at those pictures?''

The first photo Nolan showed them was the one Vicky had taken of a red lizard handbag. The second featured Cole jogging past a litter barrel at the train station. Todd Hamilton was clearly visible in the background. He was stuffing the same handbag into the litter barrel.

''That camera was an excellent piece of equipment,'' Abernathy said. ''If you look closely, you can even pick out the monogram in the corner of the purse Hamilton's throwing away. I hope your bosses won't mind if I keep this picture, Miss Rand. I have a feeling the prosecutor may have a pressing need for it in the not-too-distant future.''

''I'm sure they'll be happy to cooperate in any way,'' she replied. ''It's going to be great publicity for the paper—'Girl Reporter Helps Nab Killer,' et cetera.''

The lieutenant then brought out two items he thought they might find of interest. One was the plastic bag containing the note Todd had given Paula at the station; the other was a plastic bag containing the note that had supposedly fallen out of Cole's pocket in the lounge.

"I'm no handwriting expert, but these sure look like they were written by the same person, don't they?"

"They certainly do," Cole murmured. "Todd probably dropped the second note when I pulled out my handkerchief. It was the perfect way to get everybody outside, wandering around aimlessly in the dark, and he didn't have to worry that Paula would see it and recognize his handwriting, since she'd already gone up to her room."

Vicky agreed. "So when I went up to change and told her about it, she probably thought that Todd had altered the script for the phony murder without telling her. That was why she was so eager to go outside and why she slipped away from us as soon as she could—she was desperate to find Todd."

"And instead he found her," Cole said quietly.

Chapter Sixteen

A week later Cole came to Vicky's apartment for dinner. He brought wine, a dozen long-stemmed yellow roses, a stuffed teddy bear and a five-pound box of chocolates.

"I'm not taking any chances," he said when she opened the door and her mouth fell open in astonishment. "I was going to bring you balloons, too, but I couldn't make up my mind whether to get the regular round ones or those shiny things with sappy messages painted on them."

"You mad, impetuous fool," she said, laughing as she took the roses and the teddy bear and led him into the kitchen. "Does the wine need to be chilled?"

"Don't ask me. I know nothing whatsoever about wine. I thought it always needed to be chilled."

She cast a suspicious glance at the bottle, then removed a vase from one of the cabinets. "Would you be offended if I asked what criteria you used to select it?"

"The man at the liquor store said it was their best-selling Illinois wine. Should I put it in the refrigerator?"

Fortunately, Vicky had an excuse to turn away. "Yes, why don't you?" she said as she stuck the vase under the faucet. "It should be properly chilled by the time we're ready for dessert."

He stayed in the kitchen and insisted on helping her put the finishing touches on the meal. They had seen each other every night for the past week, but they hadn't gone to bed together yet. It wasn't that they hadn't wanted to. Sparks flew every time they touched or their eyes met. Skyrockets exploded and cymbals crashed when they kissed. But they had an unspoken agreement to spend some time getting to know each other better. They weren't in any hurry, because they both knew it would be fantastic when it finally happened, and the waiting only heightened their sense of anticipation.

And the instant Vicky had opened the door, they'd both known that tonight would be the night.

They took their time over the meal. Vicky told Cole that Lieutenant Abernathy had called her at work to say that the Chicago police had managed to retrieve Erica Wagner's handbag from the city sanitation department. It had contained four torn photographs of Todd and Paula *in flagrante delicto*. When confronted with the pictures, Todd had broken down and confessed to both murders.

Cole had some news for her, too. His brother, Bob, had admitted that the toupee on Vicky's dinner plate had been arranged in advance, as sort of an icebreaker to help the mystery-weekend participants loosen up and get into the mood. She told Cole to tell Bob that he owed her one roast beef dinner. Cole replied that he already had and that they were invited to Bob and Zoe's house next Friday night.

"His wife's name is Zoe?"

"Yes, and you'll like her. She plays the oboe and the gong."

"Did you say the *gong*?"

"That's right. My mother will also be there," he added casually.

"Your mother?"

"Mmm, she's flying in from Dubuque. She wants to meet you. You'll like her, too. She's a lot like me, or I suppose I should say I'm a lot like her."

"You mean she's stubborn?" Vicky asked dryly.

Cole smiled. "No, she's tenacious."

After dinner they settled on the sofa for coffee and dessert. The wine Cole had brought was so awful that he took it back into the kitchen and poured it down the sink. Groucho, the cat, decided to make an appearance about ten o'clock. He jumped on the arm of the sofa and gave Cole a long, yellow-eyed stare. Cole stared back, then reached out to rub his ears before Vicky could warn him not to. The cat started purring so loudly that she thought her friend Alicia could probably hear him next door.

"I don't believe it," she said when Groucho finally jumped down. "He usually doesn't take to strangers. It's a wonder he didn't claw your hand to ribbons."

"I told you, I get along well with all animals and most children," Cole murmured as he pulled her into his arms. "Are you going to let me stay all night?"

"And tomorrow night, too, if you want."

He kissed her throat, then her ears, and her temples and eyelids and nose and chin, making her wait. When his lips finally settled on hers, the passion that flared between them took her breath away.

"I accept the invitation," he whispered, easing her down onto the sofa cushions.

His hands moved over her slowly, gently, caressing and exploring, lighting fires up and down her body as he leisurely bared it to his teasing fingers and tormenting mouth. By the time he removed her panties, Vicky was writhing with desperate need.

"Cole!" His name was little more than a gasp on her lips. She reached for him, and he smiled as he leaned down to meet her. Vicky wound her arms around his neck and fastened her mouth on his. Then he slid an arm beneath her knees and suddenly swept her up off the sofa, cradling her high against his chest.

She pulled back in surprise. "What are you doing?"

His dimple winked at her. "Earning points for romance and finesse, of course. Where's the bedroom?"

She tilted her head toward it. "But this really isn't necessary, you know," she murmured in his ear. "You already have all the points you'll ever need." She nibbled at his ear and the side of his neck as he carried her across the living room and through the bedroom door.

Cole stopped beside her bed. "I do? Since when?"

"Since you became a hero. A zillion points come with the title."

"Now you tell me." He glanced down at the bed. "Oh, well, since I've already made the effort . . ."

Vicky laughed softly as he released her legs and let her slide down his body. She undressed him in half the time it had taken him to undress her, then stood back and looked at him. From top to bottom, every golden inch.

"My God, Cole, but you're beautiful," she whispered.

"No." His voice was a soft rasp. "You're the one who's beautiful."

She felt her whole body flush with pleasure. "I'm glad you think so, but you are, too."

He'd never had a woman look at him the way she was looking at him—the way a man looks at a woman when he wants her to know how desirable she is. Cole discovered that he liked having Vicky look at him that way. It was exciting. Almost too exciting. He closed his eyes and swallowed hard. "You're embarrassing me."

Her rich, throaty chuckle made the hair on his arms stand up. "Strange, you don't look embarrassed," she murmured wickedly. Her cool fingers glided across his hip and closed around the part of him that was already hard and aching for her. A thick groan rose in his throat. He reached for her blindly.

"Yes," Vicky urged as he pulled her down on the bed. "Oh, yes, Cole. Please." She scattered hot little kisses across his throat and shoulders and chest, suddenly impatient to have all of him, to give him all of herself. "I need you. I want you. Hurry, please."

Despite her pleas, he didn't hurry. Nor did he love her quite as slowly and leisurely as he'd intended. Her name started as a sighing whisper on his lips, then became a gasp of wonder, and finally a shuddering moan as her soft, ecstatic voice cried out to him at the end.

Long minutes later, Vicky lay curled up against Cole's side, blissfully content and more thoroughly satisfied than she'd ever believed it was possible for a human being to be.

"I thought you'd led a very sheltered life," she remarked with a dreamy smile.

Cole nipped at her shoulder. "You bring out the beast in me. You do realize that we have something extra special, don't you?"

"Oh, yes. Super-duper extra special. But we'll probably have to really work to keep it this special," she teased as she ran a lazy finger down his chest. "You know ... find ways to keep the excitement alive."

"I'm certainly willing to do my part." He rolled over to cover her with his body, his blue eyes glowing with tenderness as they caressed her face. "Do you think you could get away next weekend?"

"I imagine so. Why, have you got something planned— other than Friday night dinner with the Madigan clan, that is?"

"Well ..." He bent his head to run the tip of his tongue around her ear. "Bob told me today that there's another mystery weekend planned, and they've had two sudden cancellations."

"Oh, no," Vicky said firmly. "Get that idea right out of your head, Cole Madigan."

"But we make such a terrific team," he coaxed, nibbling at the lobe of her ear.

"Stop that. You think I don't know what you're doing? You're *not* going to seduce me into going on another of those trips, Cole.'' Her little speech lost some of its effectiveness when his tongue dipped into her ear just as she said his name, so that it came out sounding rather breathless and weak.

"How can you accuse me of such a thing?" he murmured. His hand closed over her breast. "Did I mention that everybody will be going as his favorite fictional detective?"

"No, Cole, and that's final. I don't care if I never set foot on a train again for the rest of my life."

"I already told Bob we'd take the canceled reservations."

"You didn't!"

"I'll be Travis McGee, and you can be…let's see, I don't suppose Lois Lane would qualify as a detective, would she?"

Vicky gave in with a resigned sigh. "I'll get you for this," she threatened, winding her arms around his neck.

Cole lifted his head to grin down at her. "We'll have a terrific time; just wait and see. And this time you won't have to be just an impartial observer."

Vicky gasped indignantly, as he'd known she would, and he immediately took advantage of her open mouth. *Travis McGee should be so lucky,* he thought as Vicky started kissing him back. *Rhett Butler, too, for that matter.*

WHAT READERS SAY ABOUT HARLEQUIN INTRIGUE . . .

Fantastic! I am looking forward to reading other Intrigue books.

*P.W.O., Anderson, SC

This is the first Harlequin Intrigue I have read . . . I'm hooked.

*C.M., Toledo, OH

I really like the suspense . . . the twists and turns of the plot.

*L.E.L., Minneapolis, MN

I'm really enjoying your Harlequin Intrigue line . . . mystery and suspense mixed with a good love story.

*B.M., Denton, TX

What the press says about Harlequin romance fiction...

"When it comes to romantic novels...
Harlequin is the indisputable king."
—*New York Times*

"...always with an upbeat, happy ending."
—*San Francisco Chronicle*

"Women have come to trust these
stories about contemporary people,
set in exciting foreign places."
—*Best Sellers*, New York

"The most popular reading matter of
American women today."
—*Detroit News*

"...a work of art."
—*Globe & Mail*, Toronto

ATTRACTIVE, SPACE SAVING BOOK RACK

Display your most prized novels on this handsome and sturdy book rack. The hand-rubbed walnut finish will blend into your library decor with quiet elegance, providing a practical organizer for your favorite hard-or soft-covered books.

Only $9.95

Approximately 16" x 8" when assembled

Assembles in seconds!

To order, rush your name, address and zip code, along with a check or money order for $10.70 ($9.95 plus 75¢ postage and handling) (New York residents add appropriate sales tax), payable to *Harlequin Reader Service* to:

In the U.S.

Harlequin Reader Service
Book Rack Offer
901 Fuhrmann Blvd.
P.O. Box 1325
Buffalo, NY 14269-1325

Offer not available in Canada.

Six exciting series for you every month... from Harlequin

Harlequin Romance ·
The series that started it all

Tender, captivating and heartwarming...
love stories that sweep you off to faraway places
and delight you with the magic of love.

◆

Harlequin Presents ·
Powerful contemporary love stories...as individual as the women who read them

The No. 1 romance series...
exciting love stories for you, the woman of today...
a rare blend of passion and dramatic realism.

◆

Harlequin Superromance®
It's more than romance... it's Harlequin Superromance

A sophisticated, contemporary romance-fiction
series, providing you with a longer,
more involving read...a richer mix of complex plots,
realism and adventure.

Harlequin American Romance™
Harlequin celebrates the American woman...

...by offering you romance stories written about American women, by American women for American women. This series offers you contemporary romances uniquely North American in flavor and appeal.

◆

Harlequin Temptation ™
Passionate stories for today's woman

An exciting series of sensual, mature stories of love...dilemmas, choices, resolutions... all contemporary issues dealt with in a true-to-life fashion by some of your favorite authors.

◆

Harlequin Intrigue™
Because romance can be quite an adventure

Harlequin Intrigue, an innovative series that blends the romance you expect... with the unexpected. Each story has an added element of intrigue that provides a new twist to the Harlequin tradition of romance excellence.

Harlequin Books·

PROD-A-2